Praise for the Mirrorscape trilogy

'It is a firework of inspiration and homage to art. Wilks' book is bubbling with ideas, tremendously fast and funny'
Der Spiegel

'An endearing hero, a cast of incredible characters and a plot that will keep you breathlessly turning the pages. Mirrorscape is magical and enthralling'
Jenny Nimmo, author of the Charlie Bone series

'Wilks has crafted an enchanting world where anything is possible in the eye of the beholder. The imagery in Mirrorscape is beautifully crafted and brought the book to life even more for me . . . Mirrorscape is a great start to a series that will have you glued to the story down to the very last page'
Fantastic Book Review

'Mirrorscape is one of the most original concepts I have ever come across. You have the ingredients for a stunning fantasy series that is guaranteed to keep you enthralled'
www.eternalnight.co.uk

'As with all the best fantasy, the real excitement is the human story, which involves betrayal, friendship and a whole range of qualities (and their opposites), a titanic struggle between good and evil, and some very fine writing'
Story Time Books for Kids

'Mirrorscape is one of the most unique and enthralling fantasy stories I've ever read . . . I heartily commend Wilks for his creative and exciting plot; there wasn't a moment in the story that failed to capture my interest'
The Book Muncher

VLAM

THE HOUSE OF THRONES

MW 2007

THE HOUSE OF MYSTERIES

THE HOUSE OF SPIRITS

Londoner Mike Wilks is an award-winning artist and bestselling author of *The Ultimate Alphabet*, *The Ultimate Noah's Ark* and *Mirrorscape*. His paintings, which have been described as 'meticulous and eye-bending', can be found in public and private collections in Europe and the USA. The Mirrorscape books transport the reader into Mike's compelling inner world.

www.mike-wilks.com
www.mirrorscape.co.uk

Other books by Mike Wilks

Pile – Petals from St. Klaed's Computer
(With Brian Aldiss)

In Granny's Garden
(With Sarah Harrison)

The Weather Works

The Ultimate Alphabet

The Annotated Ultimate Alphabet

The BBC Drawing Course

The Ultimate Noah's Ark

The Ultimate Spot-The-Difference Book
(Metamorphosis)

Mirrorscape

Mirrorstorm

MIKE WILKS

MirrorShade

EGMONT

For my teachers.
For Terence Horney and Victor Freeborn who taught me
to draw and paint, for Herman Hecht who taught me to
design and for Cally Poplak who taught me to write.

EGMONT

We bring stories to life

Mirrorshade first published in Great Britain 2010
by Egmont UK Limited
239 Kensington High Street
London W8 6SA

ISBN 978 1 4052 5373 4
1 3 5 7 9 10 8 6 4 2

A CIP catalogue record for this title is available from the
British Library

Typeset by Avon DataSet Ltd, Bidford on Avon
Printed and bound in Great Britain by the CPI Group

Contents

Spiracle, Blinker, Gusset and Flob

As Mel stirred in his sleep and hovered on the lip of wakefulness he became aware of an unusual sound in the dormitory. It sounded like a whisper. Curious, he opened his eyes and nearly jumped out of his skin. A surprised gasp escaped his throat. There, at the foot of his bed, stood six figures. Two of them he recognised. His best friends and fellow apprentices, Ludo and Wren, shivering in their nightclothes, their eyes wide with alarm, were bound and gagged and being held fast by an enormous creature covered in shaggy, ginger fur. A pair of miniature, flesh-covered horn-buds protruded from his bald forehead and a number of small, beaked creatures poked their heads out from his tangled pelt. Mel knew at once that the being was a figment, an inhabitant of the Mirrorscape – the strange and secret world that exists inside paintings. But what was he doing here, in the real world?

Standing to his left, his companion was no less weird. He was tall and skinny and dressed from head to foot in a heavy and somewhat rusty suit of armour, covered with a multitude of small, latched doors of all shapes and sizes.

The third figment was very short and stocky. He also wore armour but it was several sizes too large. His pudding-basin helmet was so big it covered his face and a pair of red, glowing eyes peeped out from a slit in the front. On top of this helmet was mounted a shuttered miner's lantern that cast the only light in the dark dormitory. He held a peacock feather quill in one hand, poised to write in the big ledger he held open in the other.

The final figure was a grotesquely fat figment with skin as white as drawing paper. He was dressed only in a leather loincloth and gladiator sandals that were bound to his substantial legs with crisscross thongs. He was covered in hundreds of coloured tattoos which, to Mel's amazement, moved about of their own accord like animated drawings.

Before Mel could promote his initial gasp to the

rank of full-blown scream, the figment leant his shaven and much-illustrated head forwards over him and quickly clamped a blubbery hand over the youngster's mouth. He wheezed into Mel's ear, 'Hello, my name is Gusset. I'll be your abductor this night.'

As Mel watched, a tattoo of a faun ambled over the man's ample chest and plucked a tattooed poppy from the bouquet depicted near his armpit. The faun held the scarlet flower in front of its face and blew a cloud of pollen that enveloped Mel. The poppy-dust made his eyes heavy and, in an instant, he was asleep once more. The last thing he saw was the short figment make a tick in his ledger.

When Mel came to he knew at once he was back in the Mirrorscape. While he had been unconscious he had also been bound and gagged. He was lying on a drawbridge suspended from huge chains with links as thick as his forearm. Mel sat up alongside Wren and Ludo and together the friends gazed around, amazed at the gargantuan space. There were other drawbridges – some raised, some lowered – linking the many walkways that spanned the canyon-deep void in the centre of the building. High above, a thunderstorm brewed amid roiling clouds. Lightning flashed and by its spectral light Mel saw colossal statues of muscular men in chains on the far side of the void. The drawbridge trembled as the thunder rolled. A steadier illumination was supplied by a great many fires, which burned inside giant spherical cages that hung on impossibly long chains. They swayed like lazy pendulums in the updraft from the depths. Doors and windows with fat, iron bars peppered most of the vertical surfaces and massive, circular grilles spewed out billows of steam. Far, far off echoed the wail of desperate cries.

'Ah, you're awake,' said the short figment, obviously the boss. 'I expect you're wondering what's happened and where you are.'

As one, Mel, Ludo and Wren nodded, making muffled *yes please* sounds inside their gags.

'We are Messrs Spiracle, Blinker, Gusset and Flob.' He used the eyed, feathery end of his long quill to identify himself, the armoured figment, the tattooed and the hairy ones in turn. 'Incorporated bounty hunters. No bounty too small, no fugitive too large. Satisfaction guaranteed or your money back. As to where you are, my young friends, well, you're in Deep Trouble, the most secure prison in the Mirrorscape.' He made a sweeping gesture with his quill, indicating the interior. 'And now, without further ado, we must hand you over to Locktight, your personal gaoler.' Spiracle half-bowed. 'It's been a pleasure apprehending you.'

Blinker threw a bundle of clothes into the air over the friends' heads as if it were a game of piggy-in-the-middle.

Mel turned, and standing behind him was yet another figment who expertly caught the bundle. 'If you'd care to follow me, I'll show you to your cell.' The friends had no choice as Locktight tossed a lasso ensnaring the three of them and set off across the drawbridge, towing them behind.

The gaoler was a large, muscular figment who wore an executioner's mask made from riveted iron that covered the top half of his head. An abundant and greasy black beard titivated with small bows of coloured ribbon protruded from beneath it. His belted black jerkin was covered in dozens of bunches of keys that hung from hooks. As he moved he sounded like an out of tune wind-chime. Locktight led them even further into Deep Trouble, occasionally stopping to operate large star-wheel winches that raised and lowered the drawbridges.

Eventually they came to a thick, iron-bound door with a small, barred window set into it. Locktight selected a bunch of keys, opened the door and pulled the friends inside. 'This will be your accommodation until the trial. The straw is changed every two years – whether it needs to be or not – and a bowl of gruel is served on alternate Sundays.' He tossed their clothes on the floor. Before Locktight untied the children and removed their gags he quickly injected all three of them with a rusty syringe.

'Ouch! Why'd you do that?' said Ludo, rubbing his arm.

'Prison regulations,' explained Locktight with a malicious grin. 'Humans get ill if they remain in the Mirrorscape for too long. And you're going to be here a long, long time. The shots will prevent you feeling sick.'

So saying, he left, slamming the door behind him. The key was turned loudly in the lock.

'Well,' said Wren. 'We all know *where* we are.'

'We're in Deep Trouble,' said Mel. 'That's where.'

'You can say that again,' added Ludo.

'And we all know *what* we are.'

'Prisoners,' said the boys miserably.

'But what we don't know is *why* we're here,' said Wren.

'It must be serious,' said Mel. 'Locktight said something about a trial.'

'And *that*, dear clients,' came a booming voice from the little window in the door, 'I believe you'll find is my domain.'

The door was unlocked and swung open. Standing there was another figment. He was tall and dressed in a voluminous black robe with long white bands at his stiff collar like an inverted letter V. Above his haughty face with its beak-like nose and extra-bushy eyebrows, resided a pale legal wig. 'Allow me to introduce myself. Mithras Periwinkle, barrister at law, at your service. And this,' he gestured behind him, 'is Shrug, my articled clerk.'

A wobbly stack of casebooks with a pair of feet beneath it tottered into the cell and lowered itself to the floor. From behind it emerged yet another figment. He was small and dressed in a black frock coat and had a face that looked like it belonged to a hundred-year-old baby with a permanently runny nose. 'Pleased to meet you, I'm sure.' He sniffed loudly.

'Now,' said Mithras Periwinkle, rubbing his hands. 'Time is short. We must begin to prepare your defence. Shrug? If you'd be so kind.'

Shrug got down on his hands and knees and the barrister sat on him as if he were a stool.

'Why do we need a defence?' said Mel. 'We haven't done anything wrong.'

Mithras Periwinkle smiled the smile of a man who had heard this a thousand times before. 'That's the spirit.'

'No. *Really* we haven't,' said Wren.

Ludo nodded vigorously.

'It matters not. Innocent or guilty, I will defend you to the limit of my considerable abilities. The case of *Mirrorscape versus Polymath* seemed hopeless until Mithras

Periwinkle was engaged. Today Mirthless Polymath is fruitfully engaged in running a very profitable concession in second-hand pedantry in Pennyweight Market. All thanks to yours truly. Shrug? The indictment, if you'd be so kind.'

There came a muffled sniff and Shrug waved a document from beneath the lawyer. Mel was amazed that the tiny, feeble-looking clerk did not collapse under the other's bulk.

Mithras Periwinkle took the papers and untied the pink ribbon securing them. He cleared his throat and read out the charge. 'In short, it is alleged that Orange 22403101, alias Melkin Womper, together with Orange 22403102, alias Ludolf Cleef, and Indigo 29990313, alias Wren Delf, employees of the Monolith in the city of Anywhere in the land of Nowhere, did wantonly disregard the Terms and Conditions of that said organisation and that each did separately and unilaterally terminate their employment in strict contravention of the aforesaid Terms and Conditions.'

From beneath the barrister Shrug said, 'You did a bunk.'

'Precisely.' Mithras Periwinkle looked up at the trio. 'Well? Is this true?'

'*Sort of*,' said Mel.

'"Sort of", dear client, is not a plea that the court will recognise. If I am to effect an acquittal, you must be frank with me.' He raised a quizzical eyebrow as thick as a hairy caterpillar.

'Well, yes, then,' said Wren. 'But –'

'In my considerable experience,' interrupted the barrister, 'there's always a "but". "But" is the mortar between the bricks. "But" is the jelly in the pork pie, the jam in the sandwich, the fluff in the belly button of any given case. "But" is the difference between spending the rest of your lives in Deep Trouble and walking free. In short, "but" will form the heart, the linchpin, nay, the very *crux* of our defence. Now, if you'd be so kind as to elucidate your particular "but".'

'He means "tell him what happened",' sniffed Shrug.

'We only took the jobs in the Monolith so that we could look for Wren,' said Ludo.

'She was being forced to marry a monster called

the Morg,' continued Mel. 'We *had* to find her and help her escape.'

'Actually, it was me who found *them*,' said Wren. 'And then we all left so that . . .' Her voice trailed off. 'If you look at it that way then we *did* ignore the Terms and Conditions.'

Mithras Periwinkle pursed his lips. 'I see, I see. So you are what we members of the bar call in legal parlance "culpable".'

'He means *guilty*,' said Shrug. He added a sniff for emphasis.

'I suppose we are,' admitted Mel with a sigh.

'Ah.' Mithras Periwinkle pursed his lips and steepled his long-fingered hands. He got to his feet and began pacing the cell. 'There's nothing I enjoy more than a challenge – and this is indubitably that. In such a hopeless case as this the only course of action open to us is the Periwinkle Defence.'

Shrug sniffed again. 'He means *a bung*.'

Mithras Periwinkle scowled at his clerk. 'That, Shrug, is not a term the court will recognise.'

'*Sniff.* It's true, though.'

11

'You mean a *bribe*?' said Wren. 'Where would we get the money for a bribe?'

'Money? Money would be of no consequence in this matter,' said Mithras Periwinkle. 'Not with a charge of such gravity as this. To ensure a satisfactory outcome to this case you would need to offer something considerably more valuable than mere currency.'

'Such as?' said Mel.

'Mmmm. This requires serious thought.' The barrister stroked his chin in a dramatic manner. Shrug got to his feet, opened a casebook and flicked through it. He ran his finger down a page and showed his finding to the barrister. Mithras Periwinkle looked up. 'Thank you, Shrug. After careful consideration, I estimate that the only thing, the *only* thing, that could possibly swing the trial in your favour would be the fruit of the mirrortree.'

'What's that?' asked Ludo.

'Where is this mirrortree?' said Wren.

'How can we get it anyway?' said Mel. 'We're stuck here in chokey.'

'Alas, dear clients,' said Mithras Periwinkle with a shrug, 'answers have I none.'

'He means *it's not our job*,' sniffed Shrug, shutting the book.

'I regret to say that my clerk is right,' said the lawyer. 'I deal in legal legerdemain. Horticulture, geography and procurement are outside my domain. I will leave you to ponder on this. Fear not, though. You are in the capable, the competent, nay the *accomplished* hands of Mithras Periwinkle, barrister at law.' He put a hand into his long legal robe, pulled out a small notebook and made a tick against an entry there. 'I bid you, for now, dear clients, a fond fare-thee-well.'

'He means *goodbye*,' said Shrug with a parting sniff.

So saying, Mithras Periwinkle, with a theatrical swirl of his robe, and Shrug, staggering beneath his pile of books, left. The door was locked after them.

Locktight's face appeared in the little window. He looked at the friends and scoffed. 'Find the mirrortree? Never in a million years.'

'Why do you say that?' asked Mel.

'In the first place, no one's ever escaped from Deep Trouble.'

'And?'

'In the second place, this mirrortree doesn't exist. We'll be seeing a lot of each other over the coming years. Ever such a lot.' The cruel smile beneath his mask widened. Locktight's laughter faded as he walked away until it was indiscernible from the anguished cries of the other inmates.

The Prisoners of the Clinch

The sky gradually paled and the sun heaved itself over the jagged blue peaks of the mountains of Herm, washing the topmost pinnacle of the House of Mysteries, the tallest building in the city of Vlam, in its butterscotch glow. Inch by inch, the light crept its way downwards until the highest spires of the House of Spirits and the House of Thrones were similarly touched by its diurnal blush. As it continued on down it animated intricate stonework with shadows and light, announcing the new morning to the lower city.

In a quarter that boasted the grandest houses and most splendid squares, the sunlight spilled across brightly tiled and frost-kissed rooftops, sending exploratory beams into the dormitory that contained the sleeping forms of the apprentices to the Seven Kingdoms' most famous artist, Ambrosius Blenk. One by one the boys stirred in response to the dawn's silent music. They rose, dressed and made their way to the refectory for breakfast. They had expected to find Mel and Ludo already there,

15

their beds being empty. When Bex, the head apprentice, sent one boy to knock on the door to Wren's room, he reported back that she too appeared to have risen early.

As the sun rose inexorably higher, it eventually seeped down to light the seven bridges that spanned the Farn. They were so overflowing with shops and inns that people crossing them were often unaware that they were on bridges at all. Clinging to one of the piers of the westernmost bridge like a giant nesting box hung the towered and turreted Clinch, Vlam's prison. It was connected to the bank by a drawbridge above the dark, soupy waters of the river.

As the members of the Day Watch, resplendent in their white-plumed helmets, arrived at the prison to relieve the black-plumed Night Watch, the sergeant in charge inspected the list of prisoners, including those that had been apprehended during the hours of darkness. The moustachioed officer of the law was surprised to see the names of three children on the list.

'What's this?' he asked the Sergeant of the Night, pointing to the entry in the ledger.

'Vandals,' replied the other.

'What kind of vandalism gets children thrown in the Clinch?'

The Sergeant of the Night cupped his hand and whispered into the other's ear.

'They did *what*?' exploded the Sergeant of the Day.

The Sergeant of the Night, blushing deep red with embarrassment, repeated his whisper.

Speechless and sporting his own high colour, the Sergeant of the Day went at once to inspect the perpetrators of this outrage. When he peered into the gloomy cell through the little barred window in the door he was taken aback. 'But . . . but these aren't street urchins. The deep blue doublets, the white silk hose – they're Ambrosius Blenk's apprentices. It's the most famous livery in Vlam.'

'It doesn't alter what they did,' said the Sergeant of the Night. 'They were caught red-handed. If we hadn't apprehended them when we did, there's no telling what Vlam would be waking up to this morning. Revolutions have been started for less.'

Two pairs of Sergeants' eyes stared into the cell in disbelief.

'What're you staring at, Goggle-Eyes?' shouted Wren.

'Yeah. Bog off. This isn't a zoo,' bawled Ludo.

A well-aimed and nearly full water jug shattered against the bars, drenching the Sergeants and peppering them with earthenware shrapnel. 'Bullseye!' cawed Mel. The eyes withdrew, leaving a trail of expletives in their wake.

After a while Ludo said, 'Are they gone?'

'Yeah,' said Wren. 'Crawled back under their stone, I expect.' They both looked at Mel. 'What now?'

'We've got to get out of here,' said Mel. 'If you two hadn't stopped to decorate that wall we wouldn't be banged up like this.'

'Couldn't resist it,' said Ludo. 'Call it an artistic urge.'

'*Huh*,' scoffed Wren. 'It didn't even look like the king.'

'Did too,' countered Ludo. 'And the pig was perfect – right down to every last anatomical detail.' He sniggered. 'Anyway, you helped.'

'Shut your gobs, both of you,' said Mel. 'You've just

cost us more time. We've got something important to do. Or have you forgotten?'

'Of course I haven't forgotten,' said Wren. 'Ludo's the one lacking brain cells, not me.'

'Scrot to you, little Miss Perfect,' said Ludo.

'But *why* do we have to find it?' whined Wren.

'We just do, that's all,' said Mel. 'So shut the skeg up! You two can fight each other later. I'll even hold your doublets. Right now we need to escape.'

'Yeah, yeah, yeah,' said Ludo, narrowing his eyes at Wren. 'What do you propose we do? Overpower the guards?'

'Get real,' said Wren, sneering back at Ludo.

'I'm the creative one around here,' said Mel. 'Just put a bung in your gobs and let me think.' He paced to the corner of the cell and sat down on a pile of old rags.

The rags spoke. 'What's it worth if I tell you how to get out of here?'

Mel jumped up as if scalded. Ludo and Wren rushed to his side, their fists clenched. The three began kicking the rags.

'Whoa. Hold your horses,' said a man's voice from inside the rags. 'Whoa. There's a body in here. *Ouch!*'

The kicking ceased.

'What're you doing here?' said Mel.

'Three guesses,' said the man. 'Or have they turned the Clinch into a luxury hotel while I've been sleeping?' The rags turned out to be the man's clothes and his sneering smile displayed a parade of broken and discoloured teeth. He got to his feet, rubbing his bruises.

'Who are you?' asked Ludo.

'People call me Scratchbeard,' said the man, unconsciously demonstrating how he earned the epithet.

'Just the beard?' said Wren, turning up her nose at the malodorous prisoner.

'In my line of work it pays to look pathetic,' said Scratchbeard. 'No one coughs up for a healthy-looking beggar.'

'You don't get thrown in the Clinch just for begging,' said Mel.

'There're no flies on you, are there, Shrimp?' said

Scratchbeard as a couple of his own escaped his rags. 'I've diversified. I'm now what you might call a *beggar-stroke-cutpurse*. It allows for a certain amount of give and take. Either people give it to me – or I take it.'

'You're not a very good cutpurse if you got caught,' observed Ludo.

Scratchbeard scowled and spat on the floor. 'You're not exactly the cream of the underworld yourselves. In case you've missed it, you're in the Clinch too.'

'We're not part of your sordid underworld,' said Wren self-importantly. 'We're on a *mission*.'

'Wren!' said Mel in a warning tone.

'What?' said Scratchbeard. The eye not covered by his black patch took on a cunning glow. 'What kind of a mission?'

'Nothing,' said Wren, looking away.

Mel quickly changed the subject. 'So, how *do* we get out of here?'

'What's it worth?' said Scratchbeard, still looking at Wren with an appraising, one-eyed stare.

'We haven't got anything,' said Ludo. 'They took it all when they booked us in.'

Scratchbeard tore his gaze off Wren and reached out a filthy hand to stroke Ludo's blue velvet doublet. 'I can see who you are. There's only one person in Vlam rich enough to dress his apprentices in such pretty duds. Your master got any nice stuff in his mansion?'

Ludo knocked the hand down and backed away from Scratchbeard's bad breath. 'Yeah, tons.'

'Such as?'

'Paintings and things,' said Wren. 'They're very valuable.'

'But not very portable,' said Scratchbeard. 'Has he got anything more *convertible*?'

'Like gold and jewels?' said Mel. 'Yeah, of course he has. But it's all locked away.'

'But I bet you know where it is,' said Scratchbeard. 'I bet you could get me into the mansion and show me where it is.'

A sly smile spread across Mel's face. 'And in return, you'll show us how to get out of here?'

'That's the deal, Shrimp. Take it or leave it.' Scratchbeard went back to his corner of the cell and sat down on the floor.

The three friends huddled together. 'What do you think?' whispered Wren.

'Old Blenko's crying out to be robbed,' said Ludo equally softly. 'It'll serve him right for being so rich. But if we have to take Stinky back to the mansion it'll delay us all the more.'

'No one's going to be taking anyone back to the mansion,' whispered Mel. 'We'll string him along. Then, as soon as we get out of the Clinch, we'll lose him and get on with what we've got to do.'

The three shared a conspiratorial smile. Mel turned and said in a normal tone, 'All right, Thatchbeard. You've got a deal. Now, how do we get out of here?'

Scratchbeard smiled a mocking smile. 'I'd tell you but it's above your heads.'

'Who're you calling stupid?' said Ludo as his face flushed with anger. Mel put out an arm to hold him back.

'You really are as dim as you look,' said Scratchbeard. 'I said "It's above your *heads*".' He looked up and the friends' eyes followed. In the centre of the ceiling was a small circular grille covering a ventilation shaft. 'The

Clinch was built to hold adults, not minnows like you. I bet Shrimp there could wiggle into that shaft and find his way outside and unlock the cell door.'

'Stop calling me a shrimp,' said a ruffled Mel. 'I'm big enough to spoil your day any time I choose.'

'But not right now, Shrimp, eh? You'll need to stand on my shoulders to get to that grille. Here, use my shiv.' He produced a home-made knife from inside his rags. 'If you weren't so green, you'd know how to hide things from the Watch.'

After an hour's work the iron grille came away from the crumbly mortar and Mel was able to haul himself into the shaft. It was a tight fit, even for someone as small as he was, but he caterpillar-wriggled along until he was looking down through another grille on to the empty room that housed the winch used to raise and lower the drawbridge. Some more work with the shiv and that grille too was removed and Mel dropped down into the room. The Day Watch were out patrolling the city and only the gaoler and his assistant were left in the little room adjacent to the winch. They were more intent on their game of cards than the possibility that an inmate was on the loose. While they were engrossed in their game Mel was able to silently snag a bunch of keys from their hook on the wall and to make his way back to the cell.

'You took your time,' complained Wren as soon as the door was opened.

'You can leave by the shaft,' said Mel. 'See how much you like it.'

'She'd never make it. She's much too fat,' said Ludo.

'Just keep it up,' warned Wren. 'Just keep it up.'

'Do you want to stay here and fight each other or would you rather escape?' asked Scratchbeard. He turned to Mel. 'Anyone about?'

'Just the gaoler and his mate.'

'That's what I figured,' said Scratchbeard. 'Your job's only half done, Shrimp. Now we need to lower the drawbridge. Did you spot the winch?'

'It's right next door to the gaoler's room,' said Mel as he led them out into the corridor. 'But we'll need a diversion, otherwise they'll see us. And don't call me "Shrimp".'

'Let's burn the place down,' said Ludo, reaching up

25

and grabbing a torch from a bracket on the wall. 'We'll start *here*.' He touched the flaming brand to Scratchbeard's ragged cloak and it caught fire immediately.

'*Hey!*' Scratchbeard whipped off his greasy cloak and beat his hands against his smouldering tunic.

'Oops. Sorry. *Accident*,' said Ludo with a wicked smile.

'What're you complaining about, Snatchbeard,' said Wren, nodding towards the still-blazing cloak on the floor. 'We've got our diversion.'

'*Fire!*' shouted Mel as white smoke began to billow. '*Fire!*' He quickly led them into a side corridor. They saw the gaoler and his assistant dash past their hiding place carrying water buckets. Then they slipped out and ran towards the winch room.

As they arrived Scratchbeard disappeared into the gaoler's room. He emerged holding a pair of handcuffs. Before Mel could react, he found himself cuffed to the beggar. Scratchbeard made a show of placing the small key into his mouth and swallowing. 'I know what you plan to do. You and me's going to be like joined twins

– at least until Mother Nature returns the key.' He smiled his broken-toothed smile. 'And I'll take that,' he said, whipping his shiv from Mel's belt. 'Just in case you have any more *accidents* planned.'

He dragged Mel to the winch room and swung a lever. There was a jarring squeal followed by a machine-gun *clank-clank-clank* as the ratchet released, and then a reverberating *thump* as the drawbridge crashed down on to the wharf. Ludo and Wren ran out over the bridge, followed by Scratchbeard and Mel. As they hurried off the wharf towards the maze of narrow streets that comprised the riverside district of Vlam the Clinch's alarm bell began to toll.

Deep Trouble

'Scrot,' swore Ludo after the friends had checked the small cell for any window or ventilation shaft. 'Locktight was telling the truth. I doubt if anyone's ever escaped from here. The only way out is through that very thick, and very locked, door.'

'I don't know about either of you two,' said Wren, 'but I'd feel better if I wasn't wearing my nightclothes. Let's get changed.'

As soon as he was dressed Mel felt in the inside pocket of his doublet and was relieved to find that his most precious possession was still there and intact. His quill made from an angel's feather shone with its own inner light and seemed to signal hope in the dingy cell.

'Listen!' said Wren. 'What was that? It sounded like tapping.'

'I heard it too,' said Mel. He tucked his quill back into his doublet as he crossed to the other side of the cell and put his ear to the wall. 'It's coming from here.'

Ludo and Wren joined him.

'What do you think it is?' asked Ludo.

'Perhaps it's someone in the next cell trying to communicate,' said Mel. 'You know. One tap for A, two for B and so on.'

'Let's answer him,' said Wren.

Ludo took off his boot and used the heel to tap several times. The other tapping stopped. 'What shall I say? I know.' He beat out eight taps followed by five taps followed by twelve and twelve and fifteen. H-E-L-L-O. There was silence so Ludo tapped it out again.

This time there was an answer. C-H-I-G-N-O-G.

'*Chignog?*' said Wren, baffled. 'What's that supposed to mean?'

'Maybe we counted wrong,' said Mel.

Ludo tapped out W-H-A-T.

S-P-A-G came the reply.

'Do you think it's another language?' said Wren.

'Or perhaps it's code,' said Mel.

'Maybe he can't spell,' said Ludo. 'I'll try again.' H-E-L-L-O.

G-U-R-B.

'*Gurb?*' Mel was nonplussed. 'This is getting us nowhere.'

As the friends listened the tapping got louder and more insistent. They counted twenty-nine taps.

'Now he's making fun of us. Do you think he's –'

Wren never finished her question. There was an extra loud tap and a hole appeared in the mortar between the stones in the cell wall. The pointed end of a slim chisel poked through. The chisel was wiggled and pulled back, the tapping recommenced and soon all of the mortar around a stone had been chipped away. With a scraping sound the loosened stone was pushed through into their cell. The three friends peered into the hole. A dusty face was looking back at them out of the darkness.

'Chignog,' said Ludo.

'*What?*' said the face with a wrinkled, uncomprehending brow.

'Spag. Gurb,' said Ludo.

'Do any of you idiots speak Nemish,' said the face, 'or have I tunnelled into a madhouse?'

'But you were . . .' Ludo closed his mouth and

looked at his friends as it dawned on him that they had been listening to random tapping, not code.

'Help me shift a few more of these stones,' said the face. 'They're really, really heavy.'

A little while later the hole was big enough for the face, and the body attached to the end of it, to crawl through. It was a figment girl a few years older than Wren. She had cropped fair hair decorated with crumbs of rubble and a very pale complexion with dark circles beneath her large, blue eyes. She stood up and stretched before dusting stone dust from her striped prison clothes. 'Nice cell,' she said with evident admiration. 'It's much bigger than mine. And you've got fresh straw too. A swanky four-star if ever I saw one. I bet it's the show-cell they print in the prospectus. You must be really, really important prisoners.'

'Never mind about us,' said Mel. 'Who're *you*?'

'My name's Prisoner 24-72149 – but my friends call me Twenty-Four.'

'What're you doing in Deep Trouble?' asked Wren. Twenty-Four rolled her eyes and gestured at her clothes. 'What a stupid question. I'm a prisoner, just like you.'

'We mean, "What did you do to get in here?"' said Mel.

'Exams.'

'You got put in here for doing exams?' said Wren. 'Did you get caught cheating or something?'

Twenty-Four looked hurt. 'Of course I didn't cheat. I *passed* my exams to get in here. I'm studying to be a professional convict. Right now I'm in the middle of my C-levels. There's just my tunnelling and informing modules to complete.'

Ludo said, 'So that tunnel was just –'

'Coursework,' said Twenty-Four. 'Everyone has to do it.'

Mel's face lit up. 'Everyone? So there must be lots of tunnels.'

Twenty-Four shrugged. 'Yes, lots of them.'

'All over Deep Trouble,' added Mel.

'Sure to be,' said Twenty-Four, 'what with the number of prisoners in here. It's a very big campus.'

'Great,' said Mel. 'We can use them to escape.'

'Escape?' Twenty-Four looked confused. 'You've probably got the nicest cell in Deep Trouble. Why would you want to escape?'

'And you thought *we* were mad,' said Wren. 'Isn't that what prisoners are meant to do?'

'Help us to escape and we'll take you with us,' offered Ludo.

'I've studied a long time to get where I am now,' said Twenty-Four. 'You're really, really asking me to throw it all away when I'm so close to graduating?'

'So you won't help us,' said Ludo.

Twenty-Four smiled apologetically.

'Just a mo,' said Mel, narrowing his eyes suspiciously. 'You mentioned informing?'

'That's easy,' said Twenty-Four. 'All I have to do is to inform on someone who's trying to –' She shut her mouth quickly.

'Escape?' offered Ludo.

Twenty-Four clamped her mouth shut even tighter.

'Look,' said Mel. 'If you help us to escape –'

'And keep quiet about it,' interrupted Wren.

'– you can have our cell.'

Twenty-Four's face brightened. 'Really, *really*?'

The friends nodded.

Her face darkened again as uncertainty gripped her. 'I don't know.'

'Twenty-Four,' said Mel. 'Why do you suppose you have to study tunnelling?'

'Because it's on the curriculum, of course.'

'But why's it on the curriculum in the first place?' asked Wren. 'Why would a prisoner need to know about tunnelling?'

'So they can know all about . . .?' Twenty-Four's face creased in concentration.

'Escaping?' prompted Ludo.

'I . . . I suppose so,' said Twenty-Four hesitantly.

'So how many other student convicts will know what it *really* feels like to escape?' said Mel.

'You'd have a head start on the others sitting the exam,' said Wren.

Twenty-Four slowly smiled. 'Yes. Yes, I would. OK, I'll help you to escape – just to see what it's like. But . . .' she hesitated. 'Deep Trouble's escape-proof.'

'That's only because no one's done it before,' said

Wren. 'There's a first time for everything.'

'Right,' said Ludo, rubbing his hands. 'Let's get cracking.'

'Not now,' said Twenty-Four. 'I've got to go or I'll be late for Inf–' She shut her mouth tight.

'Look,' said Mel. 'If you inform on us then we won't be able to escape.'

'And if we don't escape . . .' said Ludo.

'. . . you can't have our cell,' finished Wren.

Twenty-Four looked very uncomfortable.

'Couldn't you make something up to use in Informing?' suggested Mel.

A smile dawned on Twenty-Four's face. 'You mean *lie*?'

The three friends nodded.

'I did get an A-plus for duplicity,' said the figment. 'I came top of the class.'

'Then it'll be a doddle,' said Mel.

'But I've still got to go,' said Twenty-Four as she began to climb into the hole. 'Put the stones into place again and I'll come back for you after my tutorial.' She took a last look around her.

'Really, *really* nice cell.' And she was gone.

The friends replaced the stones and then sat down on the floor with their back to them just in case Locktight looked in through the little window.

'Do you think Twenty-Four will come back for us?' said Wren.

'It's a cert,' said Ludo. 'Did you see the expression on her face when we offered her the cell?'

'But she did get that A-plus for duplicity,' said Mel.

After what seemed like an age, the stones popped back into their cell and Twenty-Four's voice called from the darkness behind, 'Come on then, if you're coming.'

Wren, then Ludo and Mel crawled into the tunnel and followed Twenty-Four as she retreated before them with a small lantern. The tunnel was surprisingly complicated and parts were obviously the work of many prisoners before Twenty-Four. They came to several T-junctions, which their guide navigated them through, until an irregular rectangle of flickering yellow light ahead signalled their destination.

But as Mel climbed from the tunnel after his friends his heart sank.

'Which part of "No one's ever escaped from Deep Trouble" didn't you understand?' smirked Locktight, standing next to Twenty-Four. 'It seems that our four-star cell was not to your liking, so this will be your home from now on. It comes without gruel.'

Mel looked at Twenty-Four. 'How could you? We trusted you.'

Twenty-Four stared at her feet, looking awkward.

'Amazing what the promise of a higher grade can do,' said Locktight, releasing Wren and Ludo.

'Sorry,' said Twenty-Four. 'But I really, *really* needed an A-plus grade for informing – to make up for my C-minus in mailbag sewing. And Professor Locktight promised me your old cell if I led you here.'

'And what are you going to do with all these high grades?' asked Wren.

'Once I've passed all my exams I'll be a professional prisoner.'

'But you're a prisoner now,' said Ludo.

'There's more to life than Deep Trouble,' said Mel.

'That's enough of that kind of talk,' scowled Locktight. 'We don't like trouble-makers in here. Upsetting things, rocking the boat, spreading *ideas*.' He said the last word as if it were the worst possible crime. 'Any more of that kind of thing and you'll be out of here and into a two-star cell.' He raised his voice. 'Smirk! Snag! More work for you in here.'

A couple of under-gaolers came in and cemented the loose blocks back into place. As he was leaving with Twenty-Four Locktight said, 'You may have lost your four-star cell but it's not all bad news. Someone's sent you a food parcel.' Another under-gaoler came in and placed a large cardboard box on the floor. The door was slammed and the friends heard five heavy locks being turned.

Their new cell was even smaller than the last one. The straw was filthy and the light much dimmer than before. Mel tried to loosen the freshly cemented blocks but they had been fixed with quick-drying mortar. Disheartened, the friends sat down on the cold, hard floor.

'At least we won't go hungry,' said Ludo as he opened the box.

'But who could've sent us food?' said Wren. 'No one knows we're in here.'

'There's a note inside,' said Mel.

Attached to a decorative ribbon around the large fruit cake was a folded slip of paper. It read:

We always knew you three couldn't keep out of trouble for long. Now it looks like you're in Deep Trouble. We thought you could use a piece of cake. It will make your stay seem less long. Write when you get the chance. ThINKing of you.

Love, Goldie and Pilfer.

Mel, Ludo and Wren beamed at each other, reassured that their friends, the golden fairground girl and the reformed invisible robber, would not let them rot in Deep Trouble. They each broke off a chunk of cake and began eating.

'Not bad,' said Wren. 'Good old Goldie.'

'You know,' said Mel, 'I think that message is a kind of code.'

'Like in "piece of cake"?' said Ludo.

'I suppose it's too much to hope that there's a file hidden in there,' said Mel.

Ludo finished his first handful of cake and grabbed

a second. His eyes opened wide in amazement. 'Actually, there is.'

They sat there, looking at the corner of a cardboard folder that peeked out from the heart of the cake. Mel pulled it out and brushed off the moist crumbs. He opened the file and inside was a blank sheet of parchment with small holes around the edge where it had once been attached to something.

'Is that what I think it is?' said Wren.

'I bet it is,' said Ludo.

Mel looked from the parchment to his friends. 'It's *Cogito*. The thinking machine from the Hollow World. Look how they've written *"ThINKing of you"*. I bet there's some ink in there as well.'

Wren and Ludo demolished the remains of the cake and found a small phial of ink with a screw-top lid.

Mel smiled. 'We can ask Cogito how to get out of here. He knows everything.'

'And we can ask him how to find the mirrortree, too,' said Wren.

'Yeah,' added Ludo. 'I bet Locktight was lying when he said it doesn't exist. Just to make us feel bad. Cogito will know how to find it.'

Mel charged his quill with ink and wrote on the parchment in his neatest handwriting *Hello, Cogito. How are you?* He took extra care with his punctuation without which he knew Cogito would not respond. The friends watched as Mel's writing faded and vanished, to be replaced by the elegant, flowing script of Cogito's answer.

I'm always well. But thanks for asking. After a moment the writing vanished.

We need to escape. Can you help us? wrote Mel.

Where are you?

We're in deep trouble.

That's a condition, not a location.

'You forgot to write capital letters,' said Wren. 'You know how pernickety he is.'

In reply to Mel's corrected version Cogito wrote, *It's said that it's impossible to escape from Deep Trouble.*

We know, wrote Mel. *But we thought that if there was a way out of here, then you would know it. Do you?*

Mel's question faded and Cogito's answer flowed on to the parchment. *Deep Trouble is riddled with tunnels.*

41

They're part of the students' curriculum.

Mel explained about what had happened.

In that case, you can escape through the ventilation shafts. Where exactly are you in Deep Trouble?

In a cell.

Which cell?

We don't know.

Describe it to me.

It's got walls, floor, straw, door, locks. Mel felt inadequate.

I need more information. And you *need a conjunction between 'door' and 'locks'.*

'It's just a cell,' said Ludo.

'No,' said Mel. 'We know more than that. It must be a three-star cell. The first one was a four star.'

'And Locktight said if we didn't behave we'd be demoted to a two star,' added Wren.

'I counted five locks,' said Ludo.

Mel conveyed all this in a well-punctuated and grammatical sentence to Cogito.

It could be one of hundreds, replied Cogito. *Each cell in Deep Trouble is unique. Please explain what's different about yours.*

'How would we know?' said Ludo.

'There is one way,' said Mel. He drew a sketch of their cell, taking especial care to get every detail right. He even made some enlargements of the pointing between the stones and some of the graffiti carved into the door.

That's better, a picture really is worth a thousand words. It looks very much like you're in cell B774539. Tunnel down vertically and you'll find a ventilation shaft. Once you get there make contact again and I'll tell you what to do next. Right now I have to go off-line.

Wait, wrote Mel. *Do you know how to find the mirrortree?*

The mirrortree is supposed not to exist.

But does it?

That's an interesting philosophical question. If we had more time – and you had a plentiful supply of ink – we might get to the bottom of it.

So it does exist?

The parchment was blank for quite a long time and Mel was sure Cogito had gone off-line before his answer appeared.

It could.

So where should we start looking?

I need to think about that. But are you not forgetting that you first need to escape? Now I really must go off-line.

Don't go, wrote Mel quickly. *We haven't any way of making a tunnel.*

But this time the parchment remained blank.

'Now what?' said Ludo.

'I guess we'll just have to wait until Cogito's finished his nap,' said Wren.

'We can't leave everything to Cogito,' said Mel. He leant back against the wall. 'That's funny. I can feel a vibration.' Mel placed his ear and his hands flat against the cell wall. 'It's like a tapping.'

'Not again,' said Wren, joining him. 'It can't be Twenty-Four.'

'That *traitor*,' spat Ludo.

'It's getting closer,' said Mel.

A short while later another chisel-point broke through. The stone was loosened and pushed into the cell. As the friends peered in they saw Twenty-Four's sad face staring back.

'You've got a nerve,' said Ludo. 'Have you come back to gloat?'

'I came back to say I'm sorry,' said Twenty-Four from the new tunnel. 'Really, *really* sorry.'

'Why are you coming from that direction?' said Wren. 'Our old cell's the other way.'

'I'm not in your old cell. Professor Locktight was lying. He demoted me to a two star for consorting with escapees. It's horrible.' She shuddered. 'Look, what you said about getting out of here.'

'You want to escape now?' said Mel.

'No, but I'll help you to escape. Just to get back at Professor Locktight,' said Twenty-Four as she climbed into the cell. 'I want to teach *him* a lesson.'

'Don't trust her,' said Ludo. 'It's another trap.'

'I said I'm sorry.'

'I think she means it,' said Wren. Then to Twenty-Four. '*Do* you mean it?'

'Yes. Look, take my hammer and chisel.'

'We've been here before,' said Ludo cynically. 'And look where it got us.'

'But this time it'll be different,' said Twenty-Four. 'You'll see.'

'All right,' said Mel.

45

'But you stay where we can keep an eye on you,' said Ludo.

Twenty-Four smiled meekly and handed Mel her hammer and chisel. He set to work at once on the mortar of the flagstone floor. One advantage of a three-star cell was that the mortar was older and weaker than that of a four star and, after an hour or two's hard work between the four of them, they broke though into the ventilation shaft, and one by one they dropped down.

The stone-lined shaft was about twice their height and completely circular. One way was light – the flickering yellow light of Deep Trouble – and the other, dark. A strong current of air was blowing from out of the darkness, causing Wren's long, auburn hair to stream out. Twenty-Four, who had never been outside of a cell or a tunnel, was clearly feeling intimidated by the long, seemingly endless space.

Mel pulled the parchment from inside his doublet and wrote, *Cogito? Are you there?* Fascinated, Twenty-Four gazed over his shoulder and gasped with amazement when Cogito answered.

Yes. I'm here. Where are you?

Mel penned an explanation then added, *Where do we go now?*

What you need is a map. A complicated tangle of lines, like a plateful of spaghetti, drew themselves on to the parchment. Then a cross appeared and the words *You are here.*

As Mel was studying the map the wind in the shaft changed direction. It now blew into the darkness.

'The map doesn't tell us which way is out,' said Ludo.

'Well, it can't be that way,' said Wren, pointing towards the light. 'That way leads us back into Deep Trouble.'

'So that means it must be that way,' said Twenty-Four, staring into the dark. She swallowed hard.

Mel took the lead and parted the darkness with his glowing angel's feather. They made their way deeper into the twisting maze of shafts, stopping when the way branched to consult Cogito's map. All the while the roaring of the wind grew louder. Eventually they saw two winking lights ahead.

When they reached them, the lights turned out to

be coming from two huge and grotesque faces that were carved into the wall of the shaft. Their cheeks were made from articulated and overlapping plates, like armadillo shells, that expanded and contracted as they alternately breathed in and breathed out. The light was coming from inside their mouths.

'Which way now?' shouted Ludo over the roaring wind. He clung on to the others to stop himself being blown away.

'This is as far as the map goes,' yelled Mel as he struggled to hold the flapping sheet open in the strong air current. 'All the other shafts will lead us back into Deep Trouble.'

'Does that mean we're lost?' asked Twenty-Four, cowering at the back of the group.

'No. I think we've arrived,' shouted Wren. 'Look.'

The map became paler and paler until the parchment was blank once more.

'It must mean we're there,' said Mel. 'I think we have to climb inside one of these mouths.'

As the right-hand face began its sucking cycle Mel stepped forwards and was quickly drawn into its mouth. One by one, and choosing their moment, the others followed.

It was cramped inside, most of the space being taken up by a tangle of fat pipes and valves. Some had hemispherical lights attached to them. There were also row upon row of giant bellows that rose and fell in synchronised waves.

'I know where we are,' said Twenty-Four.

'I thought you'd been locked up all your life,' said Ludo. Then, to the others, 'Don't trust her.'

'No,' said Twenty-Four. 'I do. I really, really do.'

'Go on,' urged Wren.

'I've never actually been here but I saw this place in an engraving in a text book. Then, later, we had a test with the question "Deep Trouble is escape-proof; discuss". I remembered the picture and wrote in my answer that the pipes in here seemed fat enough to hold a person and –'

'That's it!' exclaimed Mel.

'No it's not,' said Twenty-Four with a sigh. 'Professor Locktight failed me. He said that ideas as stupid as that earned students a one-way ticket to a one-star cell.'

'No, Twenty-Four,' said Wren. 'Don't you see? It's not stupid. It's brilliant! Really, *really* brilliant.'

'It is?' Twenty-Four's face was a picture of confusion.

'He failed you because it *would* work,' said Mel. 'You've worked out what's probably the only way out of Deep Trouble.'

'I have?'

Mel nodded. 'So, tell us how your plan worked.'

After they had listened to Twenty-Four's explanation they began searching for two adjacent inspection hatches set into the T-junction of a fat pipe.

'Here they are,' called Ludo. One was marked 'Inspiration' and the other 'Expiration'. Together, the friends unscrewed and lifted off the latter.

'Are you sure you won't come with us?' said Wren.

Twenty-Four shook her head. 'Deep Trouble's all I know. And with all this escaping experience I'm now bound to get a good grade.'

'But what about Locktight?' said Wren.

Twenty-Four smiled. 'Don't worry about me. He'll never know I helped you. Don't forget I came top of the class in duplicity. Besides, I'm dying to see the look on his face when he learns that you've escaped. I'll get back through the "Inspiration" hatch. If my grades are as good as I hope I might even get your old cell for real this time.'

'Thanks, Twenty-Four. We couldn't have done this without you.' Mel sat on the pipe and lowered his legs into the strong wind blowing inside the hatch. 'Well, here goes. See you on the outside.' He pushed off and was instantly sucked away.

'Thanks,' said Ludo. 'I'm sorry I thought . . . you know. You're all right.' Ludo disappeared into the pipe after Mel.

'Goodbye, Twenty-Four,' said Wren. 'I hope you pass your exams and everything turns out well for you.' She followed her friends.

'Oh, I almost forgot,' shouted Twenty-Four into the open hatch. 'Look out for the firedrakes! They're dangerous. Really, *really* dangerous.'

The Crippled Toad

The narrow streets of Vlam were crowded with people jostling each other but they readily parted as Scratchbeard and his three unwilling companions hurried through. If anyone made any connection between the beggar, the handcuffs, the richly dressed youngsters and the Clinch's tolling alarm bell they knew better than to show it.

Neither Mel nor Wren nor Ludo knew where they were in the disreputable riverside quarter. No one from the better parts of the city ever ventured there out of choice. But Scratchbeard evidently knew exactly where he was and he led them ever deeper into a maze of steep alleys lined with pawnbrokers, rag-and-bone merchants and murky shop fronts that displayed stolen articles so worthless that even the most disreputable of fences had rejected them. When he came to a low doorway that gave on to a descending flight of uneven stairs, Scratchbeard pushed Wren and Ludo down into the darkness and pulled Mel after him. Above the doorway, dangling drunkenly from one corner, hung the peeling sign of the Crippled Toad.

The dismal ale-house smelt of acrid tobacco smoke, stale beer and unwashed bodies. The only light came from a narrow strip of grimy windows near the ceiling, augmented by one or two smoking oil lamps. A paltry fire smouldered in a dirty grate, adding more smoke than heat to the already fetid atmosphere. Small, unidentifiable animals scampered about on the low beams overhead.

'Give me a drink, Mange,' shouted Scratchbeard as he approached the bar. 'My mouth's dryer than a mummy's shroud.'

The barman slammed a battered tankard of ale in front of Scratchbeard, spilling some of the short measure on the puddle-strewn counter. 'Your credit's being stretched mighty thin these days, Scratchbeard. When are you going to settle your tab?'

Scratchbeard drained the tankard with one long pull and belched. 'Very soon now, Mange.' He cocked his head at Mel and his companions and winked at the barman. 'Very soon. The Doc in?'

By way of an answer Mange nodded towards the darkest corner of the inn.

Scratchbeard increased his tab by the price of another tankard of the scummy ale and dragged it and Mel into the gloom. Ludo and Wren followed.

'Who've you got there, Scratchbeard?' asked a shadowy figure seated at a table. The shadow blew a string of blue-grey smoke rings from a clay pipe into the light of the oil lamp that rested on the scarred tabletop.

'Business, Doc. Just business.'

'Anything in it for me?' The shadow leant forwards into the light. He was a large man with greasy, black hair that hung in long ringlets about a plump, dark face that was topped with a dirty turban, middled with a bulbous nose and tailed with a ratty goatee beard. He wore a threadbare brocade coat with matted fur trim around the collar and cuffs and a superabundance of oversized and clearly fake jewellery. As he leant forwards his coat fell open, revealing dozens of small pockets covering the inside lining. There were more on his gaudy waistcoat. From each protruded the tops of ornate phials and bottles. He smelt of cheap perfume that was almost worse than the foul atmosphere in the cellar.

'Happens there is,' Scratchbeard replied. 'I got something planned could use an extra pair of hands.'

The Doc's glittering eyes took in the children's deep blue velvet doublets with an appraising glance. 'That'll be the Blenk mansion?'

'For starters, Doc,' smiled Scratchbeard. 'But I think these three might have something bigger planned. A *mission*.'

Mel, Ludo and Wren exchanged glances.

'A mission, you say,' said the man. 'In that case, you'd better introduce us.'

Scratchbeard tugged on the handcuffs, pulling Mel close to the table. 'This is the Shrimp.' He nodded towards Wren and Ludo. 'They're Missy Perfect and Smoky Joe, the fire-raiser.'

Mel said through gritted teeth, 'Don't call me a shrimp.'

'Bottle it, Shrimp,' said Scratchbeard. 'Only a fool uses their real name in the Crippled Toad.'

'In that case why can't I be Viper or Shark?'

'And I want to be Tiger,' said Ludo.

'I rather like Missy Perfect,' simpered Wren. 'It suits me.'

'He's joking,' said Ludo.

'Shut it!' spat Scratchbeard. 'All of you. You'll take what you're given and like it.'

'So what's he call himself?' said Mel, looking at the greasy man.

'That there's Doctor Sarcophagus,' said Scratchbeard.

'If he's a doctor, then I'm the King of Nem,' said Mel.

The doctor smiled a greeting, displaying several gold teeth a richer shade of yellow than those surrounding them. 'OK, Scratchbeard, that's the niceties over with. You'd better start by telling me about this Blenk job of yours.'

When Scratchbeard had finished he sat back in his chair. 'Well, what do you think?'

Doctor Sarcophagus puffed on his long clay pipe. 'Sounds like a four-hander to me. Not counting the youngsters. They'll be inside. One of them showing the way, the other two making sure we can work undisturbed. Someone like Blenk's bound to have a lot of busybody servants snooping around that mansion of his.'

At that moment the sound of a vicious argument exploded from the top of the stairs, accompanied by the barking of a dog. Then a bundle of rags tumbled down into the cellar. They contained another beggar. This one wore small, blackened glasses and carried a white stick. He got to his feet and swore at the figure that followed him down the stairs. She wore a tattered, satin ball gown with a moth-eaten bodice that pinched her ample waist and puffed out a wrinkled bosom above. Her face was lathered with thick, white make-up and her cheeks and lips were heavily and crudely rouged. To top everything off she wore a fiery ginger wig from which many strands of hair had escaped and hung, gorgon-like, about her face. A black-and-white spotted mongrel with one wooden leg hobbled down the stairs after her. The woman was drawn to the children like a moth to a flame. Up close she smelt of mice.

'Who do these little dearies belong to?' she said.

Scratchbeard raised his hand and rattled the handcuffs.

'How much?' asked the woman. 'I could use good-looking kids like these.'

'They're not for sale, Nelly,' said Scratchbeard. 'At least, not yet.'

'Pity,' said Nelly. 'They'd cripple up nicely. Get rid of those fancy clothes and the odd limb or eye and they'd earn their owner a fortune.'

'A fortune's just what I've got in mind,' said Scratchbeard. 'But a quicker one than can be made from begging.' He turned to Doctor Sarcophagus. 'What do you think, Doc? Shall we cut Nelly Buboes and Canker in on this?'

'What?' said the blind beggar, tapping his way over to them. 'I heard my name. And something about a fortune.'

'Why not,' said the doctor. 'It's always best to keep things in the family, as it were.'

The newcomers sat down and leant close. Scratchbeard repeated his plan.

* * *

Ambrosius Blenk sat in his private studio on the top floor of his mansion, a frown overshadowing his piercing blue eyes. He wore a long, embroidered robe the colour of midnight and a matching skullcap that covered his ears. He was twiddling his long grey beard round and round in the fingers of one hand. The other drummed on the carved arm of the chair. Those that knew him well took this as a sure sign the great master was agitated. There was a knock at the door.

'Come.'

Dirk Tot, dressed in the deep blue household livery, entered the room, ducking his enormously tall frame to fit through the door. His face, the left side dreadfully scarred, required little animation to contort itself into that of a fearsome monster. The master was used to this and did not need to be told that his steward was as worried by the news conveyed by the Sergeant of the Day as he was. 'No sign of them, master. Their beds had been slept in but no one has seen them since last night. How did they get out and end up in the Clinch?'

'Therein lies the mystery. It must have been them. Their descriptions matched perfectly and they were

59

dressed in my livery. But it's the vandalism that doesn't add up. Those three can certainly be wayward but I can't believe that an apprentice of mine would stoop to painting graffiti.'

'But the Sergeant said they were caught red-handed.'

The master shook his head. 'I don't care what the Sergeant said.' He tapped his nose with a long finger. 'This doesn't smell right. It doesn't smell right at all.'

'Maybe they did it for a dare – or a bet? Or perhaps they were coerced into doing it? Could they have been kidnapped and drugged? Shall I ask Green and Blue to see what they can find out?' asked Dirk Tot. 'They have contacts everywhere.'

'Please do. Something's going on and I'd dearly like to know what.'

As the great clock on the facade of the Blenk mansion struck midnight, eight dark forms, careful to keep to the inky shadows, slunk into the square as smoothly as the water flowing in the fountain that stood at the centre. The smallest shadow sniffed a lamp post and cocked a wooden leg before hobbling hurriedly to join the larger forms, which had taken up station in a doorway that boasted a good view of the gilded gates that led to the courtyard at the heart of the Blenk mansion. Their breath blew small, pale clouds in the chill night air.

Doctor Sarcophagus removed a small phial from a waistcoat pocket and dabbed a few drops of his cheap scent behind his ears. As he replaced the stopper he nodded to Nelly Buboes. 'Off you go. See what you can find out.' She detached herself from the group and returned several minutes later.

'Two watchmen inside the gates and neither of them wanted to chat to a beautiful wench.'

'They must be blind,' said Ludo, rolling his eyes.

'The mansion covers the entire block, you say?' said the doctor.

Mel nodded.

'So there'll be side doors,' said Scratchbeard.

'A couple,' said Wren. 'I'll show you. Follow me.'

'Will it be locked?' asked Canker as Doctor Sarcophagus led him after the others down a street that ran alongside the grand house.

'No,' said Mel. 'They always leave a door open so that any of Vlam's toe-rags who want to rob the place can get in.'

'Put a sock in it, Shrimp,' said Scratchbeard. 'This the door?'

'That's it,' said Wren.

'Over to you, Doc.' Scratchbeard and the others moved aside.

'Here. One of you hold this.' Ludo took the candle stump Doctor Sarcophagus proffered while Scratch-beard lit it. 'Hold it close so I can see what's needed.' The Doctor knelt and examined the heavy lock. 'Doesn't take any chances, your master. That's a Turnkey Limpet. It's a nine-lever mortise lock with a multi-spring reciprocating cylinder mechanism.'

'Can you open it, Doc?'

'Course I can, Canker. It's just a question of applying the right potion. I have one for every occasion.' The doctor opened his coat and selected a phial. 'A couple of drops of this should do the trick.' He unscrewed the silver cap and pulled out the glass pipette attached to it. As he poked it inside the keyhole and squeezed the bulb a strong smell of rotten eggs and wisps of yellow smoke snaked out. There came the sound of spring-loaded metal flying apart. When the doctor put his hand to the door it swung inwards.

'Right,' said Scratchbeard. 'Smoky and Missy, you go on ahead. If you meet any of the servants, one of you come and warn us while the other keeps them busy. And don't get any fancy ideas about making a run for it. We'll find you easy enough – and then I'll cut out your livers and feed them to Canker's mutt. Got it?'

Wren and Ludo scowled and nodded.

'Canker, you and your mutt keep watch at the door,' continued Scratchbeard. 'Any trouble, you know the signal. And you, Shrimp, will show us where your master keeps his treasure.' The thieves slipped into the mansion.

The mansion was quiet and the lamps turned down low for the night. Mel led them along corridors until they came to the grand staircase that rose to the many galleries that overlooked the main entrance hall. 'There's one of the doors to the service passages,' he said, pointing to a section of wooden panelling with a tiny keyhole just visible. 'We can go all over the mansion without being seen. You should be able to open this with some of that pong-potion.'

It was accomplished in a trice and the band entered, pulling the door closed after them. They smelt even worse in the confined space of the dark passage – especially Doctor Sarcophagus's perfume. Nelly Buboes produced a candle stump for each of them which Scratchbeard lit.

'Look,' said Mel. 'It gets very narrow further on. How about freeing me from these handcuffs?'

'Nice try, Shrimp,' said Scratchbeard. 'But you and me's staying together until this little caper's over. Now lead on.'

Mel could barely suppress his annoyance as he led them through the cramped passages and up flights of rickety stairs. After a while Scratchbeard tugged on the handcuffs, bringing their guide to a halt. 'We're passing an awful lot of doors here, Shrimp. You wouldn't be trying to lead us a dance, would you?'

'No,' said Mel. 'I want to get out of here as soon as you like. The door to the treasury's just down here.'

When Mel brought them to a halt Doctor Sarcophagus squeezed past and raised his candle. Attached to each door was a sign that indicated what lay beyond. 'The Shrimp's trying to make a fool out of us. This says "Linen Store". There's not even a lock on it.'

'Old Blenko's hardly likely to advertise where he keeps his gold now, is he?' said Mel. 'If there was a lock then all the servants who use these passages would know there's something valuable on the other side. It's fooled you easily enough.'

Nelly Buboes said, 'You'd better be telling us the truth. Otherwise your life's going to take a nasty turn for the worse. Do we understand each other?'

'Sure,' said Mel with a sneer. 'Through that door's more gold and jewels than you can carry.'

'OK,' said Scratchbeard. 'You first. And any monkey business . . .' He drew his shiv and held it to Mel's back.

As Mel lifted the latch and opened the door his candle illuminated a world made from white linen. Large bed sheets were draped on stretched clothes lines around the walls and more were neatly folded and piled on shelves. In front of them were several large wicker hampers overflowing with yet more white linen. He turned and saw the suspicious looks on the thieves' faces. 'The hampers all have false bottoms. Dig down in the linen and you'll find them.'

Scratchbeard put his shiv away and yanked Mel to one of the hampers. He began to pull out the linen. Nelly Buboes and Doctor Sarcophagus each dived into other baskets. As they were busy delving around, Mel pulled aside the doctor's coat and lifted out the silver-topped phial. 'Keep going,' he urged. 'In just a few moments you'll be as rich as Ambrosius Blenk.' He removed the stopper and squeezed a few drops into the lock of the iron handcuffs. It fizzed and the cuffs fell open.

'I can't find anything,' said the upended Nelly from deep down in her hamper.

'Just keep looking,' said Mel. 'It's really well hidden, right at the very bottom.' As he slipped out of the linen store he touched his candle to the draped sheets. They caught fire immediately.

The Firedrakes

From out of a misty, stinking moat rose the massive black fist of rock upon which Deep Trouble was built. Above this the body of the prison rose, tier upon tier, tower upon tower, spire upon spire, into a swirling sky the colour of ancient pewter. Here and there the dark silhouette of the building was punctured by the flickering yellow slits of windows. There were three dull, popping sounds, followed by three splashes as the friends, insignificantly tiny in comparison to the bulk of the prison, shot from a hole near the base of the rock and splashed down into the moat.

Mel was the first to surface. Dark weed draped his head like a witch's wig. 'Wren! Ludo! Where are you?' His voice echoed in the still air as he trod water the colour and consistency of pea soup.

'Here,' said Wren as she and Ludo swam up to him.

'Which way's the shore?' said Ludo.

'Just keep swimming away from Deep Trouble,' said Mel. 'We'll be bound to come to it.'

The others followed him into the mist. They swam for what seemed like a long way when Mel said, 'What's that wailing sound?'

Wren looked over her shoulder. 'It's coming from over there.'

Ludo turned and squinted into the mist as white shapes emerged. 'They look like . . . like *swans*.'

'Swans?' said Mel. 'Swans don't wail.'

'And they're way too big,' said Wren.

'They must be the firedrakes that Twenty-Four shouted after us about,' said Mel. 'Swim for your lives!'

Occasional glances over his shoulder as he swam told Mel that the three firedrakes were getting closer. He could now see that their resemblance to swans was only superficial. Each was as big as a barge and their long, white necks towered above them, scanning to and fro as they searched for the escapees. A foaming wake extended behind them as if they were driven by powerful propellers. But it was their heads that were so unnerving. Hollow, eyeless sockets were set into bone-white swan skulls. Their bills were blackened around the edges where sharp teeth protruded. Then the lead firedrake threw back its head and howled a screeching siren wail. The other two joined in.

'They've spotted us,' said Wren.

'Wait for me,' called Ludo, lagging behind. 'Why do you think they're called firedrakes?'

By way of an answer the lead firedrake opened its bill and sent a searing tongue of flame roaring over the moat towards the swimmers. The water a few feet behind them erupted in a hissing cloud of steam.

'Now we know,' said Wren.

'They don't have any eyes,' said Mel. 'I think they must be blind.'

'Blind?' said Ludo, as he caught up with the others. 'But they're coming straight for us.'

'That can only be because they can hear us,' said Wren. Then, as realisation dawned, 'Oh.'

Fighting an almost overwhelming impulse to flee, they all stopped swimming and trod water as silently as they could. The firedrakes slowed and came to a halt. They swivelled their long necks backwards and forwards as they tried to relocate their quarry. Their eyeless skulls seemed to stare right at the friends but, after a moment, they turned away to continue their search. Slowly they zigzagged back towards the mist in a wide V formation.

When he felt the firedrakes were out of earshot, Mel let out the breath he had been holding. 'Phew. That was close.'

They began swimming as quietly as they could towards what they hoped was the shore, but Ludo suddenly made a clumsy stroke and gulped in a great mouthful of water and floating moat-weed. He made a loud choking sound as he spat it out.

The firedrakes turned and sped towards them, sweeping the surface of the moat with arcs of roaring flame.

'Look, there's the edge of the moat,' said Wren.

They had reached a sheer wall made from the same black rock as the prison and streaked with rivulets of green slime. The top was out of reach even for a giant.

'Can you see a ladder or something?' said Ludo.

Wren looked both ways. 'No.'

'Just keep quiet and still,' said Mel. 'Maybe they won't find us.'

But Mel's optimism was misplaced. The firedrakes swam remorselessly towards the frightened and helpless friends. The leader belched a huge tongue of fire. Mel could feel the fierce heat as if it were a slap in the face. He bit his lips to keep from crying out. Then the other two firedrakes also spat flames.

'Dive!' cried Mel, taking a deep breath.

The friends ducked down beneath the waters as the searing fireballs enveloped the surface of the moat where they had been only moments earlier. From his temporary haven underwater Mel could see the glow of the conflagration above through the murk. The firedrakes came closer still and he saw the foam churned by their huge webbed feet. He could feel a pain in his chest as his lungs protested at the lack of air. The future looked like an unenviable choice between drowning and being roasted alive.

The firedrakes were now so close that the friends were buffeted about by the turbulence of their thrashing feet. Then a dark shape as big as a whale glided beneath them through the murky waters, almost close enough to touch. It swam away to Mel's right, trailing bubbles in its wake. He added being eaten by a giant fish to his list of unenviable choices. Just when he felt he could hold his breath no longer, the firedrakes swam away in the same direction as the enormous fish.

Mel was the first to surface. He gulped in a huge lungful of air, blinked the dirty water from his eyes and looked about. He saw the firedrakes speeding to a point further along the moat wall. Then Wren and Ludo broke surface.

'What was that?' said Wren.

'I don't know,' said Ludo. 'But it's attracted the firedrakes.'

They all watched the huge creatures swimming about as they searched fruitlessly for the giant fish. After a while the firedrakes gave up and disappeared back into the mist.

'Let's try and get out of this stinking moat,' said Ludo, sneezing as quietly as he could. 'I don't know about you, but I can't swim for much longer.'

At that moment a trail of bubbles erupted on the surface of the moat near to them and a bent tube with a glass lens set into the end of it rose through the foam.

It swivelled towards the friends. As Mel looked back at the tube it withdrew into the moat and a moment later the three of them were engulfed in a mass of bubbles. Then Mel felt something solid beneath his feet and slowly he and his friends rose out of the water.

They found themselves standing on the curved metal deck of some kind of underwater craft. In the centre of the vessel was a squat, circular tower complete with miniature battlements. It was streaked with orange rust. On the side was a tall, red symbol like a giant's handprint with an eye in its palm. The bent tube projected from the top of the tower like a flagpole.

There was a metallic squeal as a round hatch opened in the side of the tower and an elderly figment stepped through on to the deck. She was dressed in a crinkled, grey-brown frock. She wore rubber boots on her feet and a wide, red hat which was covered in white spots. From beneath her flat headgear spilled masses of straggly grey hair and her kindly face was adorned with half-moon spectacles that were perched on the end of her nose. Her skin was completely grey. Mel looked harder and saw that what he had taken to be her hat was actually a part of her head.

'Have those beastly firedrakes gone?' asked the figment.

'Was it you who led them away?' said Mel.

'Happy to help.' The figment smiled. 'You must be escaping from Deep Trouble. And you're soaking wet. Come inside and dry off before you catch cold.'

'You're not going to turn us in, are you?' said Ludo.

'Turn you in? I wouldn't dream of it. Now come along before you catch your deaths.' She turned and ducked back through the hatch.

'She reminds me of my granny,' whispered Wren.

'She reminds *me* of a mushroom,' said Mel.

Inside the tower was an iron ladder that led down through another hatch in the floor. At the bottom the long, curved-roofed cabin seemed very business-like, except for an ornately carved organ with fat pipes protruding from the top that stood at one end. Almost everywhere else was crowded with a maze of pipes, valves, gauges, wheels and levers.

'And look at these,' said Mel. On any available space

were the kind of wooden plaques that hunters mount trophies on. But instead of animal heads these bore a bewildering variety of fungi. There were small plaques displaying tiny, delicate mushrooms and larger ones with vividly coloured toadstools. Others bore clusters like typewriter keys or flat, sulphurous yellow ones that jutted out like shelves.

'You retrieved them intact, I see. They must be parched.' Another grey-haired, elderly figment entered the cabin carrying a tea tray. She also looked like a mushroom but one of the white, lacy variety. She set the tray down and began to pour out five cups from a mushroom-shaped teapot. 'I expect you'll be needing this after your exertions.' She handed them round.

'Thank you.' Mel was not altogether surprised to find that his tea tasted of mushrooms.

'Better?' smiled the first lady.

'Yes, thank you,' said Wren.

Ludo also nodded his thanks as they sipped their steaming drinks.

'Good. We'd better introduce ourselves,' said the first lady as she handed round fluffy towels. 'My name's

Mrs Morel and my companion here is Mrs Wood-Blewit.'

'We're very grateful for being rescued,' said Mel. 'Without you we'd be fried firedrake fodder by now.' He introduced himself and his friends.

'How did you come to escape from Deep Trouble?' asked Mrs Morel.

Wren, with interruptions from Ludo, explained. 'And now we have to find this mirrortree to bribe the court.'

'A mirrortree?' said Mrs Morel. 'Whatever's that?'

'We don't know,' shrugged Wren. 'But it must be very rare.'

'Rare, you say,' said Mrs Wood-Blewit, with a twinkle in her eyes. 'That sounds just our cup of tea.'

'What are you doing in the moat?' asked Mel.

'Doing?' said Mrs Wood-Blewit. 'Why, we're hunting.'

'Hunting fungi,' added Mrs Morel. 'We're collectors. It's our passion. We're hoping to bag a pallid puffball. They grow on the backs of firedrakes, you know. We've come all the way here especially.'

'Why don't you join us on the hunt?' said Mrs Wood-Blewit. 'It promises to be oodles of fun.'

'Firedrakes?' said Ludo with a nervous laugh. 'If it's all the same with you, we'd rather you just dropped us off somewhere safe. Besides, as soon as Deep Trouble finds we're missing, they'll raise the alarm.'

'I doubt there is an alarm, they've never needed one. No one's ever escaped from Deep Trouble. Until now, that is.' Mrs Wood-Blewit collected up the empty teacups and replaced them on the tray. 'There's more than enough time for our hunt.'

Ludo opened his mouth to protest but was cut off by Mrs Morel.

'We won't take no for an answer. And afterwards, we'll help you to find your mirrortree.' She slapped Wren heartily on the back. 'It sounds like it might be quite an adventure. And who knows what kinds of exciting fungi we might find around this mirrortree? Come along now.' She led them along the cabin and through a hatch at the end.

Beyond the hatch was a kind of small internal dock made from the same plates of riveted metal as the rest of the vessel. Reflections of the lapping water painted ripple patterns on the walls and ceiling. Floating in the dock were two paddle-wheeled launches and a small dinghy. On the launches were mounted what looked like elaborate polished cannons. Projecting from each of their barrels was a harpoon with a many-pronged tip. Ropes were attached near the ends with the rest curled up on the deck underneath like tightly coiled snail's shells. In the dinghy was a wind-up gramophone with a large, curved horn.

'Mrs Wood-Blewit, if you'll take Wren, I'll take Mel in the other launch. Ludo can man the dinghy.' Mrs Morel's voice echoed around the metal chamber. She jumped down into one of the paddle boats. 'Come along now.'

'If it's all the same with you, I'll stay here,' said Ludo.

'Stuff and nonsense,' said Mrs Morel. 'The hunt will put roses in your cheeks. A growing boy can't get too much exercise. Now hop in.'

Ludo reluctantly stepped into the dinghy. Mrs Wood-Blewit threw a lever on the dockside and a large hatch in the submarine's side swung upwards with a rusty squeal. She jumped down into her launch and started the motor. Mrs Wood-Blewit took the wheel and Wren manned the harpoon gun. The second launch, steered by Mrs Morel with Mel at the harpoon, followed them out on to the moat. Ludo was towed along behind. The paddle wheels made a rapid *slap-slap-slap* sound as they turned, seeming very loud on the still water.

A short distance from the submarine Mrs Wood-Blewit operated a lever on her boat and the hatch closed before the vessel blew a cloud of bubbles and sank back beneath the moat. 'Just in case there are any prying eyes about,' said Mrs Wood-Blewit.

The paddle-wheeled craft showed a surprising turn of speed as they sped off on their hunt. After a while they stopped.

'Now,' said Mrs Morel, calling to Ludo, 'I'm going to cast you off. We'll be waiting in the mist just out of sight. When I fire a green flare, pull the handle on the music machine and it will start.'

'*Music?*' said Ludo, alarmed. 'Won't that attract the firedrakes?'

'That's just what we want. But we won't let anything happen to you. Now don't forget. When you see my green flare, start the music. And not before. That's very important.' The two launches paddled away and disappeared into the mist.

Ludo sat in the small boat as it bobbed on the wakes of the departing craft. He felt very alone and very vulnerable. He pursed his lips to whistle himself a tune but realised that making noise was not a good idea. 'Start the music?' he muttered to himself. 'Not skegging likely.'

'Will Ludo be all right on his own?' asked Mel.

'Oh, I'm sure he will be,' said Mrs Morel. 'Just as long as he does what I asked and doesn't go jumping the gun.'

'Or in this case, the harpoon,' said Mel.

Mrs Morel chuckled. 'I can see we're going to get along famously. Now, no more talking and keep your eyes peeled. I expect Mrs Wood-Blewit's in position by now.'

Mel looked along the gleaming barrel of the

harpoon gun and practised aiming it at clumps of floating moat-weed. Mrs Morel had instructed him how to fire it and described the patches of pallid puffballs that grew on the firedrakes' backs which he was to aim for. She had assured him that the small boats could easily outrun the firedrakes and that, once back aboard the submarine, they would be safe from attack. He hoped she was right.

They did not have long to wait. Three paler patches in the mist grew larger until Mel's sharp eyes could make out the patrolling firedrakes. '*Pssttt!*' He pointed their quarry out and Mrs Morel nodded and readied her flare gun.

Ludo sat dejectedly in the dinghy, sniffing and trying not to make any noise. He nervously scanned the mist for signs of the firedrakes. Then he sneezed. 'Achoo!' Fearful that the noise might have alerted the firedrakes, he stood to try and get a better view of the moat. But the craft wobbled alarmingly under him. He put out a foot to steady himself and caught his toe on a coil of rope in the bottom of the boat. He tottered and fell backwards, jogging the lever on the gramophone as he did so. The turntable sprang into life and the scratchy and strident strains of a brass band shattered the silence.

'*Oh, no!*'

At the sudden sound of the music the firedrakes turned and sped back into the mist towards the dinghy. Mel and Mrs Morel exchanged a worried look.

'Why didn't he wait for my signal?' Mrs Morel shook her head.

Behind them came a *slap-slap-slap* as the other launch raced up to them. 'What's happened? I didn't see your green flare,' said Mrs Wood-Blewit.

'That young man's rather pre-empted things,' said Mrs Morel. 'Come on. Follow me.' The two boats paddled off at high speed after the firedrakes, the music growing louder all the time.

'There they are, up ahead,' called Wren. 'We're gaining on them.'

'Harpoons ready,' said Mrs Wood-Blewit. 'We may bag our pallid puffball yet.'

At the sound of the launches two of the firedrakes slowed, turned and then sped towards them.

'Where's the other firedrake?' called Wren.

'It's still going after Ludo,' said Mel. 'Hurry!'

'All right, we'll save Ludo. But take a glancing shot as the other two go past,' said Mrs Morel. 'You'll only have one chance. Get me my puffball.'

Mel wiped his sweaty hands on his hose, grasped the harpoon gun and squinted along its sight. The firedrakes were nearly upon them before Mrs Morel and Mrs Wood-Blewit revved their motors and sped away.

'What are you waiting for?' asked Mrs Morel urgently.

'I'll get a better shot if I . . .' Mel fired at the nearest firedrake '. . . aim from behind.' There was a loud pop as the harpoon flew from the barrel, the rope flying after it like a writhing snake. It hit the nearest firedrake. 'Bullseye!'

At the same moment, Wren, in the second launch, also fired, scoring a direct hit on the other firedrake. The fearsome creatures yelped like scolded puppies and fled into the mist. Their long necks were bent back over their bodies, tending to the featherless bare patches left by Mel's and Wren's grasping harpoons.

'Did you bag it?' called Mrs Morel over her shoulder as she piloted the launch towards Ludo. 'Reel it in, reel it in.' Nearby, Mrs Wood-Blewit was doing the same.

'Hurry,' said Mel as he pulled frantically hand over hand at the trailing rope, hauling the harpoon into the boat. He plucked the spherical fungus from the jaws of the harpoon and showed it to Mrs Morel.

'A fine specimen. Looks like Mrs Wood-Blewit and Wren have bagged one as well.'

Both boats sped into the mist towards the sound of the brass band. It got louder and louder and then there came the remaining firedrake's siren wail. This was instantly followed by a rending crunch, a resounding splash and the elongated *zzziiiippppp!* of a needle skidding across a record. The music stopped abruptly.

'What was that?' said Mel. A terrible feeling stirred in the pit of his stomach.

'Oh dear,' said Mrs Morel. 'Oh dear, oh dear, oh dear.'

'There!' said Wren, pointing. 'I can see the dinghy.'

But when Mrs Morel brought her craft to a halt there was only half a dinghy surrounded by a mat of floating firedrake feathers.

Of Ludo there was no sign.

Spandangle

Mel, Ludo and Wren stood on the far side of the square, smiling as they watched tongues of orange flame in the window on an upper floor of Ambrosius Blenk's mansion leaping into the night sky. They saw more windows light up as lamps were lit and the alarm spread through the household. Then a servant, still in his nightshirt, unlocked the gates and sprinted off in the direction of the firehouse.

'Let's stay and watch the place burn to the ground,' said Ludo. 'It'll be fun.'

'I want to see them carry Scratchbeard and the others out,' said Wren. 'I've never seen toasted beggar.'

'We don't have time,' said Mel. 'Let's get on with our search.'

'So where're we going to start looking?' said Ludo.

'Something as valuable as the mirrortree could be in any of the Great Houses,' said Mel. 'But we'll start at the House of Thrones.'

'It's the kind of thing only a king could afford,' said Wren.

'Let's get on with it,' said Ludo. 'Remember, if the others find it before we do, we'll be snuffed out like candles. We have to find it first and destroy it. Then they'll be snuffed and we'll be free.'

They had not gone far before they heard more running feet.

'That sounds like the Night Watch,' said Mel. 'We mustn't be caught again.'

'This way,' said Ludo as he led them up a side street.

'You *idiot*!' barked Wren. 'It's a dead end.' They stood staring at the poster-covered wall that blocked their escape.

'Hide!' said Mel. They flattened themselves into a shallow doorway as a detachment of the Watch ran past the end of the street in the direction of the mansion.

'Everyone will be on alert now,' said Ludo.

'We'll be picked up as soon as we're spotted wearing these,' said Wren, plucking at her doublet. As the noise of running feet died away they crept out of the doorway.

Just then there was a dull thud from behind them. They turned and, sitting spread-legged on the cobbles, looking dazed and confused, was a plump and elderly man with a big, white beard. He was dressed in the strangest of clothes. In the pool of light cast by a street lamp they could see that the man was wearing a bright red jacket and trousers. They were trimmed in white fur, as was his soft cap. He wore a wide black belt and knee-high boots. A sprig of holly was pinned to his breast and fresh snow dusted his shoulders.

'Who're you?' demanded Mel.

'I'm . . .' The ruddy-faced man scratched his head. He looked up at his questioner. 'I can't remember.'

'How can you've forgotten your own name?' said Ludo. 'Are you some kind of half-wit?'

'I . . . I don't think so,' said the man as he pulled at his beard. Then, distractedly to himself, 'Who *am* I?'

'Maybe there's a letter or something with your name and address on in your pocket,' said Wren.

The man fumbled in his pockets and pulled out a small black book the size of a pocket diary. He opened it and began to read. 'Ah, yes.' He read some more.

'Apparently, my mode of travel frequently makes me lose my memory. I've made all kinds of notes to myself. Here it is.' He looked up. 'My name's Spandangle.'

Mel looked hard at the man. 'That's not a Nemish name. Where've you come from?'

Spandangle consulted his book again. 'Somewhere called the "North Pole". It seems I was on some kind of job.'

'What's he talking about?' said Ludo. 'There's no such place.'

'What kind of job?' said Wren.

'Something seasonal to do with delivery, it says here. And . . .' Spandangle glanced down and noticed his clothes for the first time. He gave a start of surprise. 'What the *skeg* am I wearing? I look like a buffoon. Hang on. It's all starting to come back to me.' He thumbed through his book again. 'Ah, yes. *That's* it!' He closed the book and put it back in his pocket. 'Can you just confirm where I am?'

'You're in Vlam, of course,' said Wren with a puzzled frown.

'And the year?'

Ludo told him. Then, to Mel, 'He *is* a half-wit.'

'From the nip in the air, late autumn would be my guess. Right place, right time,' said Spandangle. 'Or maybe just a little early – but better that than miss all the fun.' With a smile of satisfaction he got to his feet. 'You wouldn't be Mel, Ludo and Wren, by any chance?'

'What *is* this?' said Mel. He looked around for something to use as a weapon.

'Please don't be alarmed,' said Spandangle. 'I can help you escape.'

'How do you know we're es–'

'Shut up, Ludo!' snapped Mel.

'What makes you think we need *your* help?' said Wren.

'A place to hide? A change of clothes?' suggested Spandangle. 'In fact, I could do with a change myself.'

'We do need a place to hold up and some disguises,' whispered Wren to Mel and Ludo. 'Maybe we should go along with him – just to get off the streets.'

'And then do a Scratchbeard on him,' added Ludo, drawing his finger across his throat.

A cruel smile curled Mel's lips. He turned to Spandangle. 'All right. Where's this hideout of yours?'

The book was briefly consulted. 'Merrydrip's Theatre. Such is my fame that the management keep accommodation for me all year round. Is it near here?'

'It's not far,' said Ludo. 'This way.'

As he followed the youngsters out of the cul-de-sac, Spandangle cast a glance over his shoulder at the snow scene depicted on one of the posters. In the foreground was a log with a singing robin perched on it. Leading back into the picture was a trail of footprints and an abandoned sleigh harnessed to a team of reindeer. Spandangle smiled to himself. 'Ho, ho, ho,' he said softly.

When they arrived at the dark theatre Spandangle led them around the side to the stage door. He tried the handle. 'It's locked.'

'Not to me it isn't.' Mel produced the phial he had stolen and squeezed a drop of Doctor Sarcophagus's potion into the keyhole. As soon as he heard the lock breaking apart he pushed the door open.

'This way,' said Spandangle as he entered. 'Mind you don't . . .'

There was a crash behind him.

'. . . trip over anything.' He took a lantern from a table and lit it. 'That's better.'

They were in a narrow corridor littered with the backstage clutter of gaudy props and sequinned costumes. Towards the end of the corridor Spandangle halted. He held the lantern to a door that displayed a tarnished star above a poster.

Merrydrip's Theatre Proudly Presents:
THE GREAT SPANDANGLE
Master of Illusion. Mind-Reader and
Mesmerist.
Prestidigitator Without Equal.
Renowned throughout the Seven Kingdoms.
For a Limited Season Only. Coming Soon.

Beneath this was an illustration of a tall, dark magician wearing a mask and dressed in black. He was depicted pulling a rabbit out of a hat, surrounded by fluttering doves and cascades of playing cards. Spandangle pushed open the door and entered. His white-haired head popped back out immediately. 'You'll find a choice of costumes in the room next door. Here, take this.' He handed Wren the lantern and closed the door behind him.

When Wren opened the door marked 'Wardrobe' the lamplight illuminated rows of colourful costumes hung on rails. Above them were arranged a wide variety of hats and, below, rows of footwear of all shapes and sizes.

'Some disguises, these,' said Ludo as he began sorting through the flamboyant garments. 'Unless you want to hide out in a circus.'

'Or a freak show,' added Mel as he held up a shaggy gorilla costume.

'I wouldn't be caught dead wearing any of these.' Wren held a garish, spangled gown trimmed with ostrich feathers in front of her as she regarded herself in a tall mirror.

'This is hopeless,' said Mel. 'Wearing any of this clobber we'd stand out even more than we do now.'

'Perhaps I can offer you something more to your taste,' said a voice from the doorway.

The trio turned to see a tall, slim man dressed in a black satin doublet, black tights and tall, black boots. He wore a narrow black mask tied around his eyes. Above this was slicked-back black hair and, below, a thin moustache and tiny goatee beard. A long black cape with a bright red lining hung from his shoulders. It was the magician from the poster.

'Spandangle?' said Wren.

The man bowed.

'But you look totally different,' said Ludo. 'You're taller and thinner. And your skin's so white.'

'Not to mention younger,' said Wren. 'And where's your long beard?'

'All a part of the conjuror's art.' He held up three costumes identical to his. 'These will be less conspicuous than anything you're likely to find in here.' Spandangle held out the costumes. 'They are for my assistants.'

'We're not your assistants,' said Wren.

Spandangle arched an eyebrow and smiled. 'You may change your minds when you hear that I will be setting up a selection of my illusions in the House of Thrones this very evening. In time for King Spen's celebrations three days hence. I believe that's where you were heading when we met?'

The children were stunned into silence. Their mouths hung open.

Mel's mind raced. How did Spandangle know that? He chewed his lip. This scrot could be useful. His disguises would get them off the street and into the House of Thrones. But Mel did not trust him – not an inch. 'All right.'

'But, Mel,' hissed Wren.

'Shut up,' said Mel. 'Leave this to me.' Then, to Spandangle. 'We'll be your assistants.'

'Splendid!' Spandangle tossed them the clothes. 'Get dressed. Then you can start loading the handcart.'

'But it's the middle of the night,' complained Ludo.

'The small hours of the morning, to be precise,' said Spandangle. 'You can sleep late.' He closed the door behind him and went back to his dressing room. He took out his little notebook and make a tick against an item listed there. 'That's the easy part achieved,' he said to himself. 'Now comes the hard part.'

* * *

In a dark street in the riverside quarter there came a fearful pounding on the door to the Crippled Toad.

'Mange! Open up, you skeg-bellied pile of scrot!'

A candle flickered into life in an upstairs window and an angry face pressed against the dirty glass. 'What the skeg do you mean by waking me at this hour?' Seeing Scratchbeard, Doctor Sarcophagus, Nelly and Canker, Mange opened the window and poked his night-capped head out. 'What are you doing here?' he said. Then he caught sight of their smouldering clothes and blackened faces. 'What've you been up to?'

'Are you going to open this door or do we have to break it down?' threatened Scratchbeard.

A short while later the door opened and the furious quartet pushed past Mange and down the stairs into the inn. The three-legged dog trotted after them.

'Get everyone a drink, Mange,' said Nelly Buboes as she sat down at a table. 'We've had one hell of a night.'

Scratchbeard strode up and down. 'Those little scrot-stains! I'll eat them alive.'

'But not before they've told us what this mission of theirs is, eh?' said Nelly. 'There's loot for us in this. I know there is. My fingers are pricking. I can almost feel the gold.'

'Just like the gold in Blenk's mansion?' scoffed Scratchbeard. 'Why didn't your fingers prick to that little charade?'

'We'll feed their livers to my dog,' added Canker.

'Shut up!' screamed Scratchbeard. '*You* were supposed to be keeping watch. What happened to you?'

'As soon as I saw the smoke I made myself scarce,' said Canker. 'I knew you'd be able to slip away in the confusion.'

'I'm touched by your loyalty, Canker.' Scratchbeard spat on the floor. 'Well, now you can make yourself useful. Go and rouse all the beggars, cutpurses, burglars, footpads, grifters and strumpets in Vlam. Tell them Scratchbeard's calling in every last favour he's owed. There's nowhere in Vlam where those scuts will be safe.'

'Hold your horses, Scratchbeard,' said Doctor Sarcophagus as he inspected his singed goatee in a cracked mirror on the wall. 'There's no need to get anyone else involved. We'll find those children ourselves.'

'They could be anywhere in the city by now,' said Nelly. 'We'll never be able to track them down.'

'Oh yes, we will,' said Doctor Sarcophagus. 'Some of us plan ahead, you see.'

'Eh?' Nelly cocked an eyebrow that had been plucked to the thinnest of pencil lines.

'While you were all busy casing the Blenk joint,' went on the doctor, 'I took the precaution of splashing a few drops of this potion on those little scrots.' He held up a small glass phial filled with blue–green liquid. 'Humans can't smell it but Canker's mutt there will get a whiff of it from halfway across Vlam. What's more, it won't wash off. I say we dress our wounds and get a bellyful of Mange's rotgut brew before we go a-hunting those vicious young tykes.'

'Brilliant, Doc,' said Canker, raising a tankard. 'I'll drink to that.'

'Me too,' said Nelly Buboes.

'What about you, Scratchbeard?' said Doctor Sarcophagus. 'Can we count you in?'

Scratchbeard withdrew his shiv from inside his rags and felt its edge. His smut-streaked face was reflected in its blade. 'Oh, you can count me in, Doc. You can count me all the way in.'

The Transmogrificators

'What's happened?' As Wren saw the wreckage and realised the horror of what had taken place, her voice trailed off to a whisper. 'Where's Ludo?'

Mel's face was ashen. He vainly scanned the moat, searching for his friend. When he tried to speak no words would come.

It was Mrs Morel who took charge. 'Now pull yourselves together. One thing's for certain. Whatever's happened to Ludo, the firedrake didn't get him.'

Mel stared at her. 'How do you know?'

'Firstly,' cut in Mrs Wood-Blewit, looking at the mess of feathers floating on the water, 'it looks very much as if the firedrake is the one that was "got".'

'And secondly,' continued Mrs Morel, 'those nasty beasts are capable of all sorts of dreadful things. But there's one thing they've never, ever been known to do.'

'What's that?' There was a tremor in Wren's voice.

'Leave a note behind.' Mrs Morel leant out of her

launch and picked up a piece of paper pinned to the wreckage.

'What's it say?' said Wren.

'"If you wish to see the boy again, return my property to me at once. You know where to find me,"' read Mrs Morel. 'It's signed, "H".'

'Who's "H"?' asked Mel.

'"H" is for Habilis,' answered Mrs Wood-Blewit.

'And what's that about returning his property?' said Mel.

'Ah. That,' said Mrs Morel. 'You see, we *borrowed* something of Mr Habilis's to get us here.'

'"Borrowed" as in took without permission?' said Wren.

'The submarine?' guessed Mel.

Mrs Morel and Mrs Wood-Blewit nodded.

'But you *are* going to return it to him?' said Mel.

'Of course we are,' said Mrs Morel. 'Now we have our puffball we've no more use for it.' She peered at Mrs Wood-Blewit over the top of her spectacles and added, 'For now.' She clapped her hands. 'Come on, let's get back to the vessel. We'll leave for Castle Habilis at once.'

'Where's that?' said Mel.

'On the far side of the forest beyond the moat,' said Mrs Wood-Blewit.

'However are we going to get there in a submarine?' asked Wren.

'Oh, our vessel isn't *just* a submarine,' said Mrs Morel.

'It's a *transmogrificator*,' said Mrs Wood-Blewit. As Mel opened his mouth to voice a whole string of questions, she added, 'Let's get back on board and we'll show you.'

Back inside the main cabin, Mrs Wood-Blewit went to the organ, lifted the lid to the stool and took out sheets of music covered in weird-looking loops, squiggles and arrows. She propped them up in front of the organ and sat down. 'Gather round. This will be interesting. This piece is entitled "The Tree-loper".'

'"The Tree-loper", Mrs Wood-Blewit?' said her companion, frowning. 'Is that altogether wise?'

'I don't know about the wisdom of it, Mrs Morel. But it'll certainly get us to Castle Habilis fast.' Mrs Wood-Blewit opened the music and flexed her fingers.

As she played the resounding first chord the music swelled and filled the cabin. A second chord and the volume increased. Mel could feel the deck vibrating through the soles of his boots. Mrs Wood-Blewit played a rapid arpeggio and the whole cabin began to tremble.

'What's happening?' Wren had to raise her voice to be heard over the music.

'That's just the introduction,' said Mrs Morel. 'Now comes the fun part.' She turned the page of music for Mrs Wood-Blewit.

Without pausing, Mrs Wood-Blewit's fingers danced over the keyboards and her feet over the bass pedals as she launched into the melody.

'Look!' shouted Mel as a panel in the front of the organ slid upwards to reveal lights around a tiny stage that flashed in time to the music. Centre stage was what looked like a fishbowl. 'It's us!' There, suspended in the centre of the sphere, hovered a miniature image of the submarine floating on the moat. It was accurate in every last detail.

The music got louder still as Mrs Wood-Blewit

played on. It was too loud to talk – or even shout – and Mel and Wren looked on with apprehension that was mounting along with the tempo of the music. The entire submarine reverberated to the deep thunder of the organ. Alarmed, Mel looked up and saw that the rivets in the wall were vibrating so much they were starting to work their way out of the iron panels. Mrs Morel just smiled and shook her head as if to say, 'Don't worry.' Then the rivets popped and the panel next to the organ came away. Mel expected to see water gushing in but instead the panel swivelled up and away to reposition itself. Soon other panels joined it and nuts began to unscrew themselves from bolts. Mel could feel the deck plates shifting beneath his feet as they changed shape. More rivets popped, more bolts unscrewed and plates, pipes and valves rearranged themselves in an intricate dance. The entire cabin was changing shape.

Inside the fishbowl the miniature submarine was changing shape too. The tower shrank into the hull and the submarine began to roll itself up into a ball. Two long mechanical arms grew from what had been the hull and reached up to the top of the moat wall, hauling the now spherical body of the transmogrificator after them on to the shore.

Then, with a final cadenza, Mrs Wood-Blewit stopped playing, the long after-notes lingering in the air. Mel looked around the cabin. What had formerly been a long, vaguely cylindrical space was now most definitely round and everything was in a new position.

'Oh dear, Mrs Morel,' said Mrs Wood-Blewit, gazing round. 'It looks like we lost one of our puffballs during the mutation.' Then to the children, 'It happens sometimes. I expect it'll turn up again when we next mutate.'

'Not to worry,' said Mrs Wood-Blewit as she pushed in the organ stops and the panel slid back into place, hiding the stage.

'That was us in the fishbowl, wasn't it?' said Wren.

Mrs Wood-Blewit nodded. 'Mr Habilis may be a cantankerous old curmudgeon, but he certainly has a wonderful collection of transmogrificators.'

'So what's a tree-loper?' asked Mel.

'Come over here to the porthole,' said Mrs Morel, 'and you'll see.'

* * *

Locktight stood staring down at the open inspection hatch. He was seething with anger. 'Word of this escape must never get out. Otherwise the reputation of Deep Trouble will be ruined. So will I.'

'No one will hear it from us. You'll be invoking the guarantee, I presume?' asked Spiracle, adjusting the lamp on his helmet as he bent to examine the hatch.

'You're skegging right I will,' said Locktight. '"Satisfaction guaranteed or your money back"; that's what you promised.'

'And you don't want your money back, I take it?'

'Just my prisoners,' said Locktight. 'When I get my hands on those little scrots I have a special no-star cell waiting for them.'

At the mention of a no-star cell, Blinker, Gusset and Flob shifted uneasily.

Spiracle made a note in his ledger. 'Very well. Consider them caught.' He snapped his fingers and the bounty hunters filed out of the room.

As he came to, lying in the dark, Ludo thought he might

be dead but the discomfort of a throbbing headache and the puddles of cold water lapping around his body insisted he was still alive. A moment later he heard a squeaky door clank open and watched as the tiny dots of two lanterns, like yellow eyes, approached, accompanied by the echoing *plip-plop* sound of rubber boots splashing through shallow water. By the dim light the lanterns cast he could see that he was in the hold of some iron vessel.

A voice behind one of the lanterns spoke. It echoed around the space. 'Is he dead, Nib? Mr Habilis will skin us alive if anything's happened to his hostage.'

'Of course he's not dead, Wick,' said a second voice. 'Can't you see he's looking at us?'

'Now we've got him, do you think the old ladies will do as they're told?' said Wick.

'They'd better, for his sake. If Mr Habilis doesn't get his vessel back he'll take it out on this boy. It'll be more than his hands he'll cut off.'

The lanterns came closer and over the top of them Ludo could see two disembodied faces against the darkness. They belonged to two figments – one short and fat, the other tall and thin – with shaven heads and exceptionally long, pointed ears. Under-lit by the lanterns they looked like ghouls. Their giant shadows loomed on the ceiling.

'Who're you?' asked Ludo in a shaky voice.

'It's us who're asking the questions,' said the fat face called Wick.

'Well?' said Nib. 'Speak up.'

'But you haven't asked me anything yet,' said Ludo, forcing himself to sit up.

'Don't try and be funny with me,' said Wick.

'He's got a point, though. You haven't actually asked him anything.'

Ignoring the finer points of Nib's argument, Wick grabbed Ludo by the arm and hauled him to his feet. His hands felt strange and, when Ludo looked, he saw that the figment's arms ended in iron hooks. Nib's did too.

'A spell cranking the spindle will show you who's boss,' said Wick. 'After that you'll pay us some respect.'

Ludo was taken to a long cabin and sat on an iron bench – one of two that ran the length of the rust-streaked and pipe-encrusted cabin from fore to aft. Down the centre ran the spindle, a long, kinked handle that was being cranked round and round by the two rows of figments that sat facing each other. All of them had ill-defined features with just the blurry suggestions of eyes, noses and mouths. Ludo recognised them as figments from the background of paintings. The other thing that made them different was that none of them had hands. Their wrists ended in mechanical sockets, which were attached to the spindle. On a gantry behind each row, Nib and Wick patrolled up and down in their squeaky rubber suits.

Just when Ludo thought he could not possibly crank any more, Wick barked, 'Stop cranking! Stand by to mutate!'

'Thank goodness for that,' said the cranker next to Ludo. In spite of the figment's blurred features Ludo could see that he was a boy with dark hair about the same age as him.

'No talking down there!' ordered Nib.

Ludo watched as Wick knelt and twirled the dial of a combination safe next to an organ just like the one he had seen on board the mushroom ladies' submarine. It struck Ludo as an odd setting for a musical recital. Wick opened the safe door and pulled out a small sack that thrashed about in his hands as if it contained a captive animal.

'What's he doing?' Ludo asked the boy.

'I thought I said *no talking*!' boomed Nib.

Wick shook the upended sack over the organ keyboard. But instead of a wild animal, out fell four hands. As if this were not surprising enough, two of the hands began to move up and down the keyboard and play. The other two formed into fists and beat up and down on the bass pedals. The deep notes of the organ reverberated around the iron cabin. Everything started to vibrate and iron plates around the cabin began to unscrew and reposition themselves. Startled, Ludo took an involuntary step backwards, bumping into the boy.

'Careful,' warned the boy. 'You don't want to stand too close to anyone while we're mutating in case –'

Suddenly, everything went dark and blackness engulfed Ludo as if a blanket had been pulled over his head. He felt the floor under him tilt alarmingly and, before he could stop himself, he was sliding down a slope on his bottom. He collided heavily with something hard that threw him in another direction. Then Ludo felt the unseen wall to his left move and push him in the small of his back. He could hear the music from the organ although it sounded further away, as if it was being played in an upstairs room of a large house. Accompanying this was a kind of metallic counterpoint of metal grinding against metal and sharper cracking sounds. The floor tilted again and Ludo was propelled in another direction. He put out his hands to stop himself and he tripped over something soft.

'Ouch!' It was the voice of the figment boy. 'I warned you not to stand too close.'

With a final flourish the music ended. So did the grinding of the plates. The walls and floor resumed a reassuring stillness.

'Feel in my shirt pocket,' said the boy. 'You'll find a candle stump and a match.'

Ludo fumbled in the darkness and found and lit the candle. By its flickering light he could see that they were in a very tall and very narrow space. It had a sloping metal floor and the riveted walls were at crazy angles like in a dream. 'What happened?' he asked. 'Where are we?'

'We're still on board the transmogrificator.'

'The *what*?'

'It's one of Mr Habilis's shape-changing machines.'

'And the hands playing that organ thing?'

'The *morphonium*,' corrected the figment. 'Those hands belonged to Mr Habilis. He owns this trans-mogrificator – and lots more, besides. My name's Shale, by the way. Sorry I can't shake your hand.'

'Mine's Ludo. Where *are* your hands, Shale?'

'At Castle Habilis. They're in the library.'

'Library?' said Ludo, even more bewildered. 'Like for books?'

Shale nodded.

'I don't understand any of this.'

'It must be confusing,' said Shale. 'Let me try and explain. Mr Habilis used to be a palm reader. He advertised for figments to come to Castle Habilis and have their palms read for free. That's how Shingle and I came to go there.'

'Who's Shingle?' asked Ludo.

'My sister. The trouble is, it was all a trick. We all ended up hand-less and enslaved. Without our hands we had no way of fighting back. All the male figments became his handymen and all the females his handmaidens.'

'Doesn't it hurt to have your hands cut off like that?'

'Not for us figments. But it's really difficult for us to do even the simplest things.'

'And where did everyone – and everything – in the trans-whatsitsname go?'

'Whenever a transmogrificator mutates it kind of folds itself up into a new shape and some bits of it vanish behind other bits, and bits that were previously hidden pop back out again,' said Shale.

'Like when you fold up a paper sculpture and then refold it into something else?'

'Just like that. Well, right now we're inside one of those folded-up bits. When we mutate again where we are now will probably be on the outside. It all depends on what we mutate into.'

'None of this makes any sense. Why was I

kidnapped?' said Ludo.

'They weren't actually after you,' said Shale. 'Nib and Wick were ordered to find the transmogrificator that was taken by his aunts.'

'His *aunts*? You mean Mr Habilis is related to the mushroom ladies?'

Shale nodded. 'And you're a kind of hostage.'

'How do you know all this?'

'Nib and Wick are forever talking about it. They think we slaves can't hear but we can.'

'Mr Habilis sounds very clever but he doesn't sound very nice.'

'He's not. And I bet that when Mr Habilis sees your hands he'll want those, too.'

'So *this* is what a tree-loper is,' said Mel.

Mel and Wren stood with Mrs Morel and Mrs Wood-Blewit at the transmogrificator's forward-facing porthole, watching the trees flash by. The long arms that the transmogrificator had grown were now being used to swing the spherical cabin through the trees like a giant mechanical gibbon. The motion was unsteadying at first until everyone learnt to flex their knees at the beginning and end of each swing. They soon became accustomed to the machine's strange gait and thrilled at its turn of speed.

'At this rate we should get to Castle Habilis in no time at all,' said Mrs Wood-Blewit. 'Tish to your fuddy-duddy notions of wisdom, Mrs Morel. You always were too cautious.'

Wren was clinging, white-knuckled, to a fat pipe. 'Are you sure we're safe? What if it misses a branch or slips off?'

'Don't worry so much,' chided Mrs Wood-Blewit. 'Enjoy the ride.'

'But what if something goes wrong with the machinery?' said Mel.

'What could possibly go wr—'

Everyone was suddenly thrown forward as the tree-loper stopped abruptly. Mel was the first to his feet. He scrambled back to the porthole.

'What is it?' said Wren. 'Have we hit something?'

'Yes, it looks like we're caught in a spider's web.'

'A spider's web?' Wren gave a nervous laugh.

'How could a flimsy spider's web stop something as big as this?'

'You don't understand,' said Mel. 'It's a very big spider's web.'

'Just how big?' said Mrs Morel. She exchanged a worried glance with Mrs Wood-Blewit.

Before Mel could answer the cabin darkened dramatically as the view outside was obscured by a giant, hairy head. Set into the head were eight glistening black eyes, each as big and inhuman as a football. They stared into the cabin.

The House of Thrones

Mel and Ludo, in their new black costumes and with their masks firmly in place, pushed a handcart heavily laden with magical props through the busy lamp-lit streets towards the House of Thrones. Over her black costume Wren wore a sandwich board bearing copies of the poster fixed to Spandangle's dressing-room door. The magician walked behind them, stopping frequently to distribute printed handbills advertising his forth-coming season at Merrydrip's Theatre to the gawking crowd.

'I thought we were supposed to be under cover,' hissed Wren. 'Now all of Vlam's staring at us.'

'The sooner we're off the street the better. Let's get a move on,' said Mel, puffing as he pushed the heavy cart up the steep Hill of Thrones. 'That means you too, Ludo, you lazy scut. I'm doing most of the pushing.'

Ludo cast an eye over his shoulder at Spandangle, who was busy signing autographs.

'How does he know so much about us?'

'I don't know,' whispered Wren. 'But the more I learn about this scrot, the less I like him.'

'Like him or not, it fits in with our plan,' said Mel. 'It's unlikely anyone will recognise us in these costumes and masks and it gets us into the House of Thrones.'

'I say we bash him over the head and hide until it's quieter,' said Ludo.

'Great thinking, Pea-Brain,' said Wren. 'And what happens if we're caught? Do we bash everyone over the head?'

'Do you have a better plan?' said Ludo.

'I say we do as Mel says,' said Wren. 'We can bash him over the head later, when no one's around. Agreed?'

'I suppose so,' said Ludo. 'But only if you promise to let me do the bashing.'

'Stop!' The approach to the House of Thrones was blocked by a detachment of the Night Watch. The Sergeant stepped forwards. 'You three children. Why are you wearing masks?' He lowered his flaming torch to see them better.

'They're my assistants,' said Spandangle. 'The masks are a part of our stage costumes.'

'There are dangerous fugitives on the run from the Clinch that match their descriptions,' said the Sergeant. 'There's a reward for their capture. Everyone must be checked. Have them remove their masks.'

'A reward, you say?' Spandangle approached the Sergeant and did something strange with his hands. It was very quick. Almost at once the Sergeant's eyes glazed over. 'They can't be who you're looking for.'

'They can't be who we're looking for.' The Sergeant's voice was a monotone.

'They don't look anything like the fugitives,' said Spandangle.

'They don't look anything like the fugitives,' repeated the Sergeant.

'You just want to let us get on about our business.'

'I just want to let you get on about your business.'

'Good evening, Sergeant.' Spandangle made another fast gesture.

'Good evening, Serg—' The Sergeant shook his head. His glazed expression vanished. 'Move along now. You're blocking the street with that handcart. Men, stand aside and let this gentleman and his assistants through.'

'How did you do that finger-flashy thing?' said Mel once they were out of earshot.

'All part of the conjuror's art,' said Spandangle with a wink.

'You could have turned us in for the reward. I would have done if I was you,' said Ludo.

'I couldn't have my assistants going astray before we set up the show, now could I?'

'Just as long as you don't try any of that hocus-pocus on us,' said Wren.

'How can you be certain I haven't already?' Spandangle smiled to himself and led them up to the massive gates to the House of Thrones. 'Now, you stay here while I announce our arrival.'

Mel, Ludo and Wren clustered together around the handcart.

'Do you think he has?' said Wren.

'I wouldn't put anything past him,' said Ludo. 'He seems to know what we're going to do almost before we do ourselves.'

'That's just a trick,' said Mel. 'He can't really read our thoughts.'

'What if it's not a trick?' said Wren as she removed the sandwich board.

'It's almost as if he's helping us,' said Ludo. 'Maybe he's after the mirrortree too?'

'But it'd be worthless to him,' said Mel. 'Even if he did know about it – which he doesn't.'

'But not worthless to the other Mel, Ludo and Wren,' added Ludo.

'Come along now. Don't dilly-dally,' called Spandangle, beckoning them.

Mel and Ludo pushed the handcart through the postern door and into the courtyard beyond.

'Look at the skegging *size* of this place,' said Ludo. 'We'll never find it here.'

The courtyard was vast and the four walls so high the children could not make out the top in the darkness. In the middle stood a five-storey guardhouse around which a detachment of the palace guards were practising marching in formation, their armour glinting in the light of the torches they carried. Peppering each of the courtyard's walls was a multitude of doorways that were joined to each other – and eventually to the ground – by hundreds of snaking stairways. They were lit by flaming gas lights and seemed like tendrils of glowing creeper as they wound upwards. Set into the base of each of the courtyard's walls there was an enormous arch that could easily have accommodated Ambrosius Blenk's mansion. Through them could be seen other, equally vast courtyards with yet more doorways and brightly lit staircases.

Inside, the House of Thrones was hardly less impressive. As bewigged footmen clad in the purple royal livery took charge of the handcart and wheeled it away, an under-chamberlain conducted them to a door, up a long flight of stairs and through a succession of lofty halls so rich in detail and so highly decorated that the trio's heads spun as they tried to take it all in.

'We might as well give up now,' whispered Wren. 'It will take years to explore everywhere in here.'

'But if the others find the mirrortree, we'll be goners,' said Ludo.

'We'll find it first,' said Mel confidently. 'We have two advantages over them.'

'And what're they?' said Wren as they turned into a corridor lined with rich paintings.

'First, they don't know *we* exist. And second . . .' Mel took out his quill from inside his doublet. It was raven-black and seemed to suck in all the light around it. As they walked he used its point to score long gashes into the canvases they passed. '. . . *they're* only interested in creating things.'

'And it's so much easier to destroy things,' said Ludo.

'And *much* more fun,' added Wren with a snigger.

The under-chamberlain showed them into the backstage area of the palace theatre and then on to the empty stage before he left them alone. The heavy curtains were drawn back and they could see rows of empty seats stretching into the darkened theatre. Around the walls hung dozens of ornate boxes.

'Ah,' said Spandangle, 'I see our handcart is already here. Now, after you three have made yourselves busy and set up the props on stage I'll help you in your search for the mirrortree.'

The trio's jaws dropped open. 'How did you know –' Mel stopped himself.

Spandangle just smiled and waited.

'There's no such thing,' said Ludo.

'Even if there was such a thing –'

'*Wren!*' warned Ludo.

Mel said, 'Supposing – just supposing – there was such a thing –'

'Which there's not,' cut in Ludo.

'– why'd you want to help us find it?'

'Let's just say that I have a certain interest in making sure you succeed in your quest,' said Spandangle. 'Or I could simply offer my services to the others and help *them* find it. Either way's fine by me.'

'What do you know about the others?' said Ludo.

Spandangle just smiled his infuriating smile again.

'Do you know where this mirrortree is?' said Wren.

More smiling. More silence.

After a while Wren nodded to Ludo and Ludo nodded to Mel.

'OK. You've got a deal.'

'Excellent,' said Spandangle. 'So let's go and find your mirrortree.'

'In there?' said Scratchbeard incredulously as he stared at the towering edifice. 'In the skegging House of Thrones?' Canker's dog was straining at the length of fraying rope that served as her leash. She had led the beggars there via Merrydrip's Theatre, hot on the trail of Mel, Ludo and Wren.

'My fingers are pricking,' said Nelly Buboes. 'There's gold in this for sure. Lots and lots of gold.'

'Gold inside the House of Thrones?' said Doctor Sarcophagus. 'Why, Nelly, you *do* surprise me. You'll be telling me the Mysteries are rich next.' He dabbed a few drops of scent behind his ears. 'I think Scratchbeard has stumbled upon something with those children that might feather all our nests very nicely if we play it right. I think we should get ourselves into the House of Thrones nice and quiet like. See just what they're up to. What do you think, Scratchbeard? Are you willing to postpone your revenge until they lead us to whatever it is they're after?'

'Sure, Doc,' said Scratchbeard. 'Business is business.' He spat. 'But when our business with those scrot-stains is done, then they'll find out just what it costs to cross me.'

Inside, Inside

Mrs Morel dashed to the morphonium and pulled out one of the stops. The front panel slid up, revealing the fishbowl sphere. 'You'd better all come and look at this.' Inside was the image of the transmogrificator caught in a giant web that had been spun between the trees. Clambering over it was an enormous, hairy spider. Their machine seemed no bigger than a fly in comparison. The spider was busy wrapping its prey in sticky, silken strands as fat as washing lines that it spun from the tip of its abdomen.

'We're moving!' cried Wren as the cabin lurched. She grabbed hold of a valve to steady herself.

'The spider-thing's carrying us away,' said Mel as he stared at the image. 'Where's it taking us?'

'There.' Mrs Wood-Blewit pointed at the fishbowl. 'I think it must be its larder.'

'*Larder?*' gasped Wren. 'Isn't that where you put things you're going to eat?'

Their destination looked like a giant silver-grey

globe that was suspended high between the tops of a number of the larger trees. Thick silken strands, like guy ropes, fastened it to the trunks and thicker boughs. The spider dragged the transmogrificator through a large opening in the base of the globe.

It was dark inside and much more irregular than it looked from the outside. Mrs Morel pulled another organ stop and the image in the fishbowl brightened enough so that they could see what was going on. Besides their own captor, there were several other giant spiders at work. Sticking to the inside wall of the globe were many lumps like mummies wrapped in sticky shrouds. They saw their spider scuttle away and join its companions who were feasting on a still-struggling bulge on the wall. For a moment it looked like a deer.

'What're those?' Wren pointed at some writhing shapes moving across the surface of the wall. 'They look like maggots.'

'They're much too big for maggots,' said Mel.

'Let's take a closer look.' Mrs Wood-Blewit pulled out another organ stop and the magnification in the fishbowl increased. The 'maggots' were actually as big as fully grown men. Their muscular torsos looked human but from the waist down they were more like huge, pale earwigs with sinuous, jointed bodies that ended in wicked pincers. Their heads bore erect crests of spiky hair and they had huge watery eyes and wide fish-mouths filled with rows of glistening, needle-sharp teeth. They moved over the inner surface of the larder by dragging themselves on their powerful forearms. Several had latched on to the exterior of the transmogrificator where it was stuck to the wall. Their snapping pincers could be heard as they arched their backs and attacked the hull through the layers of spider silk.

'Ugh,' said Mrs Morel. 'They're *fear-wigs*.'

'I feel sick,' said Wren.

'They're trying to get in,' cried Mel.

'No need to be alarmed,' said Mrs Morel calmly. 'I'll have us out of here in a trice.'

'You will?' said Wren, brightening.

Mrs Wood-Blewit nodded. 'We simply need to mutate into something suitable, burst out of this larder and be on our way. We'll return the transmogrificator, collect Ludo and be off searching for your mirrortree.'

'What'll it be?' said Mrs Morel as she opened the stool and sorted through the music.

'What about the Crab Concerto, Mrs Morel? We could use its big pincers to cut our way out.'

'A splendid choice, Mrs Wood-Blewit. And the central section is so melodic.' Mrs Morel set the music on the morphonium as she hummed to herself.

'We'll be free in a jiffy.' Mrs Wood-Blewit took her seat and started to play.

As before, the plates of the hull began to rearrange themselves in answer to the thundering morphonium. The walls bulged and contracted. The image of the transmogrificator in the fishbowl could be seen to strain against the binding cocoon as it changed shape. First one huge pincered crab arm grew and snipped itself free and then another. One by one the legs followed. Then the transmogrificator's body stretched as the crab continued to wrench itself from its bindings.

Suddenly, without warning, the music stopped. Mrs Wood-Blewit was sitting on her bottom on the floor.

'Are you all right?' asked Wren.

'Nothing bruised except my dignity,' said Mrs Wood-Blewit as her companion helped her to her feet. 'However, my stool appears to have vanished in the mutation.'

'Don't worry. We'll fetch you a chair,' said Wren.

Mrs Wood-Blewit looked very worried. 'But you don't understand. All the mutation music was in the stool. Without a score we can no longer change shape.'

'And, beautiful as the Crab Concerto is, it's unfinished,' said Mrs Morel.

'But you've still got the music for that,' said Wren. 'Can't you just carry on with the piece?'

'It won't work,' said Mrs Morel, wringing her hands. 'Once the tempo is broken, so is the mutation. And you can't mutate into the same mode twice in a row. We need to start over with something completely new. But now that the music has been swallowed up, I do believe we're stuck here.'

'What's more,' added Mrs Wood-Blewit, 'stopping in mid-mutation has made the transmogrificator soft and unstable. It's only a matter of time before a tear appears in the hull and those creatures outside will be able to get in.' The blood appeared to drain from her already pale face.

'But can't you just play something from memory?' said Mel.

'Or improvise,' said Wren.

'I'm afraid not,' said Mrs Wood-Blewit. 'You see, every note in a piece corresponds to the mutation of a small part of the transmogrificator. It must be note-perfect for it all to work. Why, if I was to play even one wrong note then we might very well become folded up ourselves. We could be crushed to death.'

'Maybe we can get the music back,' said Mel. 'Is it possible to get inside the folded-up bit?'

'In theory,' said Mrs Morel. She cupped a hand to her ear. 'Just a minute. Can you hear something?'

'You mean that scratching sound?' said Wren.

'It's coming from all around us,' said Mel.

'Oh dear,' said Mrs Wood-Blewit. 'You know what this means, don't you?'

'I'm very much afraid I do,' said Mrs Morel. 'One of those fear-wigs has got inside the transmogrificator.'

'More than one by the sound of it,' said Wren.

Mel looked around nervously. 'Where are they?'

'They'll be trapped in the bits that are still folded up – for a while, at least,' said Mrs Wood-Blewit.

'So there's time to get the music back?' said Mel.

'Yes, but we need a suitable duct,' said Mrs Wood-Blewit.

'Like this one?' said Wren. She knelt and peered into a grille. 'It looks like it leads somewhere.'

'Let's unscrew these nuts holding it in place,' said Mel.

'There's a narrow passage,' said Wren, squinting into the darkness. The ominous scratching noise of the trapped fear-wigs echoed down it.

'I'll go,' said Mel. 'I'm the smallest.'

'Are you aware of what you're letting yourself in for?' said Mrs Wood-Blewit. 'The transmogrificator is very unstable, not to mention the fear-wigs. And if we start mutating again everything will be . . . *rearranged*.'

'I'll be all right,' said Mel. 'Here, Wren, take Cogito . . . Just in case.'

Wren tucked the roll of parchment into the inside pocket of her doublet. 'Promise me you'll be careful.'

Mel smiled bravely and squeezed himself head-first into the passage. Even for him it was a tight fit.

'Wait,' said Mrs Morel. 'It'll be dark in there. Take a candle.'

'No need.' Mel took out his glowing angel feather.

Mrs Morel, Mrs Wood-Blewit and Wren watched as the light haloing his retreating body got smaller and smaller. Then it went out as he turned a corner at the end.

The hull gave another mighty shudder, throwing Mrs Morel to the floor. 'He'd better be quick,' she said. 'From the sound of it, the hull won't remain in one piece for much longer.'

Mel's feather only lit his way a short distance ahead. It was like being inside a scrunched-up sheet of paper except that everything was made of metal. At intervals pencil-thin beams of light shone as bright as laser beams into the narrow, cramped space through vacant rivet holes. Mel was constantly aware of the noise of the shifting hull and the slithery scratching sounds of the fear-wigs.

As he crawled further he heard a different sound. It was the noise of paper rustling and tearing. It was coming from beyond the fold just ahead of him. Mel put his feather back inside his doublet and very carefully inched forwards and peered around the fold. Everything was lit by the crisscross beams from rivet holes. There, in a cavity formed from the mad angles of the folded-up hull, was a fear-wig. So was the organ stool. It lay on its side and the sheets of music lay sprawled across the sloping floor. The creature was grasping handfuls of the precious music and chewing them to shreds with its vicious jaws.

Then Mel heard something behind him. There was just enough space for him to turn his head and peer back the way he had come. His heart seemed to stop as he saw another fear-wig crawling towards him. Its hideous face was briefly illuminated as it passed a rivet hole, bright shafts of light glinting off its teeth. The sudden glare startled the hideous beast and it let out a blood-curdling screech of alarm. On hearing this, the creature ahead of Mel answered with a terrifying screech of its own. It looked up and saw Mel.

Fighting back panic, Mel used his sharp eyes to search for a way out. As he studied the scene in front of him he saw that the fear-wig chewing the music was trapped, caught by a fold where the wall met the floor. Mel hauled himself forwards into the cramped cavity. The trapped creature in front of him screamed louder. It lunged for the intruder but its powerful arms grasped thin air mere inches from Mel. Pressing himself to the wall of the eccentric space, Mel edged around the periphery of the cavity, feeling with his hands for another way out. He came up against a solid, folded wall and could go no further when the second fear-wig squirmed into the space. Its body was covered in scrapes and cuts from the narrow passage. It soon spotted Mel and started dragging itself towards him.

Mel groped among the stray items that littered the floor, searching for anything to defend himself. His hand touched something soft and spongy. There was just enough light for him to see that it was the pallid puffball that had vanished during their previous mutation. Just then a strong hand grasped his ankle. With horror, Mel saw that the second fear-wig had hold of him. Without thinking, he threw the puffball at the creature as he kicked out with his legs. The puffball hit his attacker full in the face and split with a wheezy hiss, releasing a cloud of stinging white spores. The fear-wig immediately let go of Mel and clawed at its exposed eyes. The spores spread and engulfed the other fear-wig too. Almost without knowing what he was doing, Mel grabbed as much of the sheet music as he could reach. He screwed up his eyes and held his breath and rapidly crawled back through the cloud. Behind him he could hear both creatures alternately choking and screaming in pain at the irritating spores.

Crawling as fast as he could, Mel retraced the way back towards the entrance to the duct. He could hear Wren's echoing voice calling, 'Mel? Mel, are you all right? What's going on?'

'It's OK. I've got the music,' he shouted. Mel followed Wren's guiding voice and he soon saw the bright rectangle at the end of the duct framing her face. Relief flooded over him. 'I can see you. I'm almost there.'

But as he reached her there was a loud metallic creak and the opening buckled. The way back into the cabin collapsed to an opening no larger than a letter box.

'*Mel!*' screamed Wren.

'I'm . . . I'm all right.' Mel stared in disbelief at the narrow slit of light. Somewhere behind him he could hear the scrabbling noise of the fear-wigs. 'Look, I've got the music – all that was left of it.' He began posting it through the hole.

'But how're *you* going to get out?' called Wren as she took the sheets.

'Don't worry about me. Take the music. I'll find another way out.'

'Stay where you are. We'll prise the hole open.'

'No, Wren. There's no time.' Mel posted the last of the music through the hole. 'I'll be fine.' He began to push himself backwards down the duct.

He had only gone a little way before he felt a hand seize his ankle.

'We should explore,' said Ludo. 'Maybe we can spy on Nib and Wick and find out what's going on. What's down that way?'

'I don't know,' answered Shale. 'Everything gets changed whenever we mutate. It's never the same.'

Ludo followed Shale as he squeezed through a narrow opening. Ludo carried a candle and stuck another to one of Shale's sockets with melted wax. As they explored they sometimes had to turn sideways to get through narrow gaps or get down on their stomachs to squirm under things. Once Ludo had to help Shale to climb a tall, narrow chimney-type space before they came out into another series of folded-up passages.

'Stop!' whispered Ludo. He put out his arm to grasp Shale's shoulder. 'Blow out the candles. There's something up ahead.'

In the darkness in front of them they could see a glowing red light. Ludo and Shale crept towards it. When they reached it they found that the light was one of a pair, the other being green and unlit. Beneath them was a closed door. Set into the door was a kind of dial formed from three concentric rings with strange symbols engraved on them.

'It's some kind of door,' said Ludo. 'Where do you think it leads?'

'I don't know,' said Shale. He pushed at it with his sockets. 'It's locked.'

'Look at this hand-shaped hollow next to it,' said Ludo.

As soon as he put his hand in it the concentric rings swivelled and there was a clicking sound which made him jump. The red light above the door went out and the green light came on. The door swung outwards. 'It's a lock.'

'There's a short crinkled corridor inside,' said Shale. 'And there's another door at the far end.'

'It's got a dial and a red light, too,' said Ludo.

They walked cautiously towards it.

Behind them there was a thump as the first door closed. The red light above it lit up.

'Oh, no! We're stuck,' cried Shale.

Ludo ran back. He slapped his hand into a similar shaped depression but the red light remained lit and the door firmly shut. 'Now what?'

'Come and listen to this,' said Shale from the other door.

Ludo walked back and put his ear to the door. 'Voices.'

Then they heard another sound. It was a long metallic *swish* like a guided blade falling from a height, followed by a dull *clunk*. Shale took a step back. 'Oh, no! It's a *separator* at work!'

Spiracle, Blinker, Gusset and Flob stood in a clearing on the shore of the moat staring out at the oily water. Thin skeins of mist curled around their ankles.

The tattoos on Gusset's chest were jumping up and down to get their host's attention. 'I see something out there on the moat,' he wheezed, squinting into the mist.

'Leave it to me, old boy.' Blinker opened a hatch in his breastplate and struck a match on the leg of his armour. He put the flame inside the hatch and out shot a rocket attached to a grappling hook with a long line. The rocket arced out into the moat, trailing orange sparks, and landed with a fizz and a loud *plop*. He reeled it back in.

'It's wreckage from a wooden dinghy and some firedrake feathers,' said Spiracle, examining the stuff the hook had snagged. He turned and stooped to examine the deep depression in the loamy forest floor.

'And it looks like they had a getaway vehicle waiting.' He stood and pointed into the trees. 'They went that way. There are marks on the branches. Flob, I believe the stare-crows are called for.'

The huge figment made a guttural noise that sounded like 'OK' and reached a hand the size of a tennis racquet into his shaggy fur. When he withdrew it he was clutching three strange birds. They were the size of ravens and as black as tar. Patches of skin showed through their unkempt feathers and they had bulging eyes that seemed many times too big for their scrawny bodies. Flob released them and they wheeled up into the sky.

'The stare-crows see everything. Once they spot the fugitives, they're as good as caught,' said Spiracle.

Pennyweight Market

'So where's the mirrortree?' said Mel.

'I don't know,' said Spandangle. 'But I know someone who does. We'll find her in Pennyweight Market.'

'Where's that?' said Ludo. 'I've never heard of it.'

Spandangle took his little black book from inside his cloak and thumbed through it. 'This evening, it should be right here, in this very building.'

'A market? In the House of Thrones?' said Wren. 'I don't believe you.'

'They'd never allow a common old market in the royal palace,' said Mel.

'Oh, it's hardly a "common old market". And I'm quite sure that no one in the palace knows anything whatsoever about Pennyweight Market,' said Spandangle. 'Its venue is a closely guarded secret and it changes from day to day. It's where the Mirrorscape comes to play and barter for things with this world.'

'The *Mirrorscape*?' said Mel, his brow creasing in thought. 'Where have I heard that name before?'

Spandangle smiled knowingly and ushered the trio along a series of winding corridors and down flight upon flight of stairs. He seemed to know exactly where he was going and how to avoid the palace staff. As they descended the staircases, it was like dropping backwards through time as the styles of the architecture became increasingly older. The lamps that lit the staircases became fewer and fewer until they ran out altogether. Spandangle conjured four lit candles from out of thin air and handed them round. After what seemed ages, they stood before an ancient door at the end of a long-neglected corridor. The floor was covered with dust and the walls made of bare, rough-hewn stone. The door was very difficult to open and creaked loudly as if it had not been used in many years. Beyond it were yet more stairs that disappeared down into darkness. 'After you.'

The air on the staircase smelt very old and stale. There were cobwebs too – lots of them.

'This is the old abandoned part of the House of Thrones, isn't it?' said Mel as if remembering a half-forgotten dream.

'Indeed,' said Spandangle.

'How much further is it anyway?' complained Wren. 'My feet ache.'

'Not too far now,' said Spandangle. 'Keep going and we'll be there soon.'

Finally they reached the bottom of the stairs and found themselves in what looked like vast, subterranean ruins. They walked for a long time, accompanied only by the echoes of their footfalls and the complaints of the children.

'Straight ahead,' said Spandangle. 'I believe I can see our destination.'

In the coal-black darkness in front of them they could see a collection of tiny lights. They looked like a busy village seen at night from a long way off. These got bigger as they approached and a faint murmuring rose in pitch and volume until it sounded like a busy throng.

Set amid ruined walls and toppled columns, Pennyweight Market was lit by the light of thousands of flaming torches and was alive with the enticing smells of cooking and the noise of merriment.

'There're more people here than in Vlam on

midwinter's eve,' said Wren, as she followed the others into the crowd. 'Where'd they all come from?'

'People?' said Mel. 'Are your eyes working right? There're not too many humans that I can see. And those I can, certainly don't come from Nem.'

'What a freak-show,' said Ludo as he gazed at the weird assortment of beings that populated the market. 'Scrot, we're the only ones that look normal. I've never seen so many tents and stalls.'

'And there's a fairground over there,' said Wren, pointing to a giant Ferris wheel covered in rainbow-coloured lights.

'So now what?' asked Mel as he wove after Spandangle through bands of acrobats, jugglers and escapologists.

'I need to speak with . . . Ah! There she is.' Spandangle led the trio towards a fortune-teller's booth. It was a very tall tent made from blue–black velvet decorated with silver signs of the zodiac. The painted sign above the door-flap said 'Madam Manto'. In front of it stood a huge, bare-chested man with crossed arms. He had mauve skin and hair. As

Spandangle approached he nodded and held the tent flap aside so they could enter.

Inside was a wrinkled, grey-haired old lady with a floral bandana tied tightly around her head. She was seated at a table and seemed to be in a trance. On the table were a skull, a crystal ball, a dog-eared pack of oversized tarot cards and a fishbowl full of tiny scraps of paper. Thin strands of blue smoke curled upwards from burning incense sticks. Without opening her eyes, she gestured Spandangle into the seat opposite her. The children stood uneasily near the door.

'What do you wish to consult, O seeker after arcane knowledge; cards, scrying-glass or mystic snow?'

'A cup of pomegranate tea would be nice.'

'*Pomegranate tea?*' One of Madam Manto's eyes shot open. 'There's only one person I ever knew who drank pomegranate tea.' Her other eye opened. '*Spandangle?*'

' It's been a long time, Madam M.'

'But . . . but you look so young. Why, the last time I saw you, you were the same age as me.'

'All part –'

'– of the conjuror's art,' finished Madam Manto.

She and Spandangle laughed. 'It *is* you.' She looked up at Mel, Ludo and Wren. 'And who're these? Wait, haven't I seen you three before?'

'Not us, you daft old bat,' said Mel.

'Do pardon my new assistants,' said Spandangle. 'They have wayward tongues.'

'Assistants?' said Madam Manto, toying with her alligator teeth necklace. 'Is this the standard of help you're forced to hire nowadays? Not like in our time, eh?'

'Madam Manto used to be my assistant,' explained Spandangle.

Wren spluttered with laughter. 'What, *her*?'

'Certainly,' said Spandangle. 'She cut a comely figure in a leotard.'

'But she must be a hundred years old,' said Ludo.

'It was all a long time ago,' said Madam Manto. 'But not quite *that* long. Spandangle used to saw me in half.'

'Enough of reminiscences,' said Spandangle, quickly changing the subject. 'I need your help, Madam M. I'm looking for something. Something very special.'

'I know better than to ask you what it is,' said Madam Manto. 'This calls for the scrying-glass.' She handed Spandangle the crystal ball and waved her hands over it. 'It's cloudy, very cloudy. Concentrate on what it is you seek.'

Beads of sweat broke out on the conjuror's brow as he concentrated on the mirrortree.

At length the fortune-teller spoke. 'There's nothing there.'

'Please keep trying,' said Spandangle. 'It's important.'

'The deepest secrets hide themselves well. There's nothing there. Just clouds . . . wait a minute.'

Spandangle and the children leant closer.

'Nothing.' The fortune-teller sat back in her chair. 'It was just a spark. That's all.'

'A spark?' said Spandangle. 'You don't mean –'

'Yes,' said Madam Manto. 'You're too early. Right place, wrong time. Whatever you're seeking has not yet arrived.'

Spandangle laughed. 'Better too early than too late.' Turning to Mel, Wren and Ludo, 'Well, it looks like we have some time on our hands. Why don't you go and enjoy yourselves in the market while Madam M and I chew over old times?'

'Where the skeg are we?' complained Canker. 'It's blacker than night down here.' He strained to hold back his dog, who was hot on the scent of Mel, Ludo and Wren.

'Try taking your dark glasses off,' said Nelly Buboes. 'You can see as well as the rest of us.'

'It still doesn't help,' said Canker. 'We must be deep underground. We were going downstairs for hours.'

Doctor Sarcophagus walked in front of the motley group of beggars. He held a phial of some glowing potion above his head to light their way. 'Astounding. Simply astounding. We must be somewhere beneath the House of Thrones. Ever hear of this place, Scratchbeard?'

'I don't give a filleted fart where the skeg we are. Are we getting any nearer to those vicious little scrots?'

'Canker's mutt's going crazy,' said Nelly. 'They can't be far now. Hey!' She stopped. 'You don't think they're leading us into a trap, do you?'

'They're certainly leading us somewhere,' said Doctor Sarcophagus. He shoved his phial back inside his coat. 'There's something going on up ahead. There's lights. Can you see them?'

'It's a skegging market,' said Scratchbeard. 'And by the way the mutt's acting up, that's where those children are.'

'So, what do you think that old bat was talking about, "Right place, wrong time"?' said Mel.

'And what *is* this place?' Wren gestured around at the strange beings thronging Pennyweight Market. 'There are monsters and stuff here. Just like the things in old Blenko's paintings.'

'Paintings can't come real,' said Mel. 'That's impossible.'

'I can see monsters too,' said Ludo. 'Maybe Spandangle *did* do that finger-flashy thing on us.'

'He hasn't done anything to us,' said Mel.

Wren huffed. 'But he could have done it to *you* and made you believe –'

'Shut up about that!' said Mel. 'Let's go and –'

'What's the matter?' said Ludo. 'You've gone as white as a sheet.'

'It's Scratchbeard. He's coming this way.'

'It *can't* be,' said Wren. 'He's dead.'

'I can see him too,' said Ludo. 'He's singed around the edges but he's definitely not dead. How did he find us?'

'Skeg!' said Wren. 'Let's get out of here!'

The three turned, but blocking their escape stood Doctor Sarcophagus, Nelly Buboes and Canker with his dog. They each grabbed one of the children.

'So we meet again,' said the doctor as he shook Mel. He slapped the boy across the face.

Canker had hold of Ludo and his dog nipped the boy painfully on his leg.

'You won't be getting away from us this time,' said Nelly as she held Wren's neck in a headlock.

'I've still got something of yours,' said Mel, struggling to remove something from inside his doublet.

A quizzical look crossed Doctor Sarcophagus's face. 'Oh yes? What's that?'

'This!' Mel tipped some of the lock-melting potion on to his captor's bare hand. With an agonised scream, the doctor released Mel, who kicked him, ducked under his arm and fled into the crowd.

Ludo bit down on to Canker's hand, at the same time kicking the dog viciously in the snout. He ran after Mel.

Wren reached back and dug her nails into Nelly Buboes' eyes and wriggled free of her grasp. But, as she tried to follow the boys, she was seized from behind by Scratchbeard. He held his shiv to her throat.

'You stupid beggars,' spat Scratchbeard. 'Can't you even hold on to three children?' Then, to Wren, 'And *you* can stop struggling, Missy.' His knife drew blood at her neck as he pressed harder.

'Where'd they go?' said Doctor Sarcophagus through gritted teeth as he bound his burnt hand with a length of rag.

'They're making for the fairground,' said Canker as he tried to soothe his yelping dog.

'Come on, Canker,' said Nelly. 'That mutt of yours found them before. She can find them again.'

'She won't be tracking anything for a while,' said Canker. 'That little scrot kicked her in the sniffer.'

'We don't need the mutt,' said Scratchbeard. 'Here, Nelly, keep hold of the girl – *properly* this time. Canker, Doc, follow me.'

Scratchbeard led them through the crowd and into the heart of the fairground. He caught sight of Mel and Ludo making for a ride near the foot of the Ferris wheel. The top of the flat, cut-out facade was painted to look like the spiky roofline of a haunted castle. Ghoulish faces peered from tall, cobwebbed windows and painted bats roosted beneath the battlements. In big letters, drawn to seem as if they were dripping with green slime, were the words:

Goldie's Ghost Train
Enter at Your Peril

Built into the right-hand side was a ticket booth with a handwritten notice in its pointed window that stated:

Temporarily Closed for Maintenance

'Look, the entrance doors are still swinging,' said Canker. 'They've gone in.'

'So they like their entertainment on the ghoulish side, do they?' said Scratchbeard. He pushed open the doors and went inside.

Professor Thinkwell

The grip tightened on Mel's ankle. With a feeling of dread he turned to look at his captor. But, by the light of his feather, he saw not a fear-wig grasping him but a disembodied hand. The hand released its grip and cocked its index finger as if to say 'follow me'. As the hand scuttled off on its fingertips like a large, pink spider, Mel crawled backwards after it down the cramped and buckled shaft.

The hand led Mel through a zigzag maze within the folds of the transmogrificator until they came to a space where he was able to turn around and face it. As Mel studied the hand he noticed that it wore four strange rings, one in the shape of an ear, one in the shape of a brain, one in the shape of a pair of lips and the other with what looked like a real, lidded eye set into it.

The eye blinked several times and the lips spoke. 'My name is Professor Thinkwell. Who are you?' The voice was thin and high pitched.

'My name's Mel. What are you doing here?'

'Trying to find my way back to Castle Habilis, of course.'

'*Castle Habilis?* That's where Ludo's being taken.'

'Who's Ludo?'

'He's my friend. I'm meant to be going to Castle Habilis with Wren – she's my other friend – and Mrs Morel and Mrs Wood-Blewit.'

'Mr Habilis's aunts?'

'They're his *aunts*?' Mel thought for a moment. 'Can you take me to Castle Habilis?'

'Normally, nothing could be simpler. But I must confess that I appear to be lost.'

'That makes two of us,' said Mel. 'Excuse me for mentioning it, but shouldn't there be a bit more of you? More than just a hand, I mean.'

The eye in the ring seemed to stare hard at him for a moment as if assessing whether he was an idiot. 'Of course there should. I'm lucky that Mr Habilis thinks my hands are so useful, otherwise they'd be locked in his library along with everybody else's.'

'He keeps hands in a library?'

'Indeed. The rest of me is back at Castle Habilis

inventing all kinds of things for Mr Habilis. I invented an artificial hand to use in my laboratory so that this, my real one,' he waggled his fingers, 'would be free to travel about on my own business. I even invented the transmogrificators, you know.'

'They're very impressive,' said Mel. 'All that travelling and shape-changing stuff.'

'Oh, but they do rather more than that. For instance, you can pass directly from one transmogrificator to another – and indeed pass to anywhere within Castle Habilis. All you need to do is to find a portal and dial the correct coordinates. The trouble is everything seems to have gone haywire and the portals have been misplaced.'

'That was probably us. We changed from a submarine to a tree-loper and then the mutation music got lost.'

'No, it's rather more fundamental than the host transmogrificator simply mutating,' said Professor Thinkwell's hand. 'If that was the case the portals would still be around.'

'Perhaps it's the fear-wigs? Those horrible half-men–half-earwig creatures.'

'Yes, I know fear-wigs. They're slow, stupid beasts. I think it unlikely.' The professor's hand was quiet for a moment. 'We need to find the power source. It's the only part of a transmogrificator that never changes. There'll be a portal there.'

'Is that all?' said Mrs Wood-Blewit, regarding the meagre pile of tattered music that Mel had rescued.

'I'm afraid so,' said Mrs Morel. 'The fear-wigs must have destroyed the rest.'

'Does that mean we're stuck here?' asked Wren.

'Not a bit of it,' said Mrs Morel. 'We have one complete piece – even if it's not the one I would have chosen in our current predicament.'

'It's the "Moth Minuet",' said Mrs Wood-Blewit. 'You know, the one in three movements.'

'A *moth*? A flimsy moth up against those huge spiders and fear-wigs?' The colour left Wren's face.

Mrs Morel shrugged. 'I'm afraid it's all we have. We'd best get on with it. We don't have much time.'

'Hold on,' said Wren. 'We can't mutate. Not until Mel's back.'

Mrs Wood-Blewit sighed. 'I'm sorry, but we have to. Mel did a very brave thing going into the folded-up part of the transmogrificator like that. But if we don't mutate and try and get out of here right away then very soon we will be on the spiders' menu. Mel's sacrifice will have been for nothing.'

'And don't forget about Ludo,' added Mrs Morel. 'We have to get the transmogrificator back for Mr Habilis to release him.'

'But you can't!' protested Wren. 'Mel will be crushed.'

'I'm afraid we must,' said Mrs Morel.

'*No!*' cried Wren. 'I won't let you.' She tried to snatch the music but Mrs Morel held it high and out of her reach. 'You mustn't do this. Please wait. Mel will be back soon. I know he will.'

'I'm truly sorry, Wren, but we have no choice and no time,' said Mrs Wood-Blewit as she dragged a straight-backed chair over to the morphonium and sat down.

'We feel just as bad about this as you,' said Mrs Morel, arranging the music. With her free hand she held Wren at arm's length.

Mrs Wood-Blewit began to play, drowning out Wren's anguished cries of protest, and the plates of the transmogrificator started to rearrange themselves.

Mel had not crawled far before he heard the music of the morphonium start up. The walls and floor of the shaft began to vibrate strongly. Professor Thinkwell's hand urgently beckoned Mel after him.

'Wait for me!' called Mel.

The walls of the shaft expanded and contracted and pushed Mel first to one side and then to the other. He saw Professor Thinkwell's hand take a left-hand fork but, just as Mel reached it, the passage vanished as an iron plate in the floor swung up like a drawbridge, sealing it with a resounding *clank*. Behind him Mel could hear the shaft collapsing. He scrabbled forwards over the shuddering plates and down the right-hand fork just instants before the mouth of the opening folded shut.

Mel crawled on, wishing with all his heart that he could get to his feet and run, but he was hampered by moving plates that dug painfully into his ribs or suddenly turned a downhill slide into an uphill climb. Worse still, in places they seemed to block his progress altogether and he was forced to retreat and take an alternative gap between the folds.

Then, suddenly, there was a hair-raising screech and Mel came face to face with another fear-wig. Its huge, watery eyes narrowed and its needle-sharp teeth gnashed as it hauled itself forwards. Mel tried to push himself back but the passage buckled again and he could feel it tighten around his body like a steel trap.

Mel uttered a panicked cry. 'Help!'

The fear-wig crawled closer and reached a powerful arm forwards to grab its prey when an exceptionally loud creak and violent shudder popped all the rivets in the right-hand wall, sending them flying into the shaft like a whining hail of bullets. Several pierced the fear-wig and Mel was painfully stung by others that had ricocheted off the walls. The wounding only seemed to enrage the hideous creature and it made a grab for Mel with its bloodied but still functioning arm.

Then the floor gave way beneath Mel and he found himself hanging head-first over a steep slope. He felt helpless as he dangled there. Sheer terror lent him strength and he squirmed and kicked with all his might. Then, suddenly, he was free and falling downwards on the chute-like surface. Above and behind him he heard the ominous creak as the shaft where he had been only moments before finally collapsed. The scream of the dying fear-wig faded behind him as he plunged on.

As Mel hurtled downwards his head span with the dizzying speed. Then he heard rushing water that grew in volume. The metal all around him was becoming increasingly clammy the further he fell and the walls were streaked with moss and rust. There seemed no end to his descent and, for a moment, he imagined himself sliding downwards forever, but then the shaft got brighter and he was spewed out of a fold, tumbling head over heels. 'Whoa!' he cried as he came to a stop, face-down, in a puddle.

Mel was deafened by water thundering down from somewhere far above him. He looked up to see the water turning a multitude of waterwheels of a great many different sizes that were attached to gears, rods and pistons around the edge of the soaring, rectangular shaft. The turning wheels finally disappeared into the darkness high overhead. The sound of their rumbling and squeaking could just be heard over the roar of the falling water.

Waiting for him, tapping his fingers impatiently, was Professor Thinkwell's hand. 'There you are at last,' shouted the hand. Mel could barely hear it. 'This is the transmogrificator's power source. We need to ascend to the top of the shaft. Would you oblige me with a lift?'

Still shaking from his narrow escape, Mel picked himself up and placed the professor's hand on his shoulder. Out of breath and with every joint in his body aching, he used iron rungs set in the side of the shaft to climb. By the time he reached the top he was soaked through from the spray and his ears were ringing from the incessant noise.

The rungs had brought him to a gantry that ran like a landing around the top of the shaft. In the centre of each side and jutting out over the dizzying drop was one of four large and ugly iron gargoyles, their sculpted wings folded across their backs. Spewing from their open beaks were the ceaseless streams of water that turned the waterwheels below. On the gantry behind each of them was an identical riveted steel door with a strange dial formed from concentric rings at its centre. Above each door was a set of two lights, one red, the other green. All of the doors were closed and the red lights lit. They cast a hellish glow around the otherwise dark gantry.

Mel put his hand out and rested it on a gargoyle as he struggled to regain his breath. The spinning waterwheels disappeared down into the bowels of the transmogrificator, making him feel giddy, but his eye was caught by something else. Riding the turning waterwheels like an escalator rose a fear-wig. It was using its muscular arms to swing from one to the other as each wheel reached the top of its arc.

'Professor, I think those fear-wigs are more clever than you thought,' shouted Mel. He felt the professor's hand inch forwards on his shoulder and peer down with its eyed ring. The hand stiffened with alarm. It tapped Mel on the shoulder and pointed insistently at one of the doors. 'That's the portal that leads to Castle Habilis?' asked Mel. The professor's hand gave a thumbs-up. Mel tried the door. 'But it's locked. There's not even a handle.' He hammered on it with all his might. 'Quick, Professor. What do I do?'

There was the sound of a dreadful screech that Mel knew only too well. Hauling itself up on to the far side of the landing was the fear-wig. Its head turned and its pitiless eyes fixed on Mel. Its fish-mouth opened, revealing rows of hundreds of needle teeth.

The professor's hand tapped urgently on Mel's shoulder. It pointed at the door next to them again.

'But it won't open,' said Mel desperately. Then he saw that there was a hand-shaped depression set into the wall alongside it. He slapped his hand into it and the rings of the dial in the centre of the door began to rotate. The red light above the door went out and the green light came on. The door swung outwards and Mel dived for the open door, ripping the sleeve of his doublet on the jamb. With a last look behind him he saw a door next to the fear-wig fly open, sending the creature tumbling backwards over the rail and down the shaft, its scream quickly lost in the roaring of the water.

In the instant before Mel's door slammed shut he saw a face he recognised appear through the other door.

* * *

'What's a "separator"?' asked Ludo as he and Shale listened at the door at the end of the crinkled corridor.

Shale held up the stumpy sockets where his hands used to be.

'Oh,' said Ludo, '*that* kind of separator.' He swallowed hard. 'Let's get out of here.'

But try as they might, Ludo and Shale could not open the door back into the transmogrificator.

'The only way out's by the other door,' said Ludo.

'We can't go that way,' said Shale.

'Then we're stuck here,' said Ludo.

'We can't stay here either,' said Shale. 'If the transmogrificator mutates, we'll be crushed.'

'Then we've got no choice. We *have* to go through the other door.'

'Are you mad?'

'We'll just have to be careful.' Ludo led Shale back to the far door. He put his hand into the hand lock and the door sprung open.

They came out on to a ledge over a cavern-sized space and dropped to their knees. Below them were a number of figments with bald heads and pointed ears.

'Handymen!' hissed Shale. 'Mr Habilis's helpers.'

The figments' shiny rubber suits squeaked as they moved and reflected the many flaming torches that lit the space. In the middle of this weird congregation was a tall guillotine-like contraption with a spinning blade. It was being cranked up by two of the handymen while another was swabbing something fresh and red from around its base. In front of the device sat a large basket full of severed hands. A terrified figment was dragged towards the machine and his hands were fastened into a holder beneath the blade.

'Come on, let's get out of –' Ludo felt something cold and sharp touch the back of his neck. He slowly turned. Standing over him and Shale was another handyman.

He looked at Ludo's hands and his eyes lit up.

Goldie's Ghost Train

Glinting in the half-light inside the ghost train, twin rails wove like a meandering river through cobweb-draped doorways and past eerie, ill-lit alcoves. In one such alcove the tableau of a skeleton family sat at a table taking tea. Green vapour slowly snaked from the spout of the teapot and lay glowing like mist in the teacups. The skeletons' bones and the crockery on the table rattled as a trapdoor beneath them slammed open and the carved and gilded head of a young figment girl rose from it. She was dressed in gypsy clothes and adorned with lots of large and fake jewellery. Lit by a lantern from below, she appeared almost as spectral as the family seated above her. 'All right, Pilfer. Try it one more time.'

There was a mechanical whirring noise, followed by a series of pops as green-tinted spotlights glowed into life, picking out the scene. Then Mummy Skeleton tilted the teapot towards Daddy Skeleton's teacup. There was a clank as the lid of the pot flew off and a bat began to unfold its wings and rise into the air from inside. The two child skeletons started to leap from their chairs in alarm. Then, with a screech and a judder, everything froze and the lights flickered out.

'How's that, Goldie?' came a male voice from somewhere amid the machinery below.

'Nope, Pilfer. It's still stuck. Have you tried wiggling the grommet?'

'I've wiggled till I've giggled but the scrot won't budge.'

'Knickers!' said Goldie. 'Everyone at Pennyweight Market clamouring for a ride on the ghost train and we're scuppered by a sticky grommet. If I ever lay my hands on that scrot who sold the ride to us . . . Why ever did you talk me into buying a ghost train from a figment you met here in the market, of all places?'

'Because it was a steal.' The scent of engine oil and a collection of grease stains defining parts of an otherwise invisible face rose from the trapdoor alongside Goldie.

'And I'd like to know what's behind that locked door with the dial and the red light over it. Didn't you even get a key when you handed over all our hard-earned dosh?'

'Wouldn't do any good if I did,' said Pilfer. 'There's no keyhole that I could see.' A rag appeared and wiped the face, leaving it completely invisible.

'And what's that great big organ at the back for? When you start to play it, it feels like the whole ghost train's going to shake apart. It's beginning to look like we flushed our money down the drain.'

'*Shhh* . . . Did you hear that?' said Pilfer, lowering his voice.

'Probably some kids,' whispered Goldie.

'I don't think so. I can hear a dog – and a man's voice.'

'I'd best go and tell them we're closed for repairs.'

'Hang on, Goldie. Something tells me they're up to no good. Call it robber's intuition.'

'I hope that's *ex*-robber's intuition?'

'Of course. Just stay put while I go and have a shufti. Dim that lantern now, and take this.' A large spanner floated into Goldie's outstretched hand. 'Just in case.' The floorboards beneath the skeletons' tea party creaked as Pilfer climbed out of the trapdoor and crept off.

Doctor Sarcophagus withdrew a crystal phial from one of his many pockets and shook it. A fierce light kindled inside it, causing the three beggars to wince and shield their eyes.

Canker blinked rapidly as his eyes grew accustomed to the sudden light and he found himself face to face with a hideous zombie. '*Ahhhh!*' He turned to flee and stumbled into the arms of a looming vampire. 'Get away from me! I don't want to die!'

'Shut up, you moron,' said Scratchbeard. 'They're only dummies. This is a ghost train.' He thumped the vampire's papier-mâché head. 'Now, where're those little pus-buckets hiding?'

'Let's split up,' said Doctor Sarcophagus. 'Take these.' He handed his accomplices a phial each. 'Don't shake them too hard and, whatever you do, don't drop them. The potion's volatile and liable to explode. I'll stay here by the entrance in case they try and get out this way. You two circle round.

Whoever finds them first, sing out.'

Scratchbeard parted some cobweb curtains and disappeared through a doorway to the left. Canker nervously shook his phial, causing it to glow. He ducked under the vampire's outstretched arms and slunk off to the right. He had only gone a short distance before he smelt a strong scent of engine oil and felt a tap on his shoulder.

'What're you up to?' said Pilfer's voice in his ear.

Eyes wide, Canker spun round. 'Who's that?' He searched back and forth with his glowing phial at arm's length but there was no sign of where the voice or smell had come from.

'What's up, Canker? Have you found them?' It was Doctor Sarcophagus's raised voice from behind him.

'Did you say something, Doc?'

'I said "What's up? Have you found them?"'

'No, before that.'

'Get a grip, Canker!' called Scratchbeard from out of the darkness to his left. 'It's just a trick they use to give customers the willies. Now get on with it.'

'I wouldn't do that if I was you,' said Pilfer

from very near Canker's other ear.

Canker turned quickly but then stopped. 'It's just a trick,' he breathed to himself. 'It's just a trick.' Then, louder, 'Yeah, very good. Very *scary*. Come on, you lazy mutt.' He tugged on his dog's leash but it resisted. When he lowered his phial to investigate, he saw that the leash was fastened to one of the rails. The dog had gone. From out of the darkness off to his right he heard a faint growling as if someone was holding the dog's muzzle shut. Then there was silence. 'Scratchbeard? Doc? Did one of you take my dog?'

'Why should we take your dog?' called Doctor Sarcophagus. 'She's no good to us at the moment anyway. Keep looking for those scuts.'

'But . . .' Canker untied the leash from the rail. 'If this is to give people the willies, then it's working.'

He came to the alcove in which the family of skeletons were at a table taking tea. Goldie was holding a large spanner and standing as still as a statue to one side. Canker was reaching out to reassure himself that she was only a dummy when she spoke.

'Keep your grubby mitts off the exhibits.' With a swing Goldie brought the spanner down on Canker's head, knocking him out cold.

'What was that?' called Doctor Sarcophagus as he peered into the darkness. 'Scratchbeard, Canker, talk to me.'

'What's going on?' Scratchbeard shouted back.

'I don't know. I heard something. Is Canker with you?'

'Pipe down, Doc! Those little scrots will hear you.'

A worried frown creased Doctor Sarcophagus's singed brow. The frown deepened when he smelt engine oil and then his eyes opened wide in alarm when he heard a voice in his left ear.

'Scary in here, ain't it?'

He turned quickly but there was no one there.

'But it's all part of the fun of the fair,' said Pilfer close by his right ear, 'don't you think?'

Doctor Sarcophagus turned the other way. There was no one there either.

'Of course, it could be that it's not a trick after all,'

came Pilfer's voice from in front of him. 'Maybe us zombies and vampires are *real.*' The dummy of the vampire began to waggle its arms.

'Real my eye. It's those skegging kids!' Doctor Sarcophagus tried to dart forwards but his shoelaces had been tied together and he pitched heavily on to his face, hitting his head on a rail. He lay still.

'Two down, one to go,' said Pilfer softly.

'Now, where would I hide if I was one of those scuts?' Scratchbeard said to himself.

He stopped in front of a tableau of a torture chamber. In the centre of the display was a rack complete with a victim stretched out on it. The large star-wheel was being operated by two dwarves with black masks covering their faces.

Scratchbeard smiled to himself and climbed into the alcove. 'Got you!' He seized the nearest figure. 'Scrot!' It was made from papier-mâché. So was the second. He sniffed and was sure he smelt engine oil.

'Find what you were looking for?' came Pilfer's voice from near at hand.

In one fluid motion Scratchbeard picked up one of the dummies and hurled it in the direction of the voice. There was a loud '*Ooof!*' followed by a string of expletives. Scratchbeard leapt over the dummy and darted away into the darkness towards the rear of the ghost train.

A red light seemed to hang suspended in the air. The light from his phial showed it to be a lamp – one of a pair – above a door. 'Must be the exit.' Scratchbeard searched for a handle but there was only a strange dial in the middle. He tried pushing the door but soon gave up. 'Looks like the only way in or out's through the front.' As he turned, something hit him hard in the stomach.

'All right, Stinky. You and me's going to have a little word,' said Pilfer.

Scratchbeard threw a few wild punches into the air around him but they connected with nothing.

'It's fisticuffs you want, is it?' said Pilfer, hitting the beggar on the jaw.

Scratchbeard spun in mid-air. As he fell towards the door, his outstretched hand landed in a half-hidden hand-shaped depression in the wall. Immediately, the dial spun, the red light above the door went out, a green one lit up and the door flew open. Scratchbeard fell headlong through it. The door slammed behind him, the dial spun again and the red light came back on.

'So that's how it opens, is it?'

Suddenly, Goldie was behind him. 'Pilfer, come quick.'

'Just a mo, Goldie. I've found out how this door opens.'

'Show me later. Just come, will you?' Goldie led Pilfer towards the front of the ghost train and opened the entrance doors just enough so that they could peer through the crack. 'Take a look through here and tell me what you see.'

There was a shuffling sound as Pilfer took up position. 'I can see those two scrots we knocked out and some singed old biddy holding a girl.' Then he gave a muffled gasp. '*It's Wren!*'

'Yeah,' said Goldie. 'It looks like she's in disguise with those black clothes and that mask, but it's her all right.'

'So Madame Manto's vision in her crystal ball was right. They *were* in Deep Trouble. That cake we sent them did the trick. They must have used Cogito to help them break out.' Pilfer was quiet while he looked some more. 'But where're Mel and Ludo? Those three are inseparable.'

'Exactly what I was thinking. I bet that bunch of scrots were looking for them in here. They must be hiding inside the ghost train.'

Just then there came a crashing and splintering sound from somewhere behind them.

'I don't like the sound of that,' said Goldie. 'Come on.'

They found a rough hole in the wooden outside wall, its edges splintered.

'They must've kicked their way out,' said Pilfer.

Goldie knelt and peered through the hole. 'No sign of them. I bet they've gone to rescue Wren.'

'Let's go and help them. You ask that hunking great doorman of Madam Manto's, too. Meanwhile, I'll treat our smelly friends out there to another demonstration of invisibility.'

* * *

'Stop struggling, you little minx!' Nelly Buboes gave an extra twist to the headlock she was using to hold Wren. The body of her prisoner went limp.

'Now look what you've done,' said Canker as he sat on the ground nursing a bump on his head the size of a goose egg. 'You've killed her.'

Doctor Sarcophagus looked no better than Canker. He dabbed at his bloody nose with the end of his turban, which had begun to unravel. 'She's just faking.' He kicked Wren in the shin.

'You stinking pile of maggot-riddled scrot!' spat Wren. 'Do that again and see what happens.'

'*See.*' Doctor Sarcophagus looked around him. 'Where's Scratchbeard got to?' Then he sniffed and winced. 'Can you smell engine oil?' Suddenly, the doctor's legs shot out from under him and he sprawled on the ground.

'That's no way to treat a lady,' said Pilfer's voice from out of thin air.

'It's the ghosts,' wailed Canker. 'They've got out!'

Just then Canker's dog hobbled out of the crowd. It

fastened its teeth into something invisible.

'Agghhh!' screamed Pilfer. 'Get off!' The dog appeared to flail about in mid-air, as Pilfer tried to kick her free.

Doctor Sarcophagus got to his feet and used his outstretched hands to probe the air above the whirling dog. They soon connected with Pilfer. 'I don't know what it is, but I've got the scrot. Help me pin it down.'

Canker joined the doctor on the ground as he bucked up and down, trying to hold on to the invisible figment.

'Get off of me, you stinking scuts!' bellowed Pilfer.

'You heard the man,' said a booming voice.

Doctor Sarcophagus and Canker looked up. Looming over them was the enormous mauve figure of Madam Manto's doorman. Goldie stood to one side, hefting her spanner.

'Mind your own business.' Canker's bravado would have been more convincing if his voice had not trembled.

The doorman picked him up by the scruff of his neck. 'I'm making it my business. Now *scram*.' He pushed Canker, who staggered forwards.

'I thought I heard him say "scram",' said Pilfer to Doctor Sarcophagus and Nelly.

'And leave the girl,' added Goldie.

Nelly Buboes thought about this for a second as she weighed up the odds. Then she sniffed loudly and thrust Wren forwards. 'Take her. We can find her again any time we choose.' She turned and, with the other two beggars close behind, fled into the crowd.

Goldie dropped her spanner and dashed forwards. 'Wren! It's so good to see you. Are you all right?' She embraced her friend.

Wren pushed her away. 'Stay away from me, you freak.'

'Wren? It's Goldie. Don't you recognise me? Pilfer's here too.'

'Hello, Wren,' said Pilfer. 'Where're Mel and Ludo?'

'Who said that?' Wren backed away.

'What's the matter?' asked Goldie. 'Have you had a knock on the head?'

'Those scrots didn't drug you, did they?' said Pilfer.

Wren stooped and picked up the spanner. 'Come

near me and I'll bash your skegging heads in.'

The mauve man took a step forwards but Goldie held up her hand to stop him. 'Wren?'

Wren threw the spanner, narrowly missing Goldie, turned on her heels and ran off into the crowd.

'What's gotten into her?' said Pilfer.

'None of this adds up,' said Goldie.

'Can I do anything?' asked the mauve man.

'No, thanks,' said Goldie. 'You've been a great help. You'd best be getting back to Madam Manto.'

'We should have held on to one of those beggars,' said Pilfer. 'We could have got some answers out of him.'

'Well, we know Wren's here in Pennyweight Market.'

'So it's a safe bet that Mel and Ludo are too.'

'Let's go and find them,' said Goldie.

'Hang on,' said Pilfer. 'One of those beggars is still in the ghost train. I was trying to tell you. He went through that locked door. I know how it opens. Come on, we'll get some answers out of him.'

'Where do you think it leads?' said Pilfer as they stood in front of the door.

The reflection of the red light glowed in Goldie's gilded face like a liquid ruby. 'Well, there's only one way we're going to find out. How does it open?'

'I saw Stinky put his mitt in that hollow.'

'This one?' Goldie placed her hand in the hand-shaped depression. The dial spun. The red light went out. The green light came on. The door swung open. Beyond the door was an eccentric corridor full of giddy angles.

Goldie stepped inside on to the sloping floor and ran her hand over the crinkled wall. 'It's empty. Are you sure he came in here?'

'He came in here, all right,' said Pilfer. 'Look, there's another door at the far end.' The sound of Pilfer's footsteps advanced down the crazy corridor.

Goldie followed. 'There's another red light above it. And another of those hand-shaped locks.' She placed her hand in the depression. The dial and lights changed and the door began to open but stopped.

'Here, Goldie, let me,' said Pilfer. He grunted as he pushed. 'It's stuck.'

Goldie lent her weight. 'Both together now.

On the count of three. One, two, *three*!'

The door exploded outwards. There was a screaming cry as whoever had been blocking the door was catapulted away and Goldie and Pilfer fell headlong through the door to the sound of roaring water.

What happened next all seemed to take place at once and it was only later that Goldie was able to piece it together into some kind of order. She and Pilfer had emerged on to a rectangular gantry or landing around the top of a deep shaft. In the middle of each side of the gantry was a large iron gargoyle spewing water from its mouth into the void in the centre. In front of them, hurtling out over the head of the nearest gargoyle, was a hideous half-man, half-earwig creature. Just visible for an instant through the door to her left before it slammed shut was a face she recognised. As the dial spun, the green light above it went out and the red light lit up, she shouted his name.

'Mel!'

Moth Mode

The thunder of the organ died away as Mrs Wood-Blewit paused at the end of the movement. The hull of the transmogrificator gave a final creak as the first phase of the mutation completed itself. In the fishbowl sphere nothing could be seen of the transmogrificator, which had sunk back beneath the silver-grey cocoon of spider silk.

Once the mutation had begun Wren realised there was nothing more she could do to help Mel and the fight went out of her. With Mrs Morel and Mrs Wood-Blewit she watched the spider's silk writhe as the newly mutated transmogrificator moved beneath it. Then two of the craft's sickle-shaped mandibles pierced the surface and, in no time at all, a large hole had appeared and the transmogrificator, in the form of a huge, metal caterpillar, emerged.

'Now for the second movement,' said Mrs Morel.

Mrs Wood-Blewit started playing again and the transmogrificator began to grate and groan around them as it changed shape in response.

Inside the fishbowl the image of the caterpillar began to spin silk of its own and to seal its body inside a new cocoon. Through the translucent pupa casing it could be seen to move about for a while and then it was still. The music became softer and softer until Mrs Wood-Blewit stopped playing altogether.

'What's happening?' said Wren. 'Why've you stopped?'

'It's the end of the second movement,' said Mrs Morel, pointing to the music. 'The score calls for a thirty-two bar pause. We must be sure and keep our nerve.'

Mrs Wood-Blewit began to count to herself under her breath. 'One . . . two . . . three . . .'

Wren pointed at the fishbowl. 'Oh, no! *Look!*'

Thirty-two legs, attached to four giant spiders, were marching over the inner surface of the larder towards the defenceless pupa. A host of fear-wigs crawled in their wake.

'. . . eight . . . nine . . . ten.'

'Can't we do something?' said Wren.

'*Shhh*. Don't distract Mrs Wood-Blewit,' whispered

Mrs Morel. 'This pause mustn't be ignored. It will ruin the mutation.'

'But . . .' Wren stared at the fishbowl as she gnawed at a fingernail.

The spiders and fear-wigs drew nearer.

'. . . sixteen . . . seventeen . . . eighteen.'

And began clambering over the pupa case.

'. . . twenty-two . . . twenty-three . . . twenty-four.'

One of the spiders wrenched a great section of the soft chrysalis away and a number of fear-wigs scrambled into the resulting hole. Wren could hear them as they scuttled about somewhere on the other side of the cabin wall. 'Those fear-wigs can't get in here,' she said, 'can they?' She touched the cabin wall and it felt soft and leathery.

'I'm afraid we remain rather vulnerable until the mutation's compete,' said Mrs Morel.

'. . . thirty-four . . . thirty-five . . . thirty-six.' Mrs Wood-Blewit began to play the third movement.

There was a loud tearing noise and a split opened in the wall next to the morphonium. A fear-wig's arm squeezed through it and began blindly snatching with its scaly, taloned hand. Wren picked up a plaque with a large, mounted mushroom and smashed it against the flailing limb as a second rent opened next to it. One arm and then the head of another fear-wig writhed through. Its eyes fixed on the occupants and it screamed as it began tearing at the rent and forcing the rest of its body into the interior.

'Allegro, I think, Mrs Wood-Blewit,' said Mrs Morel as she picked up another plaque and used it to bash at the fear-wig while she turned the music with her other hand. 'Or even presto.'

The tempo of the music increased.

More rents appeared in the wall and another in the ceiling. Giant fangs and then a huge, hairy spider's limb as thick as a tree trunk forced their way through. All around the cabin new rips pierced the fabric of the transmogrificator as more and more fear-wigs opened gashes. The walls were now a mass of writhing fear-wig arms and heads, their screams a jarring counterpoint to the music of the morphonium.

'Prestissimo, Mrs Wood-Blewit, prestissimo!' shouted Mrs Morel.

Wren took off her doublet and wrapped it around her arm in readiness to fight the invaders.

The tempo of the music increased even more.

'Look!' cried Wren. 'The walls. They're solidifying.'

The fear-wigs screamed louder as the leathery walls hardened back into their customary iron and the gashes healed as new plates swung into place. Those creatures that could beat a hasty retreat. A long, hairy spider's leg was pinched off and twitched convulsively on the floor. The slower and less fortunate fear-wigs left their hands and arms and, in one case, a severed head behind. It rolled, open-mouthed, on the deck as the resounding finale of the final movement sounded and the creaking of the mutation ceased.

The image in the fishbowl now revealed the transmogrificator as a giant, iron moth forcing its way from the cocoon. For a long moment it perched on the end of the empty pupa case, flexing its new wings. The spiders and remaining fear-wigs regrouped and began to advance once more but, as they got within striking distance, the transmogrificator spread its wings and took to the air. The frustrated screams of the fear-wigs echoed around the larder and the spiders shot strands of sticky silk from the tips of their abdomens at the escaping transmogrificator. The craft made one circuit of the vast space before diving through the entrance hole and, with slow beats of its massive wings, soared up through the forest canopy into the clear sky.

Mrs Wood-Blewit shut the lid of the morphonium. 'Oh no, not *another* one!'

'What are you talking about?' said Mrs Morel as she turned to look where her companion was pointing. Lying in the middle of the deck was Wren's empty doublet. 'Oh dear. She must have been folded up in the mutation.'

'To lose one child was a tragedy,' said Mrs Wood-Blewit, shaking her head. 'To lose two was a calamity,' she sighed. 'But to lose *three*.'

Unseen high above the forest wheeled three birds with oily, black feathers. As the transmogrificator-moth flew from the mouth of the larder, one of the stare-crows detached itself from the motley flock, wheeled about, and headed back towards Deep Trouble to report to Spiracle, Blinker, Gusset and Flob.

The seething cauldron of terror, grief and anger that bubbled inside Wren was suddenly displaced by shock as she landed hard on her bottom. She quickly worked out what had happened and where she was. A thought crystallised. *If I've survived falling into a mutating hull, then perhaps Mel has too.* 'Mel! Mel, where are you?' she called.

She listened hard for a reply but at first all she could hear was the faint music of the morphonium and, louder, the metallic creaks and groans of the hull. Then she discerned other sounds too: the sound of falling water and the squeaking of machinery. Deciding to investigate, she began navigating the eccentric passages by the light beams from rivet holes and by her fingertips, heading in the direction of the sounds.

The darkness paled until she could see again and she came out at the foot of the waterwheels. With no other obvious way forwards, she climbed the rungs and eventually hauled herself on to the landing with the gargoyles. Her white silk shirt and hose were soaked through and clung to her slender frame. Her long, auburn hair lay limp against her head. She tried the four doors she found there but they were all locked, their dials immobile and their red lights glowing steadily. Caught between the door and its frame in the last she tried was a shred of deep blue velvet. Her heart leapt. *Mel must have gone through the door.* She spotted the hand-shaped depression and instinctively placed her hand in the lock, stepping through the moment the door opened.

Wren found herself in a mad-angled, crinkly corridor with yet another door at the far end that opened the same way. As this door closed behind her, Wren stepped into the back of a large pantry, leaving a trail of wet footprints. All around her were stacked casks and sacks of foodstuffs and shelves piled with straw-lined baskets. The darkened room was lit by stripes of orange light seeping through the louvred slats of the large door at the front of the pantry. There were also pyramid stacks of mottled eggs as big as rugby balls, rainbow-plumed poultry and sides of what might have been dinosaur meat hanging on s-shaped hooks from the ceiling. Beyond the door she could hear the buzz of voices, the clinking of crockery and the rattle of pots and pans. There was the smell of bread baking and meat roasting. They were sounds and smells she remembered well, if not fondly, from her time as a kitchen girl in Ambrosius Blenk's mansion before she became an apprentice.

Wren crept forwards so that she could peep between the louvres in the door. Through them she could see the hustle and bustle of the kitchen. But one thing was very different from any kitchen she had ever seen. Although all of the kitchen staff wore white aprons and tall chefs hats, none of them had any hands. Their arms all ended in utensils appropriate to the tasks they were engaged in. Pastry makers' wrists had rolling pins or pastry cutters attached, soup stirrers' arms ended in spoons or ladles and dishwashers' in scrubbing brushes.

Standing in the middle of all this activity was another fat female figment. Unlike the others, she had an air of authority and seemed to be in charge. In place of hands she had two large and very sharp cleavers.

Set into a sweaty face, her glittering, black eyes missed nothing as she surveyed her domain. A bead of sweat trembled on the end of her nose. There was no sign of Mel.

Just then Wren heard something soft falling behind her. She turned and saw several honey-coloured apples rolling across the floor. 'Mel? Is that you?' She edged towards them and just saw the toe of a shoe being withdrawn into a hiding place between two casks. Wren knelt and peered in. 'Mel?'

Staring back at her from the deep shadows was not her friend but the frightened face of a dark-haired girl a little younger than she was. She had the blurred features of a figment from the background of a painting. The girl tried to cover her pale and indistinct face. With a shock, Wren realised that she had hooks in place of hands. On one of the hooks was speared a half-eaten apple.

'Please, I just wanted something to eat,' said the girl. 'They never feed us enough. You won't tell the cook I'm here, will you?'

'No, I won't tell anyone,' said Wren. 'I promise.'

Then, to make the girl feel more at ease, 'I'm not supposed to be here either. What's your name?'

The girl stared at Wren for a while, trying to make up her mind if she could trust her. Then her blurry features formed into a wan smile. 'My name's Shingle.'

'And mine's Wren. Where are we?'

Shingle crawled from her hiding place and stood up. She was a head shorter than Wren and wore a grey dress embroidered with silver fingerprint swirls that reached to the floor. A silver circlet sat on her head and her long, dark hair draped her shoulders. 'You don't know where you are?' She took a bite of her apple.

Wren shook her head.

'We're in the kitchens, of course. Or the pantry, to be exact.'

'Have you seen my friend? He's a boy with blond hair. He'll be wearing a blue doublet. His name's Mel.'

'Here? In Castle Habilis?'

'*Castle Habilis?*' Then it struck her. 'Ludo!'

'What?'

'My other friend. If this is Castle Habilis, then he's here too. Have you seen another boy – about

196

my age – with dark hair and hazel eyes?'

'Have they come here to have their palms read by Mr Habilis?'

'Have their palms read?'

'Why else would you and your friends come here?' Shingle explained about Mr Habilis's trickery and how he was amassing a library of hands.

'What a terrible thing to do.'

Shingle nodded. 'Bumnote thinks that – *Shhh*! Someone's coming. It'll be the cook. We mustn't be caught here.'

'Quickly, come with me.' Wren grabbed one of Shingle's hooks and dragged her back to the door. She placed her hand inside the hand-lock, the dials spun and the door opened. Wren and Shingle fled through it and it closed behind them just as the door to the kitchen opened.

'Where are we?' said Shingle.

'See the door at the far end of the corridor? That's how I got here. It leads back into a transmogrificator. Here, I'll show you.' The door opened as soon as Wren pressed her hand into the lock.

'This is a transmogrificator?' Shingle asked.

'No, it's not,' said Wren, regarding the strange scene. 'I don't understand.'

The handyman prodded Ludo and Shale with the point of his trident down from the ledge and into the odd space below. The sounds of the separator's bacon-slicer blade falling and the resulting howl seemed abnormally loud to Ludo as he and Shale were marched to the far side of the folded cavern-like space.

'Why couldn't I have stayed put on the spindle?' said Shale, shaking his head.

'I'm sorry,' said Ludo. 'This is all my fault. There must be a way out of here.'

'Even if there was, we don't have any time,' said Shale. 'Look.'

Several handymen were swabbing the base of the separator clean, while another was putting an edge on the spinning blade with a hand-stone. A fountain of sparks whizzed into the air.

'But I can't just let them separate me.' Ludo swallowed with an audible gulp.

'Think yourself lucky,' said Shale. 'This time it'll be my *head* that's separated.'

Ludo and Shale were led towards the separator. The edge of its spinning blade glinted like diamonds.

Ludo was forced to his knees and his outstretched hands fixed into the vice-like holder beneath the blade. He tried to fight back but the handymen were too strong. One of them turned a handle at the side and the blade began to rise. The blood drained from Ludo's face and he felt faint. He looked desperately at Shale, who was being held fast between another two handymen. Higher and higher rose the spinning blade. When it reached the top of the structure it stopped. Ludo was terrified. He was sure he was going to be sick. The operator's hand moved towards the lever that released the blade.

All Part of the Conjuror's Art

'Perhaps we should go back and get Wren,' said Ludo, scanning the Pennyweight Market crowd for signs of the beggars.

'What for?' said Mel. 'Serves her right for getting caught. Let's go and find Spandangle. Perhaps he and that stupid old rat-bag have worked out where we'll find the mirrortree.'

'And *when*. I'm so looking forward to bashing his scrotty head in once we've found it.'

When Mel and Ludo pushed aside the flap and entered Madam Manto's tent Spandangle and the fortune-teller were still seated at the table. They were so deep in conversation that they did not notice the boys' return.

To one side slouched Wren. 'So nice of you to come back and help me,' she sneered. 'I'll make sure I do the same for you some time.'

'How'd you get away?' asked Mel.

'As if you care.' Wren huffed and folded her arms. 'The mauvey-man and some freak girl with golden skin helped me. She seemed to think she knew me. She acted as if we were old friends.'

'You haven't got any friends,' said Mel. 'No one's that desperate.'

The conjuror finally looked up. 'Ah, you're back. Been keeping out of trouble?'

'Mind your own business,' said Ludo, picking his nose.

'So, have you and old prune-features worked out how long we're going to have to hang around this scrotheap of a market?' said Mel. 'It's a skegging freak-show, that's what it is.'

'Such charm. Such eloquence,' said Madam Manto. 'All will be revealed in time. These things can't be rushed.'

'You'd better get a move on,' said Wren. 'We can't wait around here all day. Someone's after us.'

Spandangle frowned. 'Who's after you and why?'

'Just some beggars. They must have followed us,'

said Ludo. 'Not that it's any of your business.' He examined the end of his nose-picking finger.

'Oh, but it is my business,' said Spandangle. 'If you're to find the mirrortree.'

'The *mirrortree*?' gasped Madam Manto, her eyes widening. She looked at Mel, Ludo and Wren as if she were seeing them for the very first time. She nodded. 'That explains a lot. It's all beginning to make sense.'

'I'm glad someone thinks it is,' said Mel. 'Would you mind telling *us* what the skeg's going on.'

'You'll find out soon enough,' said Madam Manto. 'If you're after the mirrortree –'

The tent flap drew aside and the face of the mauve doorman appeared. 'Sorry to interrupt, Madam Manto, but those beggars are skulking around outside. It might be wise if your visitors left by the back.'

'Let me see,' said Spandangle. He rose and peeped through the flap. 'Three of the most unsavoury characters that ever graced Pennyweight Market – and that's saying something.'

'Three?' said Mel. 'There should be four.' He joined Spandangle.

'How did they manage to follow us here?' said Spandangle. 'I made sure we left no trail.'

'They've been after us since one of them helped us escape from the Clinch,' said Wren. 'Before we even met you.'

Spandangle and Madam Manto exchanged a glance.

'This is a strange business you've landed yourself in this time, Spandangle,' said Madam Manto. 'And no mistake.'

'Strange or not, I've got to see it through.' Spandangle thought for a while. 'Those beggars' interest in these three might prove useful.' Turning to the children, he asked, 'What does this absent beggar look like?'

Spandangle listened to Mel's description, then swirled his black cloak in front of him like a crow's wing. When he lowered it he looked like Scratchbeard.

'How'd you do *that*?' said Ludo.

'All part of the conjuror's art,' said Spandangle. 'Is it like him?'

'You're too tall,' said Wren.

Spandangle seemed to shrink.

'And his beard was singed,' said Mel. 'With bits of food stuck in it.'

Spandangle's beard changed. 'Teeth?'

'Yellow and broken,' said Wren, turning up her nose.

'Voice?'

'Kind of gravelly. And he wore a black eye patch,' said Ludo.

'The other eye,' said Mel. 'And he had a homemade knife.'

'Not so long,' said Wren. 'And his clothes were filthy.'

'How's this?' Another swirl of the cloak.

'No. Even dirtier,' said Mel. 'And a bit burnt.'

'Whatever did you do to him?' said Spandangle with Scratchbeard's voice as he completed his transformation. 'And I bet he hasn't washed in years – but smells are too complicated to conjure in a hurry.' Apart from his black magician's cloak over the rags, he looked and sounded the image of Scratchbeard. 'Now, you three are not going to like this, but you're going to have to trust me.' He magicked a lasso into his hands and tossed it over Mel, Ludo and Wren. In a flash he had them bound and gagged. 'That's it, keep struggling. And that look of outrage on your faces is *perfect*.'

Madam Manto cackled with laughter. 'There's nothing so convincing as the real thing.'

Keeping firm hold of the end of the rope, Spandangle bowed to his hostess. 'Madam M, it's been wonderful seeing you again after all these years. We'll talk some more when business is less pressing.'

'Take this,' said Madam Manto. She handed the conjuror a small crystal sphere no bigger than a hen's egg. 'I know I shouldn't, but I'll help you all I can. I'll keep looking in the scrying glass and let you know what I find. Just for old times' sake.'

Spandangle looked at the crystal and pocketed it. 'For old times' sake. Thank you, Madam M.' He turned and left the tent, dragging his struggling captives after him.

'Scratchbeard!' said Nelly Buboes. 'Where've you been?'

'Doing *your* job,' said Spandangle, cocking his head at his prisoners. 'That's where.'

'See, Nelly,' said Canker. 'I told you Scratchbeard would find them.'

'Nice cloak,' said Doctor Sarcophagus. 'Where'd you find it?'

'Ask me no questions, I'll tell you no lies,' said Spandangle.

'Same place Scratchbeard finds all his stuff, Doc,' said Nelly with a wink.

'Someone take a hold of these scrotty kids,' said Spandangle.

'Canker, give Scratchbeard a hand,' said Doctor Sarcophagus.

As Canker took the children from Spandangle he sniffed. 'A new cloak and you've had a wash. Is it your birthday or something? You usually smell like a rancid badger – no offence.'

'Now, let's take these little scrots somewhere quiet,' said Doctor Sarcophagus. 'I think they've got something they want to tell us.'

'No need, Doc,' said Spandangle. 'I've already

made them spill the beans.'

'I'm impressed,' said Doctor Sarcophagus. 'How about letting us in on the secret?'

'It's gold, isn't it?' said Nelly. 'I just know it's gold.'

'You couldn't be more wrong,' said Spandangle, scratching his new beard. 'It's something a lot more valuable than mere gold. A *lot* more valuable.'

'It *was* Mel,' said Goldie. She had to shout to be heard above the roar of the falling water. 'He went through that door.'

'Let's go and see if he needs any help,' said Pilfer.

Goldie placed her hand in the hand-lock. 'It won't open.' She slapped her hand harder in the depression but the door remained resolutely shut. 'It opened to let Mel through. So why won't it open for us?'

'I've never seen a lock like this one,' said Pilfer. 'But my guess is that it's got some sort of time delay. We probably just need to wait until it resets itself.'

'All right,' said Goldie. 'Let's go back and see if we can find Wren and Ludo back at Pennyweight Market. Then we'll go after Mel together.' She went back to the door they had entered by and put her hand into the hand-lock. 'Oh, no! This one's not working either.'

'Be patient,' said Pilfer. There was a soft clunking sound. 'Hear that? That's our lock resetting itself.'

The door back to the ghost train opened. Goldie led Pilfer down the folded corridor and opened the door at the far end.

'What the *skeg's* going on?' gasped Pilfer. 'Where's our ghost train?'

'More to the point,' said Goldie, 'where's Pennyweight Market?'

Monkey-Vlam

'That was my friend Goldie,' said Mel as he stood in the crinkled corridor. 'We've got to rescue her from that fear-wig.' He placed his hand in the hand-lock to the door back to the gantry but nothing happened. 'Why won't it open?'

'The time-lock will take a minute to reset itself,' said Professor Thinkwell's hand.

As soon as he heard a dull *clunk*, Mel again fitted his hand into the depression and the door swung open. It was a moment before he could speak. 'Where *are* we?'

'I don't know.' Then, after a long pause while the professor's eyed ring blinked and swivelled, 'Hold me up to the dial please.'

Mel lifted the professor's hand back on to his shoulder and together they stared at the dial on the portal. The dial's triple rings were pierced with fingertip-sized holes, each like those of an old-fashioned telephone, but with many more holes. Incised beneath each was a strange symbol.

After a moment Professor Thinkwell's hand spoke. 'Normally you can pass from any one of my transmogrificators to another by means of these portals. You simply have to dial the correct symbols. These indicate that it opens on to the gantry above the power source inside the transmogrificator. Something's gone wrong. We must investigate further.'

Mel stepped through the door into a wood-panelled room. The room, already small and dark, seemed even smaller and darker because of the thick tree trunk that grew up through the floor and out through the ceiling. A sturdy bough forked from the trunk and passed out of the window. Coming from outside were the jungle hoots and howls of many monkeys.

Mel squeezed himself between the tree trunk and the wall, stepped over an upturned desk and looked out of the window. His eyes threatened to pop out of his head as he stared hard at the view. When he finally found his voice he said in a whisper, 'It's *Vlam*! But . . .'

Every door or window of Mel's adopted city seemed to have huge roots, boughs or branches spilling from it. In places they had even shattered bricks and burst through walls. Nearly every vertical surface was draped in vines, and sweeping loops of creeper hung everywhere. Ground-hugging vegetation thrust its way between the cobblestones of the street. Some trees had toppled and now formed bridges from rooftop to shattered rooftop. Even the towering facades of the Great Houses were overwhelmed with vegetation. Green-tinted daylight filtered down through the forest canopy in dusty shafts, and everywhere – lining the countless trees, filling the buildings and thronging the streets – were hordes of monkeys. As Mel stared in disbelief at this scene, a troupe of baboons marched single-file along the overgrown street beneath his window. They were wearing plumed hats and velvet waistcoats plundered from a nearby outfitters. Above them a family of gibbons in brightly coloured doublets swung from creeper to creeper and a bewigged gaggle of small black-and-white monkeys jabbered excitedly and showered the baboons with broken twigs and roof tiles. There was not a human to be seen.

'What's Vlam?' asked Professor Thinkwell's hand.

'It's not a *what*, it's a *where*. It's the city where I live.

Except, this isn't it. Vlam's usually full of people, not monkeys. And there's no forest in Vlam.'

'Extraordinary! The coordinates on the door dial clearly indicate that we should be back above the waterwheels.'

'Perhaps your invention's not working properly.'

'My inventions always work perfectly. There can only be one explanation. This is Bumnote's doing!'

'Who's Bumnote?'

'My assistant. The trouble is he's an incompetent dabbler. We must get back to Castle Habilis without delay. Take me back down the corridor to the other door. At least I know that one leads back to the castle.'

Mel retraced his steps back down the crinkled corridor. He placed his hand in the lock to the second door. The door opened and . . . 'We're back in the room with the tree!'

'All the portals must be jammed. We must get back to my laboratory and undo whatever mischief Bumnote's created.'

'But how are we going to do that?' asked Mel. 'We can't even get back into the transmogrificator.

We're stuck here in . . . wherever *this* place is.'

The professor's hand drummed its fingers. Eventually, he said, 'You know this city. Is there a laboratory or a workshop that I could use?'

Mel thought for a moment. 'There's Dirk Tot's workshop. It's in my master's mansion. We could go there.'

'We must make haste before the portals become permanently jammed.'

'This is Vlam,' said Goldie as she took in the strange scene.

'They should sack their gardener,' said Pilfer. 'He's let the shrubs get out of hand. And where're all the people? The gaff's full of monkeys.'

Goldie and Pilfer were in a room crowded with thick branches. Through the open window they could see the overgrown city and its throng of monkeys. They tried to retrace their steps back to the gantry several times but on each occasion ended up back where they had started.

'So, what do we do now?' said Pilfer.

Goldie chewed her gilded lip for a moment. 'We should go to Ambrosius Blenk. He's a wise old bird. Maybe he knows what the skeg's going on in his city. Perhaps Mel's gone there, too.'

'I don't think this is a transmogrificator,' said Shingle as she stood with Wren, staring out of the door at the end of the crinkly corridor that led from the kitchen in Castle Habilis.

'Me neither,' said Wren. She picked her way through the jumble of twisted roots that clogged the spiral staircase leading up from the wine cellar they had arrived in. When she reached the top and found a doorway to look out of she drew in her breath sharply. 'We're in Vlam!' Then, after a while, 'And we're not too far from my master's mansion.'

Above Ludo the bacon-slicer blade of the separator spun faster, its edge diamond-bright, its hum low and sinister. He tugged frantically at his hands but they were firmly locked in the vice-like holder at the foot of the contraption. Ludo looked across at Shale and opened his mouth in a silent howl of despair.

Suddenly, there was a blinding flash as a glowing phial exploded at the operator's feet, showering him with glass. A huge ball of light like a miniature sun blossomed and, as one, the assembled handymen raised their arms to shield their eyes from the dazzling eruption.

Ludo was temporarily blinded as well. He felt the holder that was gripping his hands release and a strong but smelly arm grab him firmly in a headlock. A gravelly voice said, 'Come on, Smoky. We've got some unfinished business, you and me.' He felt himself being dragged away from the separator.

'Not without Shale,' shouted Ludo.

'Ludo?' It was Shale's voice from near at hand. 'Where are you? I can't see.'

Ludo grabbed one of Shale's sockets and the two boys were hurried away by their rescuer.

As Ludo's vision returned he could just make out that they were being taken back towards the ledge and the door they had entered by. By the look and smell of him, his captor was some beggar with a straggly beard and a black eye patch. He was wearing singed rags. Ludo was sure he wasn't a figment – only a human could smell that bad.

The beggar placed his free hand into the hand-lock then manhandled Ludo and Shale through the door. It clanked shut after them.

'What the *skeg's* going on?' said Scratchbeard as he dragged the boys through the second door at the end of the crumpled corridor. 'Where's that ghost train?' He pulled Ludo and Shale past a jumble of branches to the nearest window. 'That looks just like –'

'Vlam!' finished Ludo, equally astounded. 'It's full of monkeys. What's happened to it?'

'Where's the transmogrificator?' said Shale.

Scratchbeard released Ludo and continued to stare in disbelief at the strange city.

Ludo cleared his throat and mustered his limited store of bravado. 'Excuse me, but would you mind telling me who you are and what you want with us?'

Scratchbeard slowly turned from the window. 'You know very well who I am.'

Ludo looked confused. 'I'm very sorry, but I don't.'

'Don't try that one on me, Smoky. I was working the old amnesia scam before you were born. You may've found yourself a change of duds and a new mate with a fuzzy fizzog but your newly acquired manners ain't fooling no one. Just as soon as I can hook back up with Nelly, Canker and the Doc, you and me's going to find the Shrimp and Missy.' Scratchbeard turned back towards the puzzling view from the window.

'Quick,' whispered Shale, digging Ludo in the ribs. 'Let's make a run for it.'

'Back to the separator,' Ludo whispered back. 'No thanks. We'll be safer here.' Then, out loud to Scratchbeard, 'The Shrimp and Missy? Who're they?'

'I told you that malarkey won't work on me. Thought you could hide in the ghost train, did you? The Shrimp might have got away for now. But he can't have got too far. You and *your* friends are going to tell me and *my* friends all about this *mission* of yours.'

'But nobody knows about –'

Scratchbeard's mouth opened wide in a yellow-toothed grin. 'Take a tip from a master, Smoky. If you're trying to fool someone, don't give the game away so easily.'

'My name's not "Smoky".'

'And you haven't got a couple of friends by the names of Mel and Wren who are apprenticed to Ambrosius Blenk and live in his fancy mansion? Pull the other one.'

Ludo was shocked. His mouth hung open. 'How do you know so much about me?'

'Give it a rest,' said Scratchbeard, turning back to the scene outside the window. 'There's something very fishy about all this monkey-business, this monkey-Vlam. We're going back to the Crippled Toad. There's bound to be someone there who knows what the skeg's going on.'

They fought their way down the branch-choked staircase and out into the street. The monkeys were everywhere but did not seem especially curious about Scratchbeard and his prisoners as they moved through the overgrown city.

Clambering over the thick roots clogging the staircase, they forced their way down into the dark cellar of the Crippled Toad. It seemed empty.

'Anyone there?' called Scratchbeard.

There was the sound of movement behind the bar and the chink of upset bottles.

'Mange?' Scratchbeard went to the bar counter and looked over. Startled, he jumped back as a couple of screeching monkeys leapt out, swung on the overhead beams as far as the doorway, then scampered up the choked staircase and off into the street.

Scratchbeard sat down and was lost in thought for a while. Then, slowly, a gleam came into his eye. 'There's one thing a beggar learns early in life in this city: how to turn disadvantage into advantage. We didn't see a soul on our way here, just stinking bands of monkeys. Now, what does that tell you?'

Ludo shrugged. 'That everyone's gone?'

Scratchbeard smiled again. It was not a pretty sight. 'Now you're beginning to think like a beggar.'

Ludo looked at Shale and then back at Scratchbeard. He shook his head. 'So?'

'So,' said Scratchbeard, helping himself to a tankard of flat, scummy ale. 'If everyone's gone, there's no one to stop me helping myself to whatever takes my fancy. We're going a-robbing. And where do you think we're going to start?'

Ludo stared back blankly.

'I think we'll pick up where we were so rudely interrupted. We're going back to the rich pickings in Ambrosius Blenk's mansion. But before we leave I'm going to pen a little note and leave it here in case Doc, Nelly and Canker drop by. Let them know where we're going. And this time, I'm not coming away empty-handed or my name's not Scratchbeard.'

Friends Reunited

The further Mel journeyed through the city with the professor's hand perched on his shoulder the more he became certain of one thing: this was not the real Vlam. They were still in the Mirrorscape.

They reached the mansion and, fighting their way through the invading plant life, they made their way to the top floor.

'OK, Professor, Dirk Tot's secret workshop is behind here.' Mel climbed up the shelving in the steward's office, pulled out a false book on the top and the bookcase occupying an entire wall of the study swung out, revealing the spacious workshop.

Mel set the professor's hand down on the nearest workbench and immediately it began scuttling up and down, avidly inspecting the rows of flasks, retorts, copper vessels and metalworking tools with its eyed ring. It found an open notebook and pencil and hastily scribbled some calculations. 'I intend to fashion a morphic interrupter to reset the dials on a portal to take us back to Castle Habilis. The first thing I need will be a metal disc about the diameter and thickness of a dinner plate.'

'I'll go and see what I can find in the kitchen.'

When he got there, Mel found that the huge, vaulted kitchen had been ransacked. Flour was strewn all over the floor like snow. It bore hundreds of monkey paw-prints. All of the food had either been eaten or spoiled and anything breakable was smashed. He selected several of the least-dented metal plates and a large skillet in case the plates were not the right size.

As he was climbing back up the stairs there came a great screeching commotion from below. He peered over the banister and at the foot of the stairs he saw monkeys leaping into the air, soaring around in wild circles and spinning off to crash into the walls as if in the grip of an invisible whirlwind.

'Get off me, you 'orrible scrots!' The voice seemed to be coming from in the middle of the mêlée.

Then a figment girl with a gilded face arrived and began laying into the monkeys with a broken chair leg.

Mel recognised her at once. '*Goldie!*' He raced back down the stairs.

Goldie broke into a broad smile as Mel reached her. But her smile vanished almost as soon as it appeared. 'Mel, quick! Pilfer's being attacked. Help me get these monkeys off him.'

Mel hurled the plates at the monkeys and wielded the skillet. He and Goldie began to bash the attacking creatures as if they were rather large and hairy tennis balls.

The attackers soon had enough and ran off screeching.

'And don't come back,' came Pilfer's voice as the last of the monkeys took to the air in a great arc like a kicked football.

As the creature's pained screech died away Mel and Goldie embraced. He felt his hand being grasped and shaken by Pilfer. 'What are you two doing here?' asked Mel.

'We're looking for Ambrosius Blenk,' said Goldie. 'And for you.'

'How'd you get here?'

'We followed you here from Pennyweight Market,' said Goldie.

'Huh?' Mel stared back, a bewildered expression on his face.

'We helped Wren get away from the beggars and then came after you,' added Goldie. 'Where's Ludo?'

'What are you talking about?' Mel looked every bit as confused as he felt. 'Wren's back in the transmogrificator with the mushroom ladies and I haven't seen Ludo since he was kidnapped.'

'Now *you're* the one talking gibberish,' said Pilfer.

'I *knew* there was something iffy about all this,' said Goldie. 'Why don't you tell us what you know and we'll tell you what's been happening to us.'

'But I *know* I've never been to this Pennyweight Market,' insisted Mel. 'How could Wren and Ludo and I have been in two places at once?'

'There's only one explanation that I can see,' said Goldie. 'You've all got spitting-image doubles.'

'You mean like *twins*?' Mel scratched his head. 'But Wren and Ludo don't have twins and *I* certainly don't.'

'Maybe this professor geezer of yours knows something about it,' said Pilfer.

'Come on, let's go and ask him.' Mel picked up the plates and led the way upstairs.

When they got back to Dirk Tot's workshop the professor's hand was busy working on a long list of equations he had made in the notebook. He barely noticed their arrival.

'Professor, this is Goldie and Pilfer, my friends,' said Mel.

The professor's hand continued writing.

'You made yourself an artificial hand,' persisted Mel. 'Did you make some artificial people as well? People that look like me and my friends?'

The professor finished his calculations, took the dinner plate and fixed it into a vice. 'I've quite enough work to do without making artificial people. Pass me a file, please.'

'What about Bumnote?' said Mel. 'Could *he* have made them?'

'Bumnote couldn't make a cup of tea without me to tell him which way to stir it. Now stop bothering me and let me get on with my work. There's no time to lose.'

After half an hour's work Professor Thinkwell's morphic interrupter was finished. 'What I've done, you see, is to cut and refashion the plate into three concentric circles that can rotate independently. The projections on the underside fit into the holes on the dials. On the other side is a handle. Once the interrupter is fitted over the dial it can be turned to force it to a new position, causing a mutation to start on the far side of the portal.'

'But the portal we came through is miles away by the House of Spirits. We'd never find our way back there through the jungle,' said Mel.

'How about your door, Goldie?' asked the professor.

'No chance. Ours is on the other side of Vlam, near that House of Mysteries. It took us hours to cross the city.'

'There's one near here.'

Mel recognised the voice behind him at once. A howl of delight burst from his lips and his heart leapt in his chest. '*Wren!*' He ran to hug his friend.

'Mel! We thought you'd been crushed when the

transmogrificator started mutating,' beamed Wren as relief washed over her.

'I very nearly was.'

'Hello, Wren,' said Goldie. 'It *is* you, isn't it?'

'Of course it's me. Who did you think it was?' Wren embraced Goldie. 'Is Pilfer here, too?'

'Stupid question,' said Pilfer, giving Wren a warm hug.

'Hello, who are you?' asked Mel, turning to Wren's companion. He knew that the young figment must have come originally from the background of a painting due to her blurred features.

'My name's Shingle. I'm one of Mr Habilis's handmaidens.'

'What happened to your hands?' asked Goldie.

'Mr Habilis took them. He tricks everyone and takes all their hands. That how he gets his handmaidens and handymen to work for him.' Shingle crossed to the workbench. 'Hello, Professor Thinkwell.'

'And where are Mrs Morel and Mrs Wood-Blewit?' asked Mel.

'Back in the transmogrificator,' said Wren.

'We got separated in all the mutating.'

'So, where'd you come from?' said Mel.

'Castle Habilis.'

'But that's where *we're* going,' said Mel.

'Not the way we came,' said Wren. 'That just keeps leading us back here.'

'That's because the dials are stuck. But now we've got Professor Thinkwell's gadget, it'll fix all that.'

'So, it wasn't you in Pennyweight Market?' Pilfer asked Wren.

'Where?'

Goldie repeated her story, much to Wren's puzzlement. 'But it *couldn't* have been me,' she said.

'There's an easy way to get to the bottom of all this,' said Mel. 'We'll ask Cogito.'

'I'm sorry, Mel, but I lost him,' said Wren. 'He's back in the transmogrificator with Mrs Morel and Mrs Wood-Blewit. We'll have to find them in Castle Habilis and get him back. Perhaps he's worked out where to search for the mirrortree by now.'

The professor tapped the end of his pencil impatiently on the tabletop. 'Talking of getting back, where's this doorway of yours? There really is no time to lose.'

'Right. Come on, everyone.' Mel picked up the newly fashioned interrupter and placed Professor Thinkwell's hand back on his shoulder. Then, followed by Goldie, Pilfer, Wren and Shingle, they left the workshop.

Or tried to.

As soon as Mel opened the door he was assaulted by a horde of angry monkeys. Pilfer and Goldie kicked at the attackers, dragged Mel back inside and slammed the door. Wren and Shingle dragged a heavy chest over to hold it shut.

'We're going to have to fight our way out,' said Pilfer.

'I've got a better idea,' said Wren. 'We'll use the service passages.'

'The what?' said Goldie.

'They're like secret passages that run all over the mansion,' said Mel. 'They'll lead us to the front door.'

'Provided the monkeys haven't found them already,' said Shingle.

'Looks clear,' said Wren as she opened a door concealed in the wooden panelling. 'I can't hear anything either. Light that candle and pass it to me. Come on.'

Wren led them through the maze of narrow, cobwebbed passages and down rickety flights of stairs towards the entrance hall.

'This is even more spooky than our ghost train, Goldie,' said Pilfer.

'It's spooky, all right,' said Goldie. Then, to Mel and Wren, 'So, tell us more about this mirrortree.'

'What exactly is it?' said Pilfer.

'We don't know,' said Wren. 'But it must be very valuable. More valuable than gold – or flowers even.'

Pilfer let out a long, low whistle. 'More valuable than flowers. That's something I've *got* to see.'

'As long as seeing is *all* you've got on your mind,' said Goldie.

'*Shhh.* Did you hear that?' whispered Pilfer. 'It sounded like a muffled cry.'

'Is it the monkeys?' said Shingle, sniffing. 'It smells as bad as they do.'

'It sounded like it came from down here.' Wren held the candle up high and peered down a side passage.

'Shall we take a look?' said Mel.

'No, it's probably nothing,' said Wren. 'This place is so old it creaks all the time. Come on, this way.'

Scratchbeard took his grubby hands from Ludo and Shale's mouths. 'Hear that, Smoky? Hear that, Fuzzy? "More valuable than gold" she said. This "mirrortree" sounds like it might be more profitable than anything we'll find here in Blenk's gaff. I think the three of us will tail them. We'll let them do all the hard work of finding. And then Scratchbeard will relieve them of their burden. Yes, that's what he'll do. Then there's the little question of a score to be settled. Now, let's go. And no tricks.'

Honour Among Thieves

Spandangle scratched himself and silently cursed the fleas in Scratchbeard's rags. Sometimes he made his transformations just too perfect. He was leading Doctor Sarcophagus and Nelly Buboes, each of them carrying a glowing phial, back up the long flight of stairs beneath the House of Thrones. Behind them came Canker, complaining and towing the tightly bound and gagged children by a stout rope. Mel, Ludo and Wren's eyes were ablaze with indignation in the phial-light. Last of all hobbled Canker's three-legged dog, sniffing at the captives and administering frequent painful nips to the children's ankles.

'How come you seem to know the way so well, Scratchbeard?' said Nelly. 'I thought you said you'd never been here before.'

'I haven't,' said Spandangle. 'I made those little scrots tell me how they got here.'

'What else they tell you?' asked Doctor Sarcophagus.

'All we need to know, Doc.' Spandangle tapped the side of his nose. 'All we need to know.'

'You're keeping very quiet about it. You wouldn't be thinking of going solo on us, would you, Scratchbeard? Cutting out your friends?'

'Yeah,' added Nelly. 'The Doc's right. We're all in this together. A four-way split.'

'That don't seem quite fair, Nelly,' said Spandangle in a low voice. 'Not *equitable*, like. Not when you, me and the Doc's been doing the hard work. All Canker's done is look out for himself.'

'You're right,' said Nelly. 'Where was he when we nearly burnt to death in the Blenk gaff? Looking out for number one, that's where.'

'You thinking a three-way split's better than four ways?' said Doctor Sarcophagus, his eyes narrowing.

'A third of a pot's better than a quarter, Doc,' said Spandangle. 'You can't argue with numbers, now, can you?'

Doctor Sarcophagus glanced at Nelly Buboes. She glanced back. Slowly, sly smiles formed on their lips.

Nelly stole a look over her shoulder at Canker. 'You

might be right again, Scratchbeard,' she murmured. 'Numbers don't lie.'

'Indeed,' said Doctor Sarcophagus. 'They never lie.'

'Mel, Ludo and Wren have been spotted, master,' puffed Dirk Tot as he ran up the stairs and into Ambrosius Blenk's private studio on the top floor of the mansion. Unfinished canvases stood stacked in one corner and sketches were pinned up, covering an entire wall. 'Green and Blue heard from Mauve, an old comrade of theirs from the Rainbow Rebels, that they were in Pennyweight Market.'

'Pennyweight Market?' Ambrosius Blenk stopped sketching.

'This time it was under the House of Thrones. And Mauve reported that Spandangle the magician was with them. They were there to see Madam Manto.'

'Spandangle?' The master put down his pencil, closed his sketchbook and rose from his chair. 'And Madam Manto, you say?' He walked to the tall window and looked out. His glittering blue eyes flitted back and forth and he absently tugged at his long beard as he always did when he was thinking hard.

'Master?' said Dirk Tot. 'What shall we do?'

'Do?'

'About Mel, Ludo and Wren?'

'We should do nothing. It's all beginning to make sense, though they're much younger than I was when Spandangle came for me.'

'I don't understand.'

'Call Green and Blue off – and thank Mauve for his help. Whatever's happening and wherever they're going, they should not be hindered. Or helped, for that matter. At least not by us.'

'You make it sound like some sort of exam.'

The master made a chuckling sound, but there was no mirth in it. 'An exam? I suppose that in its own way, it is. The rewards for passing will be great. As great as the perils if they fail.'

'Perils? What kind of perils?'

'The gravest kind. If they fail, they will forfeit their lives.'

* * *

'You keeping a tight hold of those little scrots?' Spand-angle dropped back from Nelly Buboes and Doctor Sarcophagus to climb the stairs alongside Canker.

'They won't get away again,' said Canker. 'What were you and Nelly and Doc muttering about up there, Scratchbeard?'

'You think we can trust them?' whispered Spandangle.

'Why? What's going on?' Canker's eyes narrowed.

'They suggested that you weren't pulling your weight in this little escapade.'

'What!' exclaimed Canker. Then in a quieter voice, 'I'm pulling *all* the weight. These kids are skegging heavy.' He yanked the rope hard for emphasis, making the children cry out beneath their gags.

'That's not what they meant. They said that splitting the loot three ways would be better than a four-way divi. They were talking about cutting you out of the deal.'

'The skegging, scrot-eating scut-buckets!' hissed Canker. 'Hold this rope. I'm going to have it out with them.'

Spandangle put a restraining hand on the beggar's

shoulder. 'Hold your horses, Canker. I told them I wanted nothing to do with it. Canker's doing all the hard work, I said. Without Canker we wouldn't have got this far, I said. Canker's the ideal beggar for this kind of job, I said.'

'You said all that, did you?'

'I did. It's no more than the truth. And . . .' Spandangle paused for effect.

'Go on.'

'It set me to thinking. Yours truly's doing all the planning and Canker's doing all the heavy work. So why not make it a *two*-way divi. Just you and me. Half each. Have a think about that, Canker.' With a nod, Spandangle dropped back and made a show of checking Mel, Ludo and Wren's bonds.

Mel gave him a questioning look.

Spandangle leant close and whispered, 'Just evening up the odds a little in our favour. Divide and conquer, it's called.' He tied their gags even tighter and climbed back to the head of the group, winking at Canker as he passed him.

* * *

When they finally reached the door to the lowest occupied parts of the House of Thrones, Spandangle cautiously opened the door a crack and peeped out. He turned back to the others. 'Right, all clear. Time to get our breath back and rest our legs.'

As they sat in the narrow shaft of yellow light spilling on to the staircase from the crack in the door, the beggars rubbed their aching legs and feet. Spandangle noted with satisfaction the suspicious glances they cast towards each other from time to time.

After a while, Nelly got to her feet and went over to the children. She kicked Mel, pinched Ludo and spat on Wren. 'So, if they've told you all they know, why do we need to keep these little scrots alive any more?'

'Yes,' said Doctor Sarcophagus. 'They'll only slow us up. Let's pay them back for what they did to us in the Blenk mansion. Then we'll toss the bodies back down the stairs. No one will ever find them down there.'

'We'll pay them back all right,' said Spandangle. 'But not now. We'll keep them as insurance for a bit. If we run into the palace guard – well, they're less likely to loose their crossbows on children than on a bunch of beggars. We'll use them as a human shield while we make our getaway. Agreed?'

'Not so fast, Scratchbeard,' said Nelly. 'Before we go any further, I think it's about time you let us in on what it is we're after. Just what this prize is that's going to make us all so rich.'

'Yeah,' added Canker.

'Come on, cough it up,' said Doctor Sarcophagus.

Spandangle seemed to think hard for a moment as if he were calculating something. 'OK, then. Fair's fair. It's a tree.'

'*A tree?*' said the others, all at once.

'What skegging good's a skegging tree?' said Canker. 'Nem's full of scrotty trees. I could get me one of those without risking my neck. You said it's "something more valuable than gold".'

'Hang on,' said Nelly. 'We've all known Scratchbeard a long time.' Doctor Sarcophagus and Canker nodded reluctantly. 'We all know he's a sly, conniving scrot.' They nodded again. 'Who'd sell his own mother for half a silver piece.'

'And then fail to deliver,' chipped in Canker.

'But,' continued Nelly, 'when it comes to thievery, he's got a nose for what's valuable and what's not. Some say an *infallible* nose. So, what is it that makes this particular tree so precious, Scratchbeard?'

'You ever heard of the Nabob of Pyrexia's Garden of Miracles?' improvised Spandangle. He looked from one to another as they shook their heads. 'Well, long, long ago, nestling in the faraway peaks of the Tondo mountains, the Nabob of –'

'Yeah, yeah, yeah,' interrupted Canker. 'Spare us the fairy tale and get on with it.'

'As you like. It's said that anyone who rubs the sap of the Nabob's tree into their skin becomes invisible. And what do you suppose an invisible beggar could help themselves to? They could take –'

'Anything they skegging well please,' finished Doctor Sarcophagus. His eyes seemed on fire. 'They'd have the pick of anything in the entire Seven Kingdoms. Scrot – in the whole skegging *world*!'

'And if the Watch ever came a-calling –' added Spandangle.

'They'd never find you,' finished Canker.

Spandangle smiled. 'Believe me, invisibility is what every villain needs.'

'And there *is* such a tree and these scrot-stains know where it is?' said Nelly. She stared hard at the captives.

Spandangle nodded.

'Whoa, back up a bit. How do we know they're not lying?' said Doctor Sarcophagus. '"Invisible sap"? It sounds like just the kind of tall yarn kids would spin. Sounds like we'd end up the saps.'

'Yeah,' said Canker. 'How come they know all this?'

'King Spen's just blown half his treasury on this here tree. And Ambrosius Blenk has been given a secret commission from old money-bags to design and decorate a pot to hold this miracle tree. Only him and his steward are supposed to know about it but these three ear-wigged what was going on and decided that they'd get their grubby mitts on it and use the sap themselves.'

'And they told you all this?' said Nelly.

'After a little persuasion,' said Spandangle.

'No offence,' said Doctor Sarcophagus, 'but I'll believe it when I hear it from their own mouths.'

'Be my guest,' said Spandangle, shaking his head sadly. He made a quick but subtle movement with his hands.

Doctor Sarcophagus loosened Mel's gag. 'Well? Is this true?'

Mel spat and formed the words, 'You evil-smelling scrot-bags will get nothing out of me.' But he found he had lost control of his voice. What actually came out of his mouth was, 'Don't hurt me. I'll tell you everything.'

'That's more like it,' said Nelly.

Ludo stared at Mel. 'Shut up! Don't tell them anything,' he cried. What everybody heard was, 'What Scratchbeard said was all true.' His eyes opened wide in disbelief at the strange words coming from his own lips.

'Stop blabbing, you idiots,' Wren tried to say. But, like the boys, she found that she too had lost control of her voice. It came out as, 'Now you know it all.'

'So where's this tree?' said Canker.

'It's hidden somewhere in Pennyweight Market,' Ludo was astounded to hear himself saying.

'You've given the game away,' Wren heard herself say.

'Just where, exactly?' said Doctor Sarcophagus.

'Somewhere in the fairground,' came out of Mel's mouth.

'Satisfied?' said Spandangle as he fastened the children's gags back in place. He leant close to the children and whispered, 'Ventriloquism: all part of the conjuror's art.'

'Come on then,' said Spandangle. 'We'll go back there and have a look-see – but first we'd better make sure there're no palace guards around to follow us. Nelly, you check the corridor to the left. Doc, you take the right. I'll take the one opposite. Canker, you stay here and keep an eye on the kids.'

Canker's eyes narrowed suspiciously. 'Why me? I should be checking out the corridor. What if none of you come back? Why can't Doc or Nelly guard the kids?'

'What's your game, Canker?' said Nelly. She shot a glance at Doc. 'Someone's got to stay behind and guard these little scrots. A pretty wench like me is less likely to arouse attention in a swanky palace than a scruffy beggar.' She toyed with the rat's-nest of her hair.

'And it can't be me,' said Doctor Sarcophagus.

'What if we need a potion or two? I'm the only one who knows how to use them.'

Canker persisted. 'I still think I should be the one to –'

'Look,' Spandangle interrupted. '*I'll* stay behind and keep an eye on the kids. Canker can take my place.'

Reluctantly, Canker agreed.

Spandangle watched their backs through the crack in the door. When he was sure they'd gone, he turned to the children and loosened their gags. 'That worked well. It won't take much now to set them at each other's throats.' He made another movement with his hands. 'You can have your voices back now.'

'Untie us, you privy-licker!' spat Mel the instant his gag was released.

'You stinking coward,' said Ludo. 'If I had my hands free, you'd be sorry.'

'That's one good reason for leaving you as you are,' said Spandangle.

'Let me go and I'll scratch your eyes out,' said Wren.

'And that's another.' Spandangle squatted alongside

them. 'Now shut up and listen to me, we don't have much time. You're going to have to grin and bear this a little longer.'

'Why'd you go and tell them about it?' moaned Ludo.

'Because seven pairs of eyes are better than four,' said Spandangle. 'And greed makes vision that much sharper, I find.'

'But they won't swallow that guff you spun them about invisibility sap for long,' said Wren.

'Oh, I think they will. Greed makes for sharper eyes but it also makes for duller brains.'

'Why not untie us now and we'll make a run for it?' said Mel.

'That's unlikely to work,' said Spandangle. 'If they found you in Pennyweight Market they could find you again.'

'And what about the others?' whined Wren. 'While we're stuck here they might find the mirrortree before we do.'

'Madam Manto said that we're too early,' said Spandangle. 'That means that *no one* will be able to find the mirrortree yet.'

'Maybe it's not too early any more,' said Ludo. 'We were climbing those stairs for ages.'

Spandangle magicked the tiny crystal sphere that Madam Manto had given him into his hand. He peered into it and nodded as if he were hearing something. After a while he looked up. 'Madam M has been trying again. It's still too early but we're to return to Pennyweight Market.'

'This sounds like another one of your tricks,' said Mel.

'*Shhh!* Someone's coming back,' said Spandangle. With a flourish of his hand the sphere vanished. He quickly fastened their gags back in place and got his fingers bitten in the process.

Doctor Sarcophagus poked his head around the door. 'Scratchbeard, a word in your ear. I've been thinking about this three-way split idea of yours.'

Spandangle raised a singed eyebrow. 'And you were thinking a *two*-way split would make more sense?'

'Great minds think alike. Canker and Nelly are just dead weight. While you and me, well, we're in a different league, wouldn't you say?'

'Supposing I go along with it,' said Spandangle. 'What's to stop *you* going solo on *me*, eh? A full share's twice as big as a half.'

'Come on, Scratchbeard. You should know that even for a pickpocket it's a two-hander: one for the dip, one for the pass-on. No, the way I see it, you and me's the minimum for this job. So, what'd you say?'

Spandangle returned Doctor Sarcophagus's sly smile. 'A beggar after my own heart. Put it there.'

Both men spat into their open hands and shook on the deal.

'Still want to pay them back and toss them down the stairs?'

Both men looked down at the children.

'Later, Scratchbeard. Later.' Doctor Sarcophagus threw back his head and laughed. Spandangle joined in.

They were still laughing when the others got back.

'What's so funny?' said Nelly Buboes.

'Yeah,' said Canker. 'Let us in on the joke.'

'You'll see,' said Doctor Sarcophagus. 'You'll see.'

Castle Habilis

'There's the door that brought us here,' said Shingle as she led the others into the wine cellar of a house in the grand square opposite Ambrosius Blenk's mansion.

'And once we've used Professor Thinkwell's gadget on it, it should take us back to Castle Habilis,' said Mel. He placed the interrupter over the dial and rotated the three circles until the projections clicked into the holes. Then, grasping the handle on the back, he began to turn it. 'It's too stiff. It won't budge. Give me a hand.'

As many hands as could fit grasped the handle and, together, they heaved. There was a metallic grating sound and slowly the rings on the interrupter slid around into their new position. The door opened as soon as Wren put her hand in the hand-lock.

'What's going on?' said Goldie. 'The corridor's moving about as if it's alive.'

'The interrupter is forcing a mutation,' said Professor Thinkwell's hand. 'We must wait until it's stopped otherwise we run the risk of being crushed.'

'Waiting's not a good idea,' said Wren. 'Look behind you.'

Everyone turned. Swarming down the staircase and into the cellar were a score of monkeys screeching loudly. They began jumping up and down and several started hurling wine bottles at the group.

Mel ducked and a bottle smashed on the wall behind where his head had been only a moment earlier. 'We can't wait. Let's go!'

Holding on to each other for support, Mel, with the professor's hand, Goldie, Pilfer, Wren and Shingle dashed along the writhing corridor. They looked like they were doing some mad dance as they fought for balance. The monkeys were hot on their heels and much more agile. With some difficulty, Mel placed the morphic interrupter on to the second door's dial and, with the help of Wren and Shingle, forced it to rotate and unlock that door while Goldie and Pilfer kicked at the monkeys. The door opened and they all ran through.

'Pilfer! Goldie! Come on!' yelled Mel.

'Quickly, the corridor's still unstable,' said Professor Thinkwell's hand.

Goldie and Pilfer lashed out at the monkeys, turned and sprinted after the others.

'Quick, shut the door,' shouted Pilfer.

Mel and Wren slammed it shut. The incensed screeching of the monkeys could be heard on the far side. Then there was a loud creak. And then silence.

'Sounds like we only just made it,' puffed Goldie.

Panting and trembling a little from the close call, Mel looked at his surroundings for the first time. 'Where are we?'

'It's a bit on the poky side for a castle,' said Goldie.

'That's because we're inside a transmogrificator,' said Shingle.

The cramped, cylindrical cabin had a row of iron benches on either side of a kinked spindle and there was a small morphonium at the far end. Everything seemed very old and worn.

'Looks like Professor Wink-well has mucked things up,' said Pilfer. 'His doodad has delivered us to the wrong place.'

'Nonsense. Take a look outside.' The Professor's hand pointed towards one of the portholes.

Shingle went over and looked out. 'No, it's worked. We *are* back at Castle Habilis. We're in one of the transmogrificator docks.'

The others crowded around the porthole. Outside it was deep night but they could see that there were ten floodlit docks. They looked like giant iron forearms that rose up as if they were bursting, elbow-deep, out of the ground far below. The transmogrificators themselves rested on top of these on platforms fashioned like cupped and upturned palms. The thumb and fingers of each dock were peppered with lit windows, and cranes and gantries projected from them. Thin wafts of steam, underlit by the floodlights, drifted from the fingertips. From their vantage point they could see that all but one of the docks were occupied with strange machines.

'Those are the other transmogrificators,' said Shingle.

'And look, that must be the one we were on before, Mel,' said Wren. 'We were mutating into moth mode just before I got swallowed up.'

'That means that Mrs Morel and Mrs Wood-Blewit are already here,' said Mel. 'I wonder if they've found

Ludo yet? I hope he's all right.'

The docks were arranged in a semicircle around the castle itself. At first glance it looked like a great, towering stalagmite. This, too, had been built to resemble a huge cluster of upward-thrusting forearms, but it was much larger than those of the docks. The towers and pinnacles occupied yet more fingers. From the topmost finger-tower flew the Habilis flag – a red handprint on a black background with an eye in the centre of the palm. They could see that the castle was a hive of activity, with figures silhouetted behind myriad lit windows.

'How do we get into the castle, Professor?' asked Wren.

'There's always the front door.'

'That's a no-no,' said Pilfer. 'I'm allergic to front doors.'

'You're beginning to talk like a robber again,' chided Goldie.

'Sorry, force of habit,' said Pilfer. 'But I don't like the look of that place. And from what I've heard about Mr Habilis, he might not be too willing to let us go once we're inside.' Pilfer was quiet for a moment.

'OK, listen up. I'll go and have a scout around and see what I can find.'

After a while, Pilfer returned. 'I've found our way in,' he reported. 'Follow me.'

Pilfer led the small band from the transmogrific-ator and down through the dock's forearm and they made their way to the base of the castle walls.

'What's that crunching noise under our feet?' whispered Wren as they crept forwards.

Mel withdrew his angel's feather and lowered it to the ground. With his free hand he scooped up a handful of the stuff they were walking on. 'It looks like . . . Ugh!'

'They're fingernail clippings,' explained Shingle. 'Mr Habilis makes us handmaidens trim the nails of all the hands in the library but they just grow back again. It's a never-ending job.'

'The clippings must be coming from here,' said Goldie.

They stood beneath a circular hole in the castle wall. Around the base was a small, pale mountain of clippings that spilled out on to the surrounding ground. When Mel held his feather inside the hole they could see an upward-sloping shaft.

'That's our way in,' said Pilfer.

Two scrawny birds with huge eyes and oily feathers as black as night alighted on the tip of one of the castle's finger-towers. They watched as, far below, Mel and his friends climbed into the shaft. Then one of the stare-crows took off and wheeled twice around the tower before it flew back to report to Spiracle, Blinker, Gusset and Flob.

At the top of the steep incline was a locked, iron grille that Pilfer used his robber's skills to deal with. When they climbed through it, the party found themselves in a cavernous library containing a labyrinth of shelves that stretched right up to the soaring ceiling. Except that instead of books the shelves were stacked with countless hands arranged side by side in pairs. Many of them were fidgeting.

Mel shifted uneasily as he looked at the constantly

moving shelves. 'This place is giving me the creeps.'

'Me too,' said Wren.

'There's nothing creepy at all,' said Shingle. 'If they were still attached to their owners, you'd think nothing of them.' She rushed to some nearby shelves and took down two pairs of hands. 'These are mine and Shale's,' she announced with delight.

'If all these belong to Mr Habilis's handymen and handmaidens then there must be thousands of the blighters,' said Pilfer.

'Indeed there are,' said Professor Thinkwell's hand. 'But time is pressing. We must get to my laboratory before the damage to the portals becomes irreversible.'

'How do we get there?' said Wren.

'We have to get out of this library first,' said Shingle as she cradled the hands. 'There's a really big lock on the door.'

'Right-o.' There was the sound of Pilfer rubbing his hands together. 'I'm just in the mood for a big lock.'

'Shale, *run*!' shouted Ludo as Scratchbeard pushed him

and the figment boy out of the fingernail chute and into the library. He sprinted off towards the maze of shelves.

'Ludo! Help!' cried Shale from behind him.

Ludo stopped and turned to see Scratchbeard holding Shale in a headlock. His shiv trembled in front of his captive's face.

'Come back here, Smoky,' said Scratchbeard. 'Unless you want me to carve Fuzzy a smile in this blurry face of his.'

Ludo's shoulders slumped and he walked back. Scratchbeard seemed wise to their every move. Even when they were attacked by the monkeys as they followed Mel, Wren and the others, the beggar had not relaxed his vigilance.

'What do you make of this place?' said Scratchbeard as he gazed around at the library. 'This caper gets stranger and stranger.' The beggar pushed Ludo and Shale before him and towards the open door. 'Right, let's go and see where the Shrimp and Missy are leading us.'

* * *

Professor Thinkwell's hand directed the friends steadily higher into one of the finger-towers. They reached the laboratory without encountering any of the castle's inhabitants.

Shingle pushed open the door.

'Whatever's happened?' said a shocked Wren.

It looked as if a whirlwind had wrecked the laboratory. Workbenches were strewn with jumbled mounds of scientific equipment and upturned jars of chemicals dotted the floor. Mountainous piles of books and papers had fallen everywhere. Upended stuffed creatures rested on shelves, and from the ceiling rafters hung many strangely shaped copper vessels. On nearly all the horizontal surfaces stood half-eaten plates of food and every vertical surface was covered in scrawled equations.

'Oh, it always looks like this,' said Shingle as she led the others into the room. 'Genius – what can you do?' She shrugged. 'Professor?'

There was the dotty, scratchy sound of someone writing on a blackboard coming from beyond a wall of stacked books at the far end of the laboratory. The sound stopped and a face appeared from behind the book-wall. It had a bald head framed by an unkempt mop of snow-white hair and matching eyebrows. Half-moon spectacles were perched on the end of its nose, from behind which stared big, pale eyes. His right hand was obviously false, with lots of visible wires and tiny pulleys.

'You must be the real professor. I think this is your hand,' said Mel, passing it over.

'My word. I've been looking everywhere for that. I swear it's got a mind of its own. Have we met before?' The professor unscrewed his false hand and put it in the pocket of his floor-length velvet robe. He fitted his real one in its place. He flexed the fingers and seemed satisfied.

'This is Professor Thinkwell,' said Shingle, introducing the elderly figment. 'Where's Bumnote? Isn't he helping you, Professor?'

'He's right here,' said Professor Thinkwell. 'Bumnote, come out and say hello to our guests. Don't be shy.'

There was a crash from somewhere behind the wall of books, followed by another, and the sound of someone falling over. Professor Thinkwell rolled his eyes.

Then, stumbling into view, came the tall and unmistakable figure of Mel's worst nightmare.

Bumnote

The blood drained from Mel's face and he fought for breath as he stared into the hated face of Groot Smert, Ambrosius Blenk's former head apprentice. There was no mistaking the pointed, rat-like features and the single dark eyebrow that ran above Groot's pale eyes. His features had been etched into Mel's memory after countless acts of cruelty. It was a face Mel had come to loathe. He took a step backwards and tripped over a pile of books. He reached out his hand as he fell and brought more tumbling down on top of him.

The tall youth rushed towards Mel. 'Whoops-a-daisy. Here, let me help you up.'

Wren snatched up a heavy candlestick and stepped defensively in front of her fallen friend. 'Don't you come near us.' She hefted the candlestick like a club.

Goldie joined her. 'You're that evil stowaway from my merry-go-anywhere-you-want-to.'

Bumnote stopped. 'I beg your pardon?'

'Don't pretend you don't know us,' said Mel, digging

himself out from under the books and scrambling to his feet.

'I'm sorry, but you must be confusing me with someone else.' Suddenly, Bumnote seemed to clamp his arms to his sides and go into a kind of a spasm. 'What's happening? Let me go!'

'It's all right,' said Pilfer. 'I've got the scrot in a bear hug.'

'Release my assistant at once,' said Professor Thinkwell. He did not seem surprised by the invisible figment. 'And please, *please* will someone be good enough to explain what's going on?'

'That's not Bumnote,' said Mel. 'He's really Groot Smert.'

'He's a bully, a cheat, a drunk *and* a liar,' said Wren.

'Look, I think there must be some mistake,' said the professor. 'Bumnote is none of those things. If he has one fault it's his over-enthusiasm. And perhaps a certain lack of expertise. And poor manual dexterity, of course. And, oh, a few others maybe . . . Anyway, I'm *sure* he's not who you think he is. Why, he even has an artistic side.'

'Oh, he's got an artistic side, all right,' said Mel. 'We've been on the receiving end of *that*.'

'Please,' said Bumnote. 'You're making a mistake. What can I do to convince you I'm not who you think I am?'

'*You?*' said Wren. 'There's *nothing* you could ever do that would convince me you've changed your ways.'

'But that's just it,' said the professor. 'There are no "ways" for Bumnote to change. He's *always* been as he is now.'

'The professor's right,' said Shingle. 'I've known Bumnote for ever such a long time. He's been at Castle Habilis as long as I have.' The hands she was holding put their thumbs up in agreement.

Wren looked at Mel. He was studying Bumnote's face hard. 'What is it?' she asked.

'His eyes are somehow different,' said Mel. 'Groot's were like a snake's. And now . . . well, now they're not. And his expression. It's not so much evil as . . . as kind of *gormless*.'

'*Gormless?*' spluttered Wren.

'Perhaps not exactly gormless,' said Mel. 'That's

a bit unkind. But certainly not evil. And Professor Thinkwell's hand called him "an incompetent dabbler". That doesn't sound like Groot.'

The professor blushed. 'Did I *really* say that? I swear sometimes my left hand doesn't know what my right hand's doing. Sorry, Bumnote.'

'Hang on, Wren,' said Goldie. 'Your double was in Pennyweight Market. Perhaps he's a double, too.'

'That Wren looked just like you,' said Pilfer. 'But in every other way she was your complete opposite. She even tried to brain Goldie with a spanner. You'd never do that.'

'So what are you saying – that this is Groot's *good* double?' said Wren.

'It's a possibility,' said Pilfer.

'But how?' Mel rubbed his temples. Then, to Bumnote, 'Do you have a double?'

'Not that I'm aware of.'

'You're the brainy one around here, Professor,' said Goldie.

'I'm afraid all this is quite outside my field.'

'If only I still had Cogito with me,' said Wren. 'He'd

know. But he's tucked in my doublet back on the transmogrificator.'

'That's all the more reason to find Mrs Morel and Mrs Wood-Blewit,' said Mel.

'Look, I can vouch for Bumnote,' said Professor Thinkwell.

'Me too,' said Shingle. 'So could Mrs Morel and Mrs Wood-Blewit, if they were here.'

'So, can I let him go?' Pilfer asked.

'I . . . I guess so.' Mel looked at Bumnote. 'I'm sorry. Especially about the "gormless" bit – but we really did think you were Groot.'

'That's all right,' said Bumnote. 'I guess I am a bit gormless sometimes. This Groot probably has my entire share of gorm. Now, if there's anything I can do to help?'

'We have to find Ludo,' said Wren.

'The professor – or his hand – promised he'd help us,' said Mel.

'Did I really?' said the professor. 'How very magnanimous of me. I really *have* given my hand too much autonomy.'

'So how come you and Bumnote are allowed to keep your hands?' said Pilfer.

'So that we could invent things for Mr Habilis,' said Professor Thinkwell. 'He's just mad about gadgets.'

'Sounds to me like he's mad about much more than that,' said Pilfer.

'Or just mad, full stop,' added Goldie.

'Professor, is it possible for you to reattach Shingle's hands?' said Wren.

'Please, if you would,' said Shingle, holding them forwards.

'Certainly,' said the professor. 'I have a little gadget that whips them on and off in a trice. Fixing them back on to a figment is relatively straightforward, but I fear that if a human becomes detached from their hands, then it's permanent – not to say, painful.'

Wren winced. 'We must find Ludo before anything happens to him.'

The professor placed Shingle's severed hands into a small, cage-like contraption that fitted over her stumps and turned a couple of knobs. When he removed it, her hooks were gone and her hands back in place.

Immediately, she began picking things up and flexing her fingers as she giggled with pleasure.

'And now we'd better search for Ludo,' said Mel. 'But where do we start?'

'We could use one of the fishbowl spheres from the transmogrificators to look for him,' said Bumnote. 'We have a spare back here.'

'Great idea,' said Mel.

Bumnote set up the sphere and wired it to a small organ keyboard. As everyone crowded around, the fishbowl began to glow and the image of Castle Habilis appeared inside it. As he manipulated some of the keys and organ stops the image flitted from scene to scene.

'*Stop!* Go back one,' cried Wren. 'Look, there's Ludo!'

'And Shale!' exclaimed Shingle, clapping her hands.

'But who's that with him?' said Goldie.

'It's one of those beggars we surprised in the ghost-train,' said Pilfer. 'And look at the way they're sneaking along. See how Stinky's holding them by the collar? The two lads are his prisoners.'

'Where are they?' said Mel.

Professor Thinkwell leant closer to the fishbowl. 'My word! I do believe they're right outside the laboratory.'

'Now, what do you suppose they're up to in there?' said Scratchbeard in a low voice. He pressed his ear against the door and screwed up his face as he tried to hear. 'I think we should take a peek inside.'

Ludo glanced at Shale but Scratchbeard intercepted the look. 'And don't even *think* about trying to warn them. Otherwise you know what'll happen.' He carefully pushed the door open a crack and peered inside. At the far end of the disordered room a group of six figures was huddled together, peering intently at something glowing on a desk in front of them, their backs to the room.

Suddenly the door flew open and someone grabbed Scratchbeard and dragged him inside.

'I've got the smelly scrot,' said Pilfer.

The others turned from the fishbowl.

'Shale!' Shingle ran and hugged her brother.

'*Ludo!*' cried Wren as she rushed towards her

friend. 'And you've still got your hands.'

'We're so glad to see you,' said Mel, slapping Ludo on the back. 'It *is* you, isn't it?'

'Of course it's me. And that one calls himself Scratchbeard.' Ludo cocked his thumb at the beggar struggling in Pilfer's bear hug. 'He saved me and Shale from – What's *he* doing here?' Ludo pointed at Bumnote.

'It's all right,' said Goldie. 'It's not Groot. Say hello to Bumnote.'

'He's Groot's double,' said Mel. 'I'd better explain.'

'That must be why Scratchbeard thought I was someone else,' said Ludo. 'He thinks you're someone called Shrimp and Wren's Missy.'

'They must be *our* doubles,' said Wren.

'What do you want done with him?' called Pilfer. His voice came from behind the chair he had bound Scratchbeard to. The beggar was mumbling angrily through his gag.

'Leave him tied up for now,' said Mel. 'We need to find Mrs Morel and Mrs Wood-Blewit and

Cogito. And then there's the mirrortree.'

'I think I've located them,' called Bumnote from the fishbowl sphere. 'They're . . .' He consulted the dials. '. . . in Mr Habilis's *guest room*.'

'I don't like the way you said "guest room",' said Goldie.

'It's really creepy,' said Shingle. 'The last thing you ever want to be is a "guest" of Mr Habilis.'

'We must get them out of there,' said Shale.

'We'll come with you,' said Shingle. 'Just as soon as the professor fixes these back on.'

'*My hands!*' Shale was beside himself with glee and hugged his sister and shook everyone's hands the moment they were reattached. 'Now we have them back, we can go back home.'

'Bumnote,' said Mel, 'is there any way we can take this fishbowl with us?'

'No, but there's a small prototype that we've been working on. We could take that.'

'Come on then,' said Mel, turning. 'Let's go – Where's Scratchbeard?'

The others turned. The chair the beggar had been

tied to was empty. Loose coils of rope lay on the floor.

Goldie stooped and picked up a piece of the rope and examined its end. 'It's been cut.'

'He had a home-made knife,' said Ludo.

'Why didn't you search the scrot, Pilfer?' said Goldie.

'Sorry, Goldie,' answered Pilfer. 'I didn't fancy putting my hands inside those filthy rags of his.'

'He'll wish he'd stayed put,' said Shale. 'If one of Mr Habilis's handymen catches him, he'll be separated as quick as you like.'

Bumnote coughed politely. 'If it would help, we could get to Mr Habilis's guest room by a transmogrification portal. They're all over the castle.'

'Are the portals working properly again?' said Goldie.

'Why shouldn't they be?' asked the professor.

'It's just that you said . . . Your hand, that is . . . After all that trouble we had getting here from Monkey-Vlam . . .' Mel trailed to a halt as he saw Bumnote blush bright red and become very busy polishing the small fishbowl sphere. 'Oh, nothing. Let's use a transmogrification portal. It's a brilliant idea.'

'What is it, Mel?' whispered Wren as everyone filed to the rear of the laboratory.

'Yeah, something up?' said Ludo, joining them.

'It's just that in the transmogrificator Professor Thinkwell's hand blamed Bumnote for the portals not working,' said Mel. 'And there's something Bumnote's not letting on about.'

'Do you think we can trust him?' said Wren.

'Perhaps he really *is* Groot,' said Ludo.

'I don't think he can be,' said Mel. 'But something's not right about him. Let's go along with him for now though.'

'But we need to keep our wits about us,' said Wren.

'And our eyes on Bumnote,' said Ludo.

'Come along, come along,' called Professor Thinkwell. 'You don't have time for idle chatter.'

The professor rotated the dials on the portal at the far end of the laboratory with the interrupter. After a short wait, the red light changed to green and the door opened to the touch of the professor's hand. The doorway at the far end of the short corridor opened just as easily.

'This is the guest room all right,' said Shingle.

'In that case,' said Mel, 'where are the guests?'

Back to the Crippled Toad

When the beggars eventually arrived at their destination, there was no sign of Pennyweight Market or even that it had ever been there. They stood with Spandangle and the bound and gagged children in a wide puddle of phial-light on the cracked, stone floor, surrounded by an ocean of impenetrable darkness. The silence was profound.

'You sure we've come back to the right place?' said Nelly in a low voice, awed by the emptiness.

'We're in the right place, sure enough,' said Doctor Sarcophagus. 'The market's gone. We've been had.'

'You don't think we imagined that market?' said Canker.

'The only imagining that's been done is these three scrot-stains thinking they could outwit us,' said Nelly. 'I'll make them sorry they were ever born.' She drew a dagger from her bodice and Mel, Ludo and Wren's eyes opened wide in terror.

As Nelly moved towards the children the sound

of barking came from out of the darkness.

'Sounds like the mutt's found something,' said Canker.

When they reached the dog she was hobbling up and down in front of the dark and abandoned ghost train.

'Why's this still here?' said Doctor Sarcophagus.

'You don't suppose the tree's hidden inside, do you?' said Nelly. 'It was all closed up the last time we were here.'

'Perhaps they were using the ghosts to scare everyone away,' said Canker. 'So that the tree would never be found.'

'How many times do you need to be told?' said Doc. 'They weren't *real* ghosts. What do you think, Scratchbeard?'

'Be good to know why they didn't strike this ghost train when the rest of the market left. That's what I think.'

'So let's go inside and take a look,' said Doc. 'And this time we'll all stick together. Remember what happened last time.'

'Just a minute,' said Nelly. 'The invisible man.'

Doc, Nelly and Canker stared at one another open-mouthed as the same thought struck them all at once.

'He must have found the miracle tree and used the sap on himself!' said Canker. 'That *proves* it's in there somewhere.' He pushed the others aside and rushed towards the ghost train.

Spandangle shoved Mel, Ludo and Wren in front of him and followed the beggars into the darkened attraction.

Together, they ransacked the entire space until they all stood in front of the strange door at the rear, next to the organ.

'We've searched the whole gaff,' said Doc. 'Behind that door's the only place left it could be.'

'Why do you suppose it's got that red light above it?' said Nelly.

'Red means danger, doesn't it?' said Canker. He looked over his shoulder and tried to pierce the darkness beyond the glow of the phials they carried.

'That's a strange-looking door,' said Doc. He rapped on it with his knuckles. 'Sounds as thick as a vault door.

Do you think that big dial in the middle's some kind of combination lock?'

'Could be,' said Spandangle. 'But my guess is it works like this.' He placed his hand in the hand-lock. The dials spun, the red light changed to green and the door opened.

'Can you see the tree?' asked Canker, the last to emerge from the door at the far end of the short, crinkly corridor.

'Trees are all we *can* see,' said Doctor Sarcophagus.

'What's happened to Vlam?' said Nelly. Her mouth hung open as she surveyed the overgrown city.

Mel, Ludo and Wren were as astonished as the beggars. They looked questioningly at Spandangle, who shrugged and shook his head.

'Are those *monkeys*?' said Canker incredulously as he joined the others looking out of the window in the small room crowded with branches.

'You've got to admit it's a pretty good place to hide a tree. In the middle of a jungle.' Spandangle looked as puzzled as everybody else by the turn of events.

'So what do we do now?' said Nelly.

'I think we should make our way to the Crippled Toad,' said Doctor Sarcophagus. 'Maybe we can find someone there who can tell us what's going on.'

They walked single file through the narrow streets, ducking under low branches and clambering over others. The children stared as they passed a street of shops where every window was choked with vegetation as if it were the season's one, must-have item everyone suddenly wanted to buy. Except that there were no customers. Only bands of monkeys dressed in plundered finery that either ran away noisily or tried to pick a fight with the ragged and perplexed group.

When they finally reached the Crippled Toad and fought their way through clinging vines and down the root-choked staircase they found the inn as deserted as the rest of the city.

'Well, *someone's* been here,' said Canker. 'They've left a note.' He picked up the scrap of paper anchored to the bar with an empty tankard. His mouth dropped open. 'It's addressed to *us*.' He looked at the others. 'And it's from you, Scratchbeard!'

The blood drained from Mel's face and he

exchanged a worried glance with Ludo and Wren, equally ashen-faced.

'*What?*' exclaimed Doctor Sarcophagus. 'Here, let me see.' He snatched the note.

'I saw it first!' Canker snatched it back.

Doctor Sarcophagus and Nelly stared at Spandangle. Mel, Ludo and Wren's eyes darted about in near-panic. The only one who did not seem concerned was Spandangle.

'There's something really odd going on here,' said Nelly.

'What's it say?' said Doc.

Canker read aloud, '"Dear Doc, Nelly and Canker, Go back to the Blenk mansion. Rich pickings. Scratchbeard."'

Spandangle made a small but quick movement with his hand and, suddenly, Canker's dog erupted in a fit of barking. She foamed at the mouth and fastened her teeth into her master's leg.

Canker screamed and Nelly and Doc made a grab for the dog. The note flew into the air and Spandangle caught it. Mel saw Spandangle pass his hand over the note and the surface of the paper became like a sheet of water. The scrawled writing floated into new positions before the surface solidified again.

'What's got into the mutt?' said Doctor Sarcophagus as he tried to pull the dog off Canker.

'She's never done that before,' said Nelly as she also tugged at the dog's collar. 'Do you think it's got something to do with her sniffing that tracking potion Doc splashed on these little scrots?'

Mel, Ludo and Wren looked at each other and lowered their heads to sniff their clothes.

Spandangle nodded to himself and then made another subtle move with his hands.

Just as suddenly as the attack started, it stopped. The dog released Canker and began sniffing around the inn as if nothing had happened. Canker sat on the floor, howling with pain and inspecting his savaged leg.

'Give me that!' said Doc, snatching the note from Spandangle. He read it. 'What are you on about, Canker? You've been doing the blind scam too long.'

'What's it say?' said Nelly. She took the note from Doctor Sarcophagus and read it out. '"Dear Doc, Nelly,

Canker and Scratchbeard, Go back to the Blenk mansion. Rich pickings." Reading and writing never was your strong point, was it, Canker?' she said.

'I know what I saw,' said Canker through gritted teeth.

'Mange must have left it for us,' said Doc. 'Come on, let's go.'

When they finally arrived outside Ambrosius Blenk's mansion they were scratched, footsore and exhausted. The beggars slouched in a doorway with a view of the mansion, regretting that the irresistible lure of gold had made them forget to bring along a bottle or two of Mange's rotgut ale.

As they were deciding the best way to get into the mansion they were startled by two monkeys that bolted out of the door behind them.

'What was that?' shrieked Canker.

'Just a couple of monkeys, you cretin,' said Nelly.

'But did you see what they were carrying?' said Doc. 'If my eyes weren't deceiving me, those apes had a bottle of wine. Let's find where they got the booze from.'

Mel, Ludo and Wren dragged their feet and generally made Canker's job of getting them down the stairs as difficult as possible.

The beggars quickly found the wine cellar and helped themselves each to a bottle of the choicest vintage.

'Ahhhhh.' Doctor Sarcophagus took a long pull from his bottle. 'That's better.' He belched and wiped his mouth with the back of his hand. 'Hey, look. There's another one of those vault doors back here.'

'Do you suppose it leads back to the ghost train?' said Nelly.

'We can find out later, after we've filled our pockets in the Blenk mansion,' said Doc. 'Drink up and let's go.'

But when they got to the stairs, they recoiled as a large band of aggressive monkeys surged towards them.

'Come here, you cowards,' said Doc as the others retreated back into the cellar. 'A few scrawny monkeys can't – *Arrrgggghhh!*' He cried out as a well-aimed wine bottle shattered against his turban.

'Quick, everyone into the vault!' shouted Nelly, slapping her hand in the hand-shaped depression.

Pursued by the enraged monkey gang, the beggars pushed the children before them and fled down the crumpled corridor and through the door at the far end.

'Help me wedge it shut,' said Spandangle as he thrust Mel, Ludo and Wren through the doorway.

'This ain't no ghost train,' said Canker, gazing about. 'Where the skeg are we?'

'My guess is it's some kind of vessel,' said Spandangle.

The others were silent for a moment and then burst out laughing.

'That's a good one, Scratchbeard,' said Doctor Sarcophagus.

'A vessel,' laughed Nelly. 'Glad you've still got a sense of humour.'

'And I suppose that's the mast,' said Canker, pointing at the kinked spindle that ran down the centre of the cylindrical space. 'And they use that strange organ to play the hornpipe?'

'Can you think of anything else that has a porthole?' said Spandangle as he peered out.

'What can you see?' said Nelly, still laughing. 'A lighthouse?'

'It's some sort of house, all right,' said Spandangle. 'A house as big as a castle. And it looks as though it's made out of *hands*.'

'If you're having one of those lucinations, then I'm having it too,' said Nelly as she joined Spandangle.

'I bet the tree's in there,' said Doctor Sarcophagus.

As the three beggars rushed out of the cabin, Spandangle held back. When he was sure they had gone he took out Madam Manto's small crystal ball and stared into it. He smiled at what he saw. He loosened the childrens' gags.

Mel exploded with rage. 'You privy-licking, scrot-eating, scut-sucking bucket of festering maggot food!'

'If I ever get my hands free I'm going to rip your ears off,' screamed Ludo. 'And that's just for starters.'

Wren spat and hissed and screamed. 'You think yourself so clever, but we nearly got caught back there. The real Scratchbeard can't be far away.'

'Keep your voices down,' said Spandangle. 'Or I'll make sure they're lost permanently.'

'Where are we anyway?' said Mel.

'I'm not sure, precisely,' said Spandangle. 'But Madam M thinks that we're very close to the mirrortree. The others are, too.'

'*What?*' snapped Ludo. 'Then we need to get out of this rust-bucket and find it before they do. Untie us.'

'If I was to do that, how could I ensure I'll keep my ears attached to my head?'

Ludo drew a resigned breath. 'All right. Untie us and I promise I won't rip your ears off.' And then he added under his breath, '*Yet*.'

'And you two?' said Spandangle. 'Do you promise, too?'

'Yeah,' said Mel. 'Whatever.'

'All right,' said Wren. 'We promise. *Satisfied?*'

'I've rarely received promises delivered with such a lack of conviction,' said Spandangle as he untied them. 'However, time's pressing.'

'So where is the mirrortree?' said Mel, rubbing his sore wrists.

'I don't know,' answered Spandangle.

'But it's near here?' said Wren. 'You said so. What's it look like?'

'I don't know that either. Its appearance is different for everyone.'

'Then how the skeg are we supposed to find it?' spat Ludo.

'No one knows what this particular mirrortree looks like – yet,' said Spandangle. 'But you do know what the other Mel, Ludo and Wren look like, don't you?'

The three nodded.

'So I suggest that we find them and let *them* do all the hard, and no doubt dangerous, work of finding it.'

'And then we take it off them?' said Mel.

'Exactly!' said Spandangle. 'Now let's get out of here before those beggars realise that we're not following them.'

Cogito Explains

'How very odd,' said Bumnote, as they stood in the guest room. 'The fishbowl clearly showed your friends here.'

'Well, they're not here any more,' said Ludo.

The room was roughly square with a very high ceiling. The walls were draped with tapestries woven with black-and-white fingerprint patterns. The lines were so close together they seemed to flicker. They hurt Mel's eyes when he tried to focus on them. There was a similar op-art patterned carpet.

Mel leant against the wall to steady himself. 'This room's making me feel sick.'

'It's designed to do that,' said Shingle. 'I told you you'd never want to be a guest of Mr Habilis's.'

'But where are Mrs Morel and Mrs Wood-Blewit?' said Wren, fighting back her own bout of nausea.

'Could they have left by the portal?' said Goldie.

Professor Thinkwell shook his head. 'Not while we were using it.'

'They must have gone this way,' said Shale, crossing to the window. 'Look, the catch has been left open.'

Mel opened the window and peered out into the darkness. 'Not unless they had parachutes. It's an awfully long way down. Wait a minute. There's a ledge.'

'Perhaps they went that way,' said Wren. 'We should follow them.'

'Clambering about on a narrow ledge in the dark,' said Professor Thinkwell. 'Is that wise?'

'The professor's right,' added Bumnote quickly. 'I vote we retrace our steps and find another way.'

'Sounds like the ledge will be the quickest way to find them,' said Pilfer. 'And then we can see about leaving this gaff for good.'

The others murmured their agreement.

'Sorry, Bumnote,' said Professor Thinkwell, 'it looks like you're outvoted.'

Mel led the way as they inched along the ledge. Below them was a dizzying drop that he tried to ignore. Suddenly, he stopped. 'Did anyone see that?'

'What was it?' called Ludo.

'It looked like a scrawny black bird with great big

eyes,' said Mel. 'I'm sure it was staring at us. It flew off that way, towards the edge of the forest.'

'This is really not the time for a spot of ornithology,' said Professor Thinkwell. 'Can we please continue? I fear I have no head for heights.'

Mel crept on. 'There's an open window up ahead. Wait here while I check it out.'

'Take care,' said Wren. 'There might be handymen.'

Cautiously, Mel advanced until he could peer in through the window. He saw no movement. He gestured to the others to follow, then edged the last few feet and climbed into a room even more chaotic and cluttered than Professor Thinkwell's laboratory. There were all kinds of contraptions which were either incomplete or clumsily held together with knotted string, rubber bands and sticky tape. On closer inspection, Mel could see that several of them were duplicated, triplicated or even quadruplicated.

'You wouldn't by any chance have some mushrooms and a teapot with you? We're absolutely parched,' said a voice.

Mel turned to see a red-and-white spotted

mushroom head peep from behind a contraption. 'Mrs Morel?'

'Have you just come from that ghastly guest room?' Emerging from the clutter was Mrs Morel. 'We couldn't bear to stay there a moment longer. Apart from the simply *hideous* decor there're no refreshment facilities.'

One by one, those following Mel climbed into the room. Bumnote came last of all and seemed reluctant to enter.

'We're so glad to see you again – and all in one piece,' beamed Mrs Wood-Blewit as she brushed off her lacy mushroom frock and joined her companion. 'You too, Ludo. And Wren. We feared we might have lost you all for good.'

'I'm fine,' said Ludo. He introduced Goldie and Pilfer. The mushroom ladies already knew Professor Thinkwell, Bumnote, Shale and Shingle. 'So, where are we?'

After a long silence Bumnote sighed and admitted, 'It's my workroom.'

'*Your* workroom?' said Professor Thinkwell as he feverishly polished his spectacles with the hem of his robe. 'I think you'd better explain.'

Bumnote looked very embarrassed and fiddled nervously with the tiny fishbowl sphere. 'Well, um, it's like this. I've been making my own inventions –'

'*Dabbling*, more like,' interrupted Professor Thinkwell.

'I had all these ideas and I just *had* to make them. I didn't want to tell the professor until I'd perfected them. But . . . but not all of them worked – at least, not properly.'

'I'd be amazed if *any* of them did,' scoffed the professor.

'More than you might think,' said Bumnote with an uncharacteristic hint of assertiveness. 'I even invented a transmogrificator.'

'*You?*' Professor Thinkwell seemed taken aback.

Bumnote, meek again, lowered his eyes and nodded. 'Well, anyway, another one of my inventions was a replificator. That's it, over there. You put something in the receptor, throw a few levers, press a few buttons, turn a few dials – that kind of thing – and out pops a perfect replica of the original.'

'Perfect?' said the professor. 'I very much doubt it.'

'Just a minute, Professor,' said Mel. 'Some of these machines are obviously identical.'

'Yes,' said Bumnote. 'They've been through the replificator.'

Professor Thinkwell examined a couple. 'Mmmm.' His tone was not as certain as before.

Wren shivered and hugged herself.

'Here,' said Mrs Wood-Blewit, handing Wren her lost doublet. 'You left this behind when you disappeared so suddenly in the transmogrificator.'

'Cogito!' Wren took the garment and felt in the inside pocket. 'Thank goodness he's still here.' She withdrew the roll of parchment.

'Now perhaps we can get some answers to all this twins business,' said Ludo.

'Twins?' said Mrs Morel and Mrs Wood-Blewit in unison.

'We'd best let Cogito explain.' Mel cleared a space on a desktop and unrolled the parchment. The others gathered round. Wren found an inkwell and Mel dipped his angel quill and began to write.

All humans have both a light and a dark side folded up inside themselves, wrote Cogito as Mel's question faded away. *These other halves are like ghosts or shades. They're called mirrorshades. They embody all the traits that humans try to hide from themselves. In Wren's case, it was her dark side that was in Pennyweight Market and in Groot's, Bumnote is his light side that he refuses to acknowledge.*

So, wrote Mel, *if Groot is twisted and rotten, then his mirrorshade – Bumnote – is kind and helpful?*

Yes.

But where did they come from?

Humans need to achieve a balance between these two sides of their nature to remain healthy. It's when this balance is broken that trouble ensues. Your mirrorshade is not normally separate from the rest of you, but, if you completely ignore it or venture into the Mirrorscape too often, it can become detached. Your suppressed side can develop a personality – and a body – of its own.

'I've observed this in humans before,' said Professor Thinkwell. 'If they disregard their dark streak an otherwise good human can create all kinds of trouble for themselves and those around them. On the other hand, wholly good people lack some kind of vital spark.'

'I must admit, I sometimes have dark thoughts,' said Mel.

'Me, too,' admitted Wren. 'Especially about Groot.' She glanced apologetically at Bumnote.

'I wonder if Mr Habilis has some human in him,' said Mrs Morel.

'It's one way to account for him being so thoroughly bad,' added Mrs Wood-Blewit.

So it's all right to have a dark side? wrote Mel.

To think these things is normal. To act them out is not.

Does that mean that Ludo and I also have mirrorshades?

Without a doubt. And what's more, if Wren's mirrorshade is abroad, then yours and Ludo's are bound to be too.

If they look like us, do they also think like us? asked Mel.

Yes. They will also have access to some of your thoughts and experiences just as you will have to theirs. When you wake from a bad dream you sometimes remember experiencing a bit of your mirrorshade's thoughts. In much the same way your mirrorshade will remember some of your thoughts. For them it's like a half-remembered dream.

293

So where are our mirrorshades now?

If you're in the Mirrorscape then your mirrorshades are likely to be in Nem, wrote Cogito.

What are they doing there?

They'll be doing the same as you are. You're both linked. That's why they're called 'mirror' shades.

'So, if we're looking for the mirrortree,' said Wren, 'then they will be too?'

'That figures,' said Goldie.

'And if they're anything like the one we met in Pennyweight Market, they'll be leaving all kinds of trouble behind them,' said Pilfer. 'Am I glad I'm not a human with a mirrorshade.'

'Talking of the mirrortree . . .' said Wren.

'I haven't forgotten,' said Mel. He penned the question and then added, *Have you come up with an answer yet?*

I can't help you. You must find the mirrortree yourselves.

So it does exist? wrote Mel.

You must work that out for yourself.

But we don't know where to start.

Start at the beginning. It's invariably the best place to start.

That's not what I meant. Can't you at least give us a clue where to look?

Mel's written question remained on the parchment.

'What's happened?' asked Professor Thinkwell.

'Cogito must have gone offline,' said Mel. 'He does this now and again.'

'Usually just when you need him most,' said Goldie.

'Hey, you lot, come and look at this,' called Pilfer's voice from behind mounds of equipment.

Everyone filed to the back of the room.

'Now, what do you make of this?' Pilfer turned a large canvas that had been propped against the wall alongside others.

'It's a painting of Monkey-Vlam!' said Wren.

'Yeah,' said Ludo. 'And look, it's signed "Bumnote". So he *does* have an artistic side.'

Mel, Ludo and Wren turned to stare at Bumnote, who blushed and shuffled his feet. They looked back and studied the painting.

Mel leant even closer. 'There's something not quite right.' He rubbed at the surface with his finger and examined the tip. 'Hah! I see what's happened.'

'Well?' prompted Pilfer. 'Explain it for the benefit of us non-artistic types.'

'It's an accident,' said Bumnote. 'You see, underneath there's an old painting of a jungle with monkeys and I tried to paint a view of Vlam directly on top of it.'

'When you want to reuse a canvas you have to seal the first image so that when you paint over it the colours don't bleed through like they've done here,' continued Mel. 'It's one of the first things you learn as an apprentice.'

'And the painting underneath must have a mirrormark,' said Wren. 'That's why Monkey-Vlam is a part of the Mirrorscape.'

'Bumnote's as bad at painting as he is at inventing.' Ludo blushed. 'Sorry, Bumnote.'

'But why Vlam?' said Wren. 'Shingle said that you've always been here in the castle.'

'I don't know,' said Bumnote. 'It just came to me.'

'Cogito said that each mirrorshade is connected to its counterpart,' said Mel. 'So, if Bumnote is Groot's good mirrorshade then, deep down inside, he might be able to experience the same things that Groot has.

And it comes out as imagination or inspiration or something like that.'

'You mean it's as if he were seeing it through Groot's eyes?' said Ludo. 'It would explain why the painting of Vlam is so accurate.'

'Even down to Dirk Tot's workshop in the mansion,' added Mel. 'You'd only know about that if you'd actually been there.'

'But where would you have got a mirrormarked painting in the first place?' said Wren. 'Only great masters can make a mirrormark that works.'

'I got it from Pennyweight Market,' admitted Bumnote. 'You can get anything there.'

'Can we discuss all this later?' said Pilfer. 'Now we've found Mrs Morel and Mrs Wood-Blewit and you've got Cogito back we need to get out of here and help you find this mirrortree of yours. We're going to need some sort of vehicle.'

'We could borrow a transmogrificator,' said Ludo.

'There's quite a choice outside in the docks,' said Mel. 'Come on.' He led the others back to the other end of the workroom.

'Who's been keeping lookout in the fishbowl sphere?' asked Goldie.

'That was your job, Bumnote,' said Professor Thinkwell.

'Sorry, Professor, I'll check now.' Bumnote crossed to the workbench where he had parked the sphere. He bent his tall frame to peer into it, gave a start and jumped back.

Mel, Ludo and Wren rushed over. As they, too, gazed into the sphere, they saw what had startled Bumnote. Staring back at them and occupying the entire volume of the sphere was a mechanical eye. It blinked and the pupil expanded.

'It's Mr Habilis,' said Bumnote. 'He's seen us!'

'Oh dear,' said Mrs Wood-Blewit. 'That's torn it. He'll know where we are now.'

'I fear you're right,' said Mrs Morel. 'Mr Habilis is capable of anything. Every mushroom patch has its toadstool and I'm afraid that Mr Habilis is the one in our family.'

A bell began tolling.

'It's the alarm,' said Shingle, clearly frightened.

'What'll we do?' said Shale.

'Hold on,' said Mel. 'Why don't we let ourselves be caught?'

'That sounds crazy to me,' said Goldie.

'Crazy? No, far from it,' said Mel. 'Here's what we'll do.'

Beggars Reunited

Spandangle, back in his magician's form, complete with black costume and mask, hefted an iron, fist-shaped knocker as big as a watermelon on the enormous main door of Castle Habilis. As it crashed down the sound was like a drum booming in the underworld and seemed to shake the very ground. After a while a Judas hole opened and a pair of eyes looked out. 'Yes?'

'My greetings to you, good sir,' said Spandangle, bowing. 'Please inform the master of this imposing residence that the great Spandangle and his troupe are here to perform feats of magical delectation and the most stupendous prestidigitation for his delight and edification.'

'Huh?'

Spandangle sighed. 'We're here to give a magic show.'

A second Judas hole opened much lower down and another set of eyes peeped out. 'Do you know anything about any magic show?' the voice belonging to the lower eyes muttered.

'No one tells me anything,' mumbled the voice behind the upper hole.

'Mr Habilis isn't expecting any magic show,' said the lower.

'I think you'll find he is.' Spandangle did something very fast with his hands and both sets of eyes seemed to glaze over.

'Oh, *that* magic show,' said the lower voice. 'Open the gates!'

The Judas holes slammed shut and, a moment later, the iron-studded gates swung open with a mighty groan.

'Thank you, my good fellow. My assistants and I know the way.'

'Why did we have to come in through the front door?' said Mel, as he followed Spandangle into the castle. 'Now that Mr Happy-Bliss will know we're here.'

'Since you three managed to get yourselves anointed with Doctor Sarcophagus's tracking potion, it seemed the wisest choice,' said Spandangle. 'They'll come after us, for sure.'

'Couldn't you have just magicked a new smell for us?' said Ludo.

'Smells take too much time and energy. At least this way the beggars will have to try and find their own way into the castle. It's bought us some valuable time.' Spandangle led them down a long passage lit with burning brands held by hand-shaped sconces. He smiled and inclined his head in a friendly bow each time they passed a handyman and received some suspicious stares at their hands in return.

'Well, now we're in, where are the others?' said Wren.

'First things first,' said Spandangle. 'It would be prudent to find out just who this Mr Habilis is before we go gallivanting around his domain.'

'And how are we going to do that?' said Mel. 'We don't exactly blend into the background. Everyone's staring at us.'

'Smells might be difficult but appearances are a trifle easier to create.' Spandangle gave a great sweep of his black cloak and when he lowered it he looked like a tall, thin handyman and Mel,

Ludo and Wren like short fat ones.

'Where're our hands?' shrieked Wren, holding her iron hooks in front of her new face.

'And hair?' complained Ludo. 'And what's happened to our ears?'

'Why are you still wearing your cloak?' said Mel.

'Because I feel the cold,' said Spandangle.

'We'd like the chance to feel something too,' said Wren bitterly.

'I won't be able to maintain a four-way illusion for long,' said Spandangle. 'We'd best get on.'

At that moment a bell began tolling, followed shortly by the sound of many running feet. At the end of the passage dozens of handymen appeared and ran towards them. Their rubber suits squeaked like a thousand angry mice.

'They've rumbled us,' said Mel. 'So much for your great disguises. Leg it!'

The three children turned on their heels and began running away from the handymen. After a second, Spandangle hurried after them.

'You shouldn't have run like that,' said Spandangle

as he drew abreast. 'There was nothing wrong with my disguises. Now you've given the game away.'

'Faster!' said Ludo, looking over his shoulder. 'They're gaining on us.'

'I can't go any faster in this rubber suit,' puffed Wren.

But, as the pursuing handymen caught up with the runners, rather than apprehend them, they carried on, bearing Spandangle, Mel, Ludo and Wren along with the pack.

'Where are we going?' Spandangle asked one of the handymen.

'To the Great Hall, of course. Didn't you hear the alarm bell?'

Spandangle and the children were drawn along by the sheer momentum as if caught in an avalanche. The mass of handymen finally came to a halt in a cavernous hall. Anyone familiar with anatomy would have recognised that the massive columns supporting the towering ceiling were carved in the shape of ulna and radius bones of the forearm. Similarly, the capitals at the top were in the shape of the numerous bones of the wrist. The ceiling vaulting resembled finger bones soaring high overhead. Cradled in a giant carving of a pair of cupped hands at the far end of the hall was a massive fishbowl sphere. It pulsed and glowed as swirling colours drifted about inside, painting the walls behind with moving patterns of rainbow light. Slowly, the coloured clouds drifted apart to reveal the image of a huge mechanical eye that filled the entire sphere. It stared at the thousands of handymen present.

The eye blinked once and a deep voice that made the walls tremble said, 'Hear the voice of Habilis. There are intruders in my castle.'

Standing to either side of Spandangle, Mel and Ludo tensed, ready to flee. The conjuror put a restraining hook on each of their shoulders and shook his head. 'Stay still,' he whispered. 'You too, Wren. It's the others he's talking about.'

The resounding voice continued, 'Guard every door and window. They are not to escape. They have been located in Bumnote's workroom. Now – to your posts!'

The assembly broke up and hurried off.

Spandangle drew Mel, Ludo and Wren into an

alcove. 'Fortune continues to smile on us,' he said. 'We now have a legitimate reason to be searching for the others. Come on.'

They followed the departing handymen and began to climb the stairs. Many of the handymen were armed with short, flat swords, multi-barbed spears, spiked knuckle-dusters, maces, battleaxes and electric whips. Several carried large nets.

The handymen kept climbing until they came to a halt in a long, torch-lit corridor with a single door at the far end. Eight more guards carrying a battering ram edged their way through the crowd.

With a roar of 'seize the intruders!', the guards wielding the battering ram charged forwards.

'Where are we?' whispered Canker as he climbed after Doctor Sarcophagus and Nelly Buboes out of the rubbish chute, his dog under one arm. Potato peelings and limp cabbage leaves draped their heads.

'*Shhh*,' cautioned Doc. 'Keep your voice down.'

'It looks like we're in the kitchens,' said Nelly. 'Smells like it, too.' She plucked pieces of cheese rind and some stringy, sticky giblets from her hair. 'Yuck!'

'I thought I told you to keep quiet,' said Doc. 'Come on.' He beckoned Nelly and Canker as he edged forwards and peered around a column.

Orange light from dancing flames in a big open fireplace bathed the kitchen. Two fat cooks, their faces glistening with sweat, were turning each end of a spit with the roasting carcass of some large animal impaled on it. Nearby, other cooks were busy kneading dough, peeling vegetables or gutting fish using attachments fixed to their wrists. Another group was occupied at a row of sinks scrubbing pots and pans. In the centre of all this bustling activity stood yet another fat female figment wearing a tall chef's hat and with sharp cleavers attached to the ends of her thick arms. She was busy directing the rest of the kitchen staff.

Canker licked his lips. 'I'm starving. I can't remember the last time I ate.' He strained to hold back his dog. She was salivating freely at the cooking smells wafting towards them.

As Canker was about to slip from his hiding place, Doctor Sarcophagus grabbed his collar and dragged him back. 'You idiot. Keep still or we'll be spotted.'

'Look,' said Nelly, pointing. 'Someone else is getting peckish.'

As the beggars watched they saw a hand appear from under a table and steal a slice of bread. A short while later the same dirty hand reappeared nearer the centre of the kitchen and took a wedge of cheese. But as the hand reached for a jug of milk a well-aimed cleaver crashed down on the tabletop, narrowly missing its fingers and shattering the jug. The fat cook screeched at the top of her voice as she wrenched her cleaver from the table. Several other cooks rushed from their tasks and raised the milk-soaked thief to his feet.

'*It's Scratchbeard!*' gasped the beggars in a single, harsh whisper.

They watched as Scratchbeard was threatened and interrogated by the head cook before he was tied to a fresh spit.

'Much as I'd like to see that double-crossing scrot roasted alive, I want some answers from him first.' Doctor Sarcophagus removed two phials from his waistcoat and handed one to Nelly. 'OK, Canker, let your mutt go.'

The dog hobbled off and made a beeline for the roasted meat on the spit, barking loudly. At the same time Nelly lobbed her phial over the heads of the kitchen figments and into the fire. It shattered against the chimney-back and a great ball of flames billowed outwards with a roar. As all eyes turned towards the conflagration and cries of alarm were shouted, Doctor Sarcophagus dashed his phial to the floor, where it smashed and erupted in billowing clouds of blue–black smoke. Amid the smokescreen and general confusion Scratchbeard, spit and all, was snatched and the beggars made their escape.

Doctor Sarcophagus and Canker carried Scratchbeard between them like a hunter's prize on a pole as they fled the kitchen. They ran down corridors, turning left and right at random.

'It's quiet in here,' said Nelly, ushering them into some kind of antechamber. Doc and Canker set their heavy burden down on the stone floor.

'Am I glad to see you,' said Scratchbeard. 'A moment later and I'd have been fricasseed. How did you know where to find me?'

'Shut up, Scratchbeard,' said Nelly.

'Come on,' said Scratchbeard, tugging at his bonds. 'Untie me.'

'I said *shut up*!' spat Nelly.

'All right, Scratchbeard,' said Doctor Sarcophagus. 'Where's the tree?'

'Tree? What tree?'

'Look, you might as well tell us,' said Canker, drawing his knife. 'It'll save you a heap of pain.'

'Come on, stop fooling around. Untie me and tell me how you found me.'

'You're not going to bluff your way out of this one,' said Doctor Sarcophagus, drawing a phial from his waistcoat and removing the stopper. 'Get ready to kiss your toes goodbye.'

'What are you talking about?' said Scratchbeard, his eyes wide with a mixture of confusion and fear.

'It won't work,' said Nelly, as she began to remove Scratchbeard's tattered boot. 'What do you think, Doc? Start with the little toe and work your way up?'

Scratchbeard struggled against his bindings. 'What's got into you? After I lost you in the ghost train in that freaky market, I ended up in a weird cavern place that looked like it was made of folded-up metal. Then I snatched Smoky from some kind of guillotine and somehow got back to Vlam – except it wasn't Vlam. The gaff was full of trees and monkeys and I took him to the Crippled Toad. I left a note for you.'

Doctor Sarcophagus stopped tilting his phial. He exchanged glances with Nelly and Canker. 'Go on.'

They listened in silence to the rest of Scratchbeard's tale.

'That's the truth,' finished Scratchbeard. 'I swear it.'

'Since when's your word been worth more than a filleted fart?' said Nelly.

'Hang on,' said Canker. He leant close to Scratchbeard and sniffed. '*Phew*. It certainly smells like him.'

'All right,' said Doctor Sarcophagus. 'If you're *really* Scratchbeard, tell us what the four of us were doing last midwinter's eve.'

'Last midwinter's eve? Why, we helped ourselves to that pile of presents in the children's hospital. Then we took them back to the Crippled Toad and sold the lot to Puke the fence.'

'One-eyed Puke?' asked Doc.

'Puke had both his eyes the last time I saw him,' said Scratchbeard. 'He's only got one leg, though.'

'Only Scratchbeard could have known that,' said Nelly.

Doctor Sarcophagus stared at Scratchbeard in silence for a full minute. Then he replaced the stopper in his phial and cut Scratchbeard free. 'There's something really weird going on here. You say those kids are upstairs in this castle?'

'Yeah,' said Scratchbeard. 'They've got themselves a change of clothes and a bunch of friends. One of them's invisible.'

'*Invisible?*' said the others, almost choking.

Disguises

The door to Bumnote's workshop exploded inwards with an almighty crash as the heavy battering ram did its business. The handymen stormed into the room. They cast their nets in a great arc, ensnaring all the room's occupants in one go. Other handymen poured in and gagged and bound the prisoners as efficiently as a spider binds a fly. The struggling and trussed-up figures were hoisted high over the handymen's heads and carried away.

'So *that's* what the others look like,' whispered Mel. He used the end of his hook to scratch his ear.

'What an ugly bunch,' said Wren. 'Apart from the girl. She's rather pretty.'

'Well, we've found them,' said Spandangle, as he and the children brought up the rear. 'And it was all much easier than I anticipated. Perhaps too easy.'

'How can anything be *too* easy?' said Ludo. 'The less I have to work, the better I like it.'

'But now those scrotty handymen have them,'

said Wren.

'Yeah,' said Mel. 'How are they going to find the mirrortree if they're prisoners?'

'One step at a time,' said Spandangle. 'Let's see where they're taking them.'

'It was the best disguise I've ever seen, Scratchbeard,' said Nelly Buboes. 'He looked just like you.'

'Fooled me, too,' said Doctor Sarcophagus. 'He was your exact double. Even up close.'

'Apart from his cloak,' said Canker. 'And his smell. He didn't have one.'

'Are you sure about this tree?' said Scratchbeard. 'Sounds like a fairy story to me.'

'We thought so too, at first,' said Doc.

'It don't seem likely,' said Nelly. 'But then none of this caper seems likely.'

'But Scratchbeard saw this invisible man,' said Canker. 'Well, not exactly *saw* him – but you know what I mean. So it must be true about this here tree.'

'Now you mention it, I did overhear them saying something about a tree,' said Scratchbeard. 'I thought they said "mirror tree". But it could have been this "miracle tree" of yours. Even if –'

'*Quiet!*' hissed Nelly. 'I can hear marching feet. Someone's coming.'

'Quick,' said Doc. 'Through here.' He opened a door off the antechamber and Scratchbeard, Nelly, Canker and his dog followed him through.

'What the skeg's *that*?' gasped Canker as he stared up at a tall guillotine that occupied the centre of the room.

'It's one of those chopper things I saved Smoky from,' said Scratchbeard.

'Come on,' said Doc. 'We can hide back here, behind these shelves.'

No sooner had the beggars concealed themselves than the door opened and the handymen carried their prisoners in and locked them in a cell that ran the length of one wall. Most of the handymen then filed out, looking satisfied, leaving three who busied themselves at the separator. Four more – three short and one tall and thin wearing a cloak – hovered in the doorway.

'Look in the cell,' whispered Scratchbeard. 'It's *them*!'

'They've changed back into their posh duds,' said Doc. 'But it's them, sure enough.'

'What a stroke of luck,' said Canker. He kept a firm hold of his dog's muzzle.

'Do we try and snatch them?' hissed Nelly.

'Not yet,' whispered Doc. 'Seven guards against four of us. And they're armed. Let's just sit tight for a bit and see if the odds get any better.'

One of the handymen turned the crank at the base of the separator and the circular blade rose slowly higher until it reached the top. Another handyman threw a lever and the bacon-slicer blade began to hum ominously as it started to spin.

The three handymen unlocked the cell, grabbed Mel, Ludo and Wren and dragged them to the separator. The children's screams of horror were muffled by their gags. Mel's hands were untied and fastened roughly into the clamp at the base of the contraption.

'What do we do?' whispered Nelly.

'Sit tight,' said Scratchbeard. 'It's their hands they're going to lose, not their tongues.'

Mel's eyes were wide with terror. Ludo and Wren stared back, ashen-faced and scarcely able to believe what was about to happen.

The four handymen by the door looked on, cruel smiles on the faces of the three short ones.

The blade was released and fell with a cold and sickening *swish*. Before it reached the bottom of its fall, Mel fainted.

A short while later, Ludo's and Wren's hands joined Mel's side by side on the shelves. They were still twitching.

'Come on,' said Spandangle, in a low voice. 'The show's over. Time to leave.'

'That was fun,' said Mel.

'Yeah,' said Ludo. 'Can't we stay and watch them do the rest of the prisoners?'

'No,' said Spandangle. 'Your disguises are beginning to vanish.'

'But what about finding the mirrortree?' said Wren.

'The others won't be going anywhere for a while,'

said Spandangle. 'We'll come back for them later.'

'Look,' hissed Nelly. 'The guards are all leaving.'

'Right,' said Scratchbeard as the door closed behind the handymen. 'Now's our chance.'

'I'll deal with the cell door,' said Doctor Sarcophagus, removing the stopper from one of his lock-melting phials. 'Nelly, help me and Scratchbeard grab the kids. They won't be any trouble the state they're in. Canker, you keep lookout.'

'The fight's gone out of you now, hasn't it, Missy?' said Nelly, as she stepped into the cell and poked Wren viciously in the ribs.

Wren stared back vacantly.

When Canker's dog sank its teeth into Ludo's leg, he did not utter a cry, and Mel was completely passive as he was pushed at knifepoint in front of Scratchbeard and out into the corridor. Those remaining in the cell appeared to be unconscious.

Canker went on ahead and beckoned them forwards with a low whistle when he saw that the coast was clear. 'Bring them out here,' he said, opening a door on to a crescent-shaped terrace at the tip of one of the finger-towers.

'Now, Shrimp, time for some answers.' Scratchbeard squatted on his haunches and loosened Mel's gag.

Nelly did the same for Ludo's and Wren's. 'One squawk out of any of you and it's over the edge you go. Got it?'

'Where's this tree?' said Scratchbeard.

Mel simply stared at the stumps where his hands had been. They had been crudely bound with strips of sacking. He did not seem to be in any pain.

Scratchbeard struck him hard across the face. 'Pay attention! Where's this tree?'

Mel looked up at his attacker. 'Tree?'

'Yeah. Where is it?'

'Tree?' repeated Mel blankly.

'You heard,' said Scratchbeard. 'Now cough up.'

'Tree?'

'You're beginning to get on my nerves,' said Scratchbeard.

'Maybe his wits left him when they chopped his hands off,' said Doctor Sarcophagus. 'It's the shock, I've seen it happen before. I'll try this one.' He knelt beside Ludo. 'So? Where is it, this tree?'

'Tree?' said Ludo.

'We're wasting time,' said Nelly. 'His mind's gone, too. OK, Missy. Where is it?'

Wren looked at her questioner. 'Tree?'

'What's got into them?' said Canker. 'They can't all have lost their wits.'

'It's one of their tricks,' said Scratchbeard. He grabbed Wren and lifted her on to the parapet to dangle over the sickening drop. The wind blew her long, auburn hair around her pale face like a veil. Scratchbeard turned to Mel and Ludo. 'Tell me where the tree is or I'll let her fall.'

Mel looked at Ludo and Ludo looked back. 'Tree?' they both said at once.

'OK. You asked for it,' said Scratchbeard. 'Say goodbye to your friend.'

'No, Scratchbeard, wait!' shouted Nelly. 'Perhaps they have lost their marbles but they're still worth something. No hands and no wits will earn their owner a fortune begging on the streets of Vlam. Together with their pretty faces, it's a money-making combination.'

Scratchbeard hesitated.

'Nelly's got a point,' said Doctor Sarcophagus. 'What if we can't find this tree? We don't want to go back empty-handed, now do we?'

'I suppose not.' Scratchbeard hauled Wren back and set her down on the terrace.

'But the tree's got to be here somewhere,' said Canker. 'Let's keep looking.'

'Maybe their friends back in the cell know where it is,' said Doctor Sarcophagus.

'I doubt it,' said Nelly. 'They looked completely out of it. Too bad one of them didn't get away.'

'But one of them must have,' said Scratchbeard. 'The *invisible* one. If anyone knows where this tree is, it'll be him.'

'Great,' said Canker sarcastically. 'So, any of you got some bright ideas about how we're going to find an invisible man?'

'Maybe we don't have to. Maybe we let him find us,' said Nelly. 'Assuming it's the same scrot that attacked us in the freak market, then he seems very attached to

Missy here.' She shook Wren. 'It strikes me that he'll come looking for her. For the other two as well, probably.'

'So we take her and her friends back to the cell, and wait for him there?' said Doctor Sarcophagus. 'Is that what you're saying, Nelly?'

'That's exactly what I'm saying.'

'Those beggars are more resourceful than I thought,' said Spandangle. 'They must have found another way into the castle.'

The conjuror and the three children, their handymen disguises now completely gone, watched the doorway to the terrace from their hiding place in a shadowy alcove.

'What's that noise?' said Mel.

'Someone's coming,' said Ludo.

Spandangle pushed the children further into the alcove. He made a movement with his hands and the shadows became darker still: as dark as the black masks and costumes they all wore. 'Quiet,' he whispered.

'Who is it?' whispered Wren.

'Hold your breath and hold your tongues,' said Spandangle.

Four figures stole out of the forest surrounding Castle Habilis and crept towards the castle walls. The only sound was the soft squeak of Blinker's visor, which kept falling shut. There was another squeak as a door opened in his breastplate and a spring-loaded grappling hook attached to a long line shot upwards. Flob gave a stout tug on the line and began to haul his massive body upwards, hand over hand. One by one, Spiracle, Blinker and Gusset followed.

The Replificated Portal

In Bumnote's deserted workroom one of the many jumbled heaps of discarded equipment moved and the topmost item tottered and fell to the floor. Slowly, a finger appeared, followed by a hand. The hand shifted some more of the debris and wiggled its way out. It then withdrew back into the pile, leaving a hole. From the dark depths of the cavity an eye surveyed the room. After a moment, the junk was pushed aside and a dusty figure stood up.

'It's OK. They're gone,' said Mel. 'You can all come out now.'

More hands, followed by arms and then figures, emerged from other piles of discarded equipment as Ludo and Wren crawled from their hiding places. They were followed from beneath still more piles of junk by Goldie, Mrs Morel, Mrs Wood-Blewit, Shale and Shingle. The last to emerge from their hides beneath the clutter were Professor Thinkwell and Bumnote.

'Brilliant idea of yours, Mel,' said Ludo.

'Thank goodness for Bumnote's untidiness,' said Wren.

'I must admit that the replifications from Bumnote's prototype were much better than I expected them to be. Their appearances were convincing even if their cognitive abilities left a lot to be desired,' said a beaming Professor Thinkwell, clapping Bumnote on the back.

'Our replicas may have been brainless, but they certainly fooled those guards,' said Mel.

'Be that as it may,' said Professor Thinkwell, 'Mr Habilis will want to interrogate the intruders and *he* won't be fooled by replicas. Not for a moment.'

'That's why Pilfer's followed the handymen to see where our replicas are being taken,' said Goldie. 'He'll come back and warn us if Mr Habilis turns up.'

'So?' said Mrs Morel. 'What are you going to do now?'

'Get out of here and start looking for the mirrortree,' said Mel.

'That will be difficult,' said Bumnote, gazing into the little fishbowl sphere. 'Mr Habilis is on the move.'

'We need to nab ourselves a transmogrificator and

get away from here at once,' said Mel.

'Can we use Bumnote's portal to get to the docks?' asked Ludo.

Bumnote looked uncomfortable. 'It's not working properly. I've, er . . . I've kind of been experimenting with it.'

Professor Thinkwell sighed an exasperated sigh. 'I guessed it was your dabbling that's been making all the portals malfunction so badly. All right, let's have a look and see what a mess you've made of it.' He followed Bumnote as he led everyone to the portal at the back of the workroom. 'What're all these wires for? They look like an explosion in a spaghetti factory.'

'They're connected to the mechanism from one of my prototype replificators,' explained Bumnote.

Professor Thinkwell raised his eyebrows. 'Why?'

Bumnote shrugged. 'Just to see if I could replificate a portal. But the trouble is, it doesn't work.'

'Intriguing. *Most* intriguing.' The professor leant forwards, screwed up his eyes and studied the mad wiring. He shook his head. 'Of *course* it doesn't work. That's because you have a negative cancelling input attached to a positive neutralising output.' He deftly switched two of the wires. 'There! It's only a temporary fix, however. We mustn't linger inside the crinkly corridors. Their stability will be even more impaired than usual until I can rewire it properly.' The professor set the dials.

'Right,' said Mel, 'if it's working, let's see if it really does lead to the transmogrificator docks.'

'You go on ahead,' said Professor Thinkwell. 'Bumnote and I will catch you up after we've prepared a little surprise for any pursuers.'

'Can we help too, Professor?' said Shale.

'Yes,' said Shingle. 'We'd love to lend you a hand, now that we have them to lend.'

'Very well, very well,' said the professor. 'Now, here's what I want you to do.'

As the professor, Bumnote, Shale and Shingle became lost in discussion Mel placed his hand in the hand-lock. The dials spun, the red light changed to green and the door opened. He led the others inside. The corridor seemed stable enough and at the end was another portal that opened to his touch in the hand-lock.

'It's dark,' whispered Wren as she followed the others, stepping carefully so as not to fall over anything.

'And quiet,' whispered Goldie.

Mel withdrew his angel feather from his doublet and its soft light illuminated an organ standing next to the door.

'A morphonium,' said Mrs Morel.

'We *are* in a transmogrificator,' said Mrs Wood-Blewit. 'But which one?'

The friends followed Mel as he crept further into the darkness.

'There!' hissed Wren. 'What's that? I can see the outline of figures.'

'It looks like . . .' Ludo made a gulping sound, '. . . a torture chamber.'

'This is no torture chamber,' said Goldie in a normal tone. 'We're back in my ghost train.' She stepped to one side, threw a switch and green-tinted spotlights came on, revealing the papier-mâché tableau.

'This must be the tenth transmogrificator,' said Mel.

'I bet it's the one Bumnote said he invented,' said Wren. 'Where did you get it?'

'We bought it off someone Pilfer met in Pennyweight Market,' answered Goldie. She sighed. 'It's never worked properly.'

'Then that *proves* it's Bumnote's,' said Ludo.

'Well, this is how we're going to get away,' said Wren.

'But how can it have got to the castle without anyone to tell it where to go?' said Mel.

'Beats me,' said Goldie. 'Let's go back and get the others.'

When they retraced their steps to the door back to Bumnote's workroom Mrs Morel placed her hand in the hand-lock and the door opened.

The others quickly followed her through the door and it slammed shut after them.

'Oh, no,' said Ludo as the green light above the door changed to red.

'Don't worry. We just have to wait for the time-lock to –'

Before Wren could finish speaking, they felt a vibration and the telltale rumble and creak of a mutation from behind it.

'Was that what I think it was?' said Ludo.

'I'm very much afraid it was,' said Mrs Wood-Blewit. 'Professor Thinkwell said the portals would be unstable.'

'We should thank our lucky spores that we weren't inside when it started to mutate,' said Mrs Morel.

'So where do you think *this* is?' said Goldie.

The portal had opened on to a soaring cylindrical space so tall they could not see the top or the bottom. Down the centre ran two very thick and irregular columns and, snaking loosely around them like vines, dozens of meandering fat tubes, the biggest as thick as the fingernail chute they had entered the castle by. Clinging to the circumference of the space was a spiral staircase that wound its way from up above right down into the dingy depths below. There was no handrail on the side towards the void. A strong updraft blew their hair around their faces and flapped at their clothing.

'It's like the inside of an arm,' said Wren, her voice reverberating off the walls.

'Yeah,' said Ludo. 'I bet we're inside one of the castle's forearms.'

Swooping around on the updraft were flocks of large, owl-like birds with scaly feathers. But instead of conventional wings they soared on outstretched hands with very long fingers. Stretched between each finger was a translucent membrane.

Wren turned at the sound of a mutation behind the portal door. A short while later the time-lock released and the portal opened. 'Oh no!'

Squeezing from the portal was a huge handyman. He seemed to be made from a complicated jumble of machinery and furniture.

'Look at the size of him!' said Ludo.

'However did he get into the portal?' said Mrs Wood-Blewit.

'Quick, this way,' said Mel, as he led them down the stairs.

Descending as fast as they dared, they eventually reached the bottom of the staircase.

A corridor lit by flaming torches held in skeletal, hand-shaped sconces disappeared off to the left. Behind them the handyman's heavy footsteps made the staircase tremble as he descended.

'He's coming after us,' said Ludo, looking back up the stairs.

'Come on,' said Wren. 'There's only one way we can go.'

They hurried down the corridor. But before they had gone far they arrived at a dead end.

'Oh, no!' said Ludo.

'Quick! Back the way we came,' said Mel.

But as he turned to retrace his steps a dark shadow filled the corridor. Standing at the end, blocking their retreat, was the enormous form of the handyman. Then he was joined by an identical handyman. The first one began to walk towards them, his footsteps shaking the floor. His shadow preceded him and cast its shade over the six figures like a dark tide rising. They backed away until they were stopped by the blank, stone wall of the dead end and could retreat no further.

Pilfer Tells All

From the deep shadows of the alcove, Spandangle, Mel, Ludo and Wren held their breath as the footsteps passed their hiding place and faded away.

'I didn't see anyone,' said Wren.

'Me neither,' said Ludo.

'That's because there was no one to see,' said Spandangle. 'Whoever it was, is invisible.'

'You mean that someone's already found the tree?' said Mel.

'Of course not,' said Spandangle. 'That story about the Nabob of Pyrexia's tree was made up on the spur of the moment purely for the benefit of those greedy beggars.' He peered around the edge of the alcove. 'Whoever it was seems to have gone into the room with the hand-chopper.'

Spandangle and the children crept from the alcove and went to the door. The conjuror put his finger to his lips and all four peeped in.

* * *

'So this is where they've taken you,' said Pilfer as he stared at the replicas of his friends lying still on the cell floor. 'You may only be copies but you fooled those handymen.' He sniffed. 'Hello, what's that pong?'

'*Gotcha!*' cried Scratchbeard as he homed in on Pilfer's voice and seized him in a bear hug. Doctor Sarcophagus, Nelly Buboes and Canker also grabbed hold of the struggling form and wrestled it to the floor.

'Let go of me, you stinking scrots!' shouted Pilfer. Canker's dog whirled about as Pilfer tried to kick her off.

'You won't get away from us this time.' Doctor Sarcophagus produced a length of rope from his coat pocket and trussed Pilfer tightly.

Panting, the beggars picked themselves up and stared down at the seemingly hollow coil of rope writhing at their feet.

'Copies, you say? So those kids in there aren't real?' said Scratchbeard, kicking Pilfer and nodding towards the replicas in the cell.

'Go and eat your underpants,' said Pilfer defiantly.

'Never mind about them,' said Doctor Sarcophagus. 'Where's the tree?'

'Go and suck on a toadstool,' said Pilfer.

'I've got a potion that will loosen your tongue.'

'I'm sure you have, Doc. But not here,' said Nelly. 'Those guards could come back at any time. Let's take Mr Invisible somewhere where we won't be disturbed.'

As the door closed behind the beggars, the shadows in the corner of the antechamber shimmered like a heat haze and lightened to reveal Spandangle, Mel, Ludo and Wren.

'So the others weren't real,' said Ludo. 'We've been chasing around after copies all this time.'

'I bet *he* did it,' said Wren, pointing at Spandangle. 'He's always changing things. It's another one of his tricks.'

'It's nothing of the kind,' said Spandangle. 'This has me as mystified as you.'

'If they're just copies then they'll never lead us to the mirrortree,' said Ludo.

'That's true,' admitted Spandangle. 'But there's one

thing you don't seem to have grasped.'

'Oh yeah, Mr Know-it-All,' sneered Wren. 'And what's that?'

Spandangle looked at Mel, Ludo and Wren in turn and shook his head sadly. 'Why did I ever agree to take this on?' he said under his breath. Then, out loud, 'For them to be copies then there must be originals. And it's obvious that the invisible man is close to them. Let's see if we can't get our hands on him and persuade him to tell us where they are.'

'If those beggars don't do it first,' said Wren.

'Their solution to everything is violence,' said Spandangle. 'That only ever gets you the answers you want to hear. There are other, more efficient ways to get at the truth.' He waved his cloak in front of him and became invisible.

'Bring him in here,' said Nelly. 'We won't be disturbed in a storeroom in the middle of the night.'

'Set Mr Invisible down,' said Doc as he selected a phial from his waistcoat. He let a few drops of his tracking potion fall on Pilfer. He replaced the phial and selected another. 'Now, which end's his toes?' He yelled in pain as his fingers were bitten.

'Other end,' said Canker unnecessarily.

Suddenly, there was a sharp *rat-tat-tat* on the door and the beggars froze. They flattened themselves against the wall and held their breath. Scratchbeard readied his shiv and pulled open the door.

'There's no one there,' said Nelly.

There was a faint flapping noise and a breeze as if someone were waving a piece of invisible fabric in the air.

'Look!' exclaimed Canker, turning.

The air was full of the kind of sparkling dust stage magicians use. It settled on Pilfer, revealing a short, fat figment with a shock of curly hair and a goatee beard.

'Where'd that come from?' said Nelly.

'From me. I'm out here,' came a voice from the corridor. 'I have the tree.'

The four beggars stepped out into the corridor.

'Catch me if you can,' said the voice. The sound of running feet disappeared down the corridor.

'It's *another* invisible man,' said Scratchbeard. 'Come on, after the scrot!'

'Canker, you stay here and keep an eye on this one,' said Doctor Sarcophagus as he followed Scratchbeard and Nelly in the direction of the footsteps.

'Why's it always *me* who has to stay behind and guard the prisoners?' said Canker. He kicked Pilfer spitefully. 'Who are you, anyway?'

'That's just what I'd like to know,' said Spandangle. He became visible with a wave of his cloak as he entered the room. Canker spun round but, before he could react, Spandangle moved his hands in front of the beggar's face. 'You're feeling very tired. You should take a nap.'

Canker's eyes glazed over and he yawned. 'I'm feeling very tired. I should take a nap.' He was fast asleep before he hit the floor. His dog curled up beside him.

'Come on,' said Spandangle, hauling Pilfer to his feet. 'Those beggars will soon work out that they're chasing their own shadows.'

'Who're you and – *Mel? Ludo? Wren?*' said Pilfer as

the three figures appeared in the doorway. 'What are you doing here?'

'Shut your gob,' spat Mel.

'Yeah,' added Ludo. 'It's none of your skegging business.'

'Wren? What's got into Mel and Ludo?' said Pilfer.

'You heard them, scrot-breath. Shut your gob.'

'*You're the mirrorshades!*' A look of realisation dawned on Pilfer's spangly face.

'So you and the others have found out about the mirrorshades, have you?' Spandangle led Pilfer down the corridor in the opposite direction to the beggars and quickly up several flights of stairs. He found an unoccupied room and urged his prisoner inside. Mel, Ludo and Wren followed them and closed the door.

Mel kicked Pilfer on the shin. 'Take that!' A small cloud of sparking dust rose into the air.

Pilfer winced. He looked at Spandangle. 'If they're mirrorshades, then who are you?'

'I'm the one asking the questions,' said Spandangle.

'I'm not telling you anything unless you tell me who you are and what you're up to.'

'Oh yes you will,' said Spandangle, waving his hands in front of Pilfer's face. 'Let's start with your name and how you came to be invisible. Then you can tell me where Mel, Ludo and Wren are.'

'Thank you, that was most informative,' said Spandangle when Pilfer had finished speaking. The conjuror fell silent, lost in thought.

'OK, now we know where the others are,' said Mel. 'But they still don't know where the mirrortree is.'

'What are we going to do with this one?' said Ludo, kicking Pilfer. He enjoyed it so much he kicked him again.

Spandangle roused himself from his reverie. 'Do? Why, we're going to send him back to his friends.'

'But as soon as he gets back he'll tell the others about us,' said Mel.

'I'll send him back without any recollection of ever seeing us or the beggars,' said Spandangle.

'What's the point of that?' said Wren. 'He said that the others don't even know where the mirrortree is.'

'Weren't you listening?' said Spandangle with just a

hint of annoyance. 'They have access to Cogito. He's bound to know where it is. They've probably asked him already. Now stop complaining and come on.'

'Wake up!' Scratchbeard kicked Canker. 'Wake up, you dozy scrot!'

'Scratchbeard?' said Canker, yawning. 'What's up?' Then, seeing the coil of rope laying next to him on the storeroom floor, '*Where's Mr Invisible?*'

'I was hoping *you* could tell *me*,' said Scratchbeard. 'Seeing as you were the one guarding him.' Another kick.

'We've been had,' said Nelly.

'It won't happen a third time,' said Doctor Sarcophagus bitterly. 'Wake your mutt up, Canker. At least we can rely on her and her nose.'

Hotchpotch

The enormous form of the handyman came to within a few feet of Mel and his friends and stopped. He spoke. 'Don't be afraid. It's me – !!!!!!!!' His voice sounded like a lot of people speaking at once and his name was just a cacophonous noise, somewhere between a very bad cough and a sack of geese falling down the stairs.

'What?' said Ludo.

'I said, it's all right. It's only – !!!!!!!' said the handyman.

'We still can't understand you,' said Wren.

'Let's try something else,' said Goldie. '*What* are you?'

'A successful experiment, that's what,' said the multi-voiced handyman. 'One of Bumnote's. It actually *worked*!'

'Just a minute,' said Mel. 'Look at the patchwork clothing. I can see bits of the professor's robe and bits of Bumnote's shirt.'

'And bits of workshop equipment and furniture,'

said Ludo. 'They're all jumbled up.'

'And his face seems to be a mixture of all of theirs,' said Mrs Wood-Blewit.

'You mean that Professor Thinkwell, Bumnote, Shingle and Shale are all inside you?' said Ludo.

'And your voice is you all talking at once?' added Mrs Morel.

'That's right,' said the handyman. 'I'm a *uni*plication! It was just a question of reversing the wiring on Bumnote's prototype replificator. Now we're all folded up inside here.'

'Then who's *he*?' asked Mel, pointing to the other huge handyman.

'He's a replification – of me, that is,' said the uniplication.

'Did you bring the fishbowl sphere?' said Mel. 'Can you see where Mr Habilis is?'

'I have it right here.' The sphere now seemed no larger than a cherry cradled in the uniplication's huge hand. He stared into it for a while. 'I can't see Mr Habilis but I can see a strange sparkly figment in the Great Hall who doesn't look like he belongs here – he still has his hands.'

'How do we get there, er . . .' Ludo hesitated.

'Why not call me Hotchpotch? As for getting to the Great Hall, it's best if we go that way.' Hotchpotch pointed to the blank, dead-end wall. 'The Great Hall's just on the far side.'

'That's solid stone,' said Mrs Morel. 'Has all that *plication* business addled your brain or something?'

'Not in the least,' said Hotchpotch. 'But it's certainly multiplied my strength. Stand aside, please.'

Mel and his friends flattened themselves against the sides of the corridor as Hotchpotch and his replification lumbered forwards. Hotchpotch swung his giant fist and the wall cracked. As the other one laid into it the wall shattered and crumbled to a pile of rubble at their feet. When the dust had settled the friends clambered through the gaping hole.

The huge fishbowl sphere at the far end of the Great Hall swirled with rainbow colours. Standing in the centre of the hall was a lone figure trying to brush spangly dust from himself.

'*It's Pilfer*,' gasped Goldie.

'What's happened to you?' said Mel as he ran up to Pilfer.

Pilfer looked up at the new arrivals. 'I . . . I don't know.'

'Did you find out what the handymen did with our copies that they captured?' said Goldie, as she helped her friend with the dusting. He quickly became invisible once more.

'I don't think so,' said Pilfer. 'The trouble is, I don't really remember anything about it. Who're these monsters?'

'His name's Hotchpotch. It's the professor and Bumnote and Shingle and Shale,' said Mel. 'The other one's his replification.'

At that moment a bell began tolling.

'It's the alarm bell,' said Mrs Wood-Blewit.

'Look!' cried Ludo. 'In the giant sphere!'

'*Mr Habilis*,' said Hotchpotch. 'Run for your lives!'

The huge mechanical eye appeared in the sphere and surveyed the assembly. It blinked once and said in its booming voice, 'Hear the voice of Habilis!' The reverberations caused small trickles of dust to fall from the ceiling. 'Seal the doors!' At his command the door to the Great Hall slammed shut. More dust fell from the ceiling, together with snowflakes of plaster.

'Let's get out of here,' said Mel, turning towards the hole they had entered by.

'Not that way,' said Mrs Morel. 'We need to get to the castle's main door.'

'Silence!' roared Mr Habilis. Bigger pieces of plaster and some heavier morsels of stone rained down. 'Stay where you are.'

'I'll put a stop to this,' said Hotchpotch. He led his replification to the far end of the hall and, together, they grabbed the giant sphere.

'How dare you touch the eye of Habilis!' screamed the voice. 'The penalty is death!' Cracks began to appear in the walls of the Great Hall.

'Lift,' ordered Hotchpotch and they lifted the sphere off its hands-shaped plinth.

'No!' screamed the voice.

'And now the door!' said Hotchpotch.

They hurled the sphere along the ground like a giant bowling ball. It slammed into the door with a resounding crash. It, and the door, shattered into a thousand pieces, releasing clouds of coloured gas into the hall. Large flakes of plaster dislodged from the walls like scabs. Mel and his friends ran towards the exit. But, as the clouds of gas cleared, they saw that in the corridor beyond the doorway stood ranks of handymen blocking the way out. The leading rank cracked their electric whips, making searing trails of blue-white sparks like loops of lightning. With a cry of, 'Seize the intruders!' they advanced into the Great Hall.

'Come on, Replification,' said Hotchpotch. 'This is what we were made for.' The two giants began to lumber forwards. But before they had taken more than a few steps, holes appeared between the vaulting in the ceiling and long ropes fell to the floor. Then, one by one, handymen burst through the holes and began to abseil down the ropes. More holes appeared in the walls and yet more handymen crawled through. 'Back the way we came. It's the only way out. We'll hold the handymen off for as long as we can,' Hotchpotch shouted to the friends.

'Quick, follow –' But Mel never finished his sentence.

At the rear of the advancing handymen he saw himself wearing black clothing and a mask and staring back at him. He saw Wren and Ludo too, dressed the same way, with a tall man also wearing a black cape and mask. The tall man waved his cape and the shadows around the quartet grew darker and they seemed to melt into them. Then they were gone.

Mel looked at Wren and Ludo. They had seen them too.

'They must be our mirrorshades,' cried Ludo.

'What're they doing here?' said Wren.

'No time for that now,' said Mel. 'Come on.'

They made it to the hole in the wall.

'Where's Hotchpotch?' said Goldie.

'Rather in the thick of it, I'm afraid,' said Mrs Wood-Blewit.

Despite their valiant efforts, Hotchpotch and his replification were falling back before the onslaught of the whip-wielding handymen. The two giants became wreathed in strands of white fire that writhed over their massive frames like neon snakes. Hotchpotch retreated, beating at the flames with his massive hands. His replification stood his ground, using his flaming clothing as a weapon of his own as he flailed at the handymen. Slowly, the handymen began to back away from the fire-giant.

Hotchpotch, his flames extinguished, lumbered towards Mel and his group. 'We won't be able to hold them for much longer. There're just too many.' Even Hotchpotch's four-fold voice sounded faint against the din of battle.

There came a resounding crash that made the castle tremble.

'Oh, no!' cried Mrs Morel.

'I'm afraid that your replification has had it, Hotchpotch,' said Pilfer.

The giant replification lay on the ground and handymen swarmed over it.

'We could do with a helping hand from somewhere,' said Ludo.

'That's it!' said Wren.

'What's it?' said Ludo, confused.

'*Hands*,' said Mel. 'Which way's the library, Hotchpotch?'

'Directly below us,' said Hotchpotch. 'Allow me.' He slammed his great fist into the flagstones several times until a hole appeared.

'Of *course*.' Ludo grabbed one of the ropes trailing from the ceiling and pulled hard until it came away. 'Hotchpotch, you hold this end while we climb down.'

'But how will we get back?' said Goldie.

'Here, take this.' Hotchpotch put his great hand inside his patchwork garment and pulled out something small.

'It's the professor's hand,' said Mel.

'It will guide you back here.'

Mel, Ludo, Wren, Goldie, Mrs Morel and Mrs Wood-Blewit slid down the rope into the library. They each found a large sack and began to fill them with pairs of hands from the shelves.

'Is Pilfer here?' asked Wren.

'He's gone for reinforcements,' said Goldie.

'Reinforcements?' said Wren. 'Where from?'

Goldie shrugged. 'Search me.'

Through the hole in the ceiling far above they could hear Hotchpotch battling the handymen.

'Right,' said Ludo as he stuffed his sack with a final pair of hands. 'Between us we should have enough hands to help Hotchpotch. Mel, ask the prof's hand how we get back to the hall.'

Mel set the hand down on the floor. 'OK, professor, which is the way back?'

The eyed ring blinked and looked hard at the friends before the lipped ring said, 'Mr Habilis is behind you. *Run for your lives!*'

Mr Habilis

Mel and his friends spun round to see a strange figment standing behind them.

'Hear the voice of Habilis!' boomed Mr Habilis in a deep and sinister tone. He was as tall as a man and wore a silver mask engraved with fingerprint curlicues tied around his shaven head. The mask had articulated lips, cheeks and jutting eyebrows from beneath which glared malevolent, mechanical eyes. As if this was not weird enough, Mr Habilis had eight arms and was dressed in a clockwork coat with metal gears and pulleys all over it. Perched on his left shoulder was one of the strange owl-like birds they had seen earlier.

'Hector, stop that tiresome "Voice of Habilis" business at once,' said Mrs Morel.

'We brought your precious transmogrificator back as you asked. The least you can do is be civil,' said Mrs Wood-Blewit.

Mel was impressed that Mrs Morel and Mrs Wood-Blewit were standing up to the terrifying figment but he could tell they were as afraid as he was.

'Silence!' bellowed Mr Habilis. He snarled and bared his clockwork teeth, making everyone jump.

'Don't do that, Hector,' said Mrs Morel bravely. 'It's bad manners to snarl.'

'If you always behave like that, what will you do when you *really* want to express your displeasure?' said Mrs Wood-Blewit.

'I'll *separate* them, that's what. Which is exactly what I do to thieves.' Mr Habilis reached out one of his arms and grabbed Mel by the wrist. He turned Mel's hand over and stared at the palm. 'Fascinating.' Another two of his arms grabbed Wren and Ludo in the same way and drew them to him. 'This is my lucky day. I've found three sets of palms that I will enjoy reading at my leisure. I'm going to separate you – all of you.' Yet another of his arms pulled a pair of giant secateurs from inside his clockwork coat.

'What are you doing?' cried Wren as her hand was forced into the jaws of the secateurs.

'Hector! Stop that this instant!' cried Mrs Morel as she tried to pull Wren free.

'Do as you're told,' said Mrs Wood-Blewit, joining her.

Mr Habilis merely laughed. It was a horrible sound. He batted away his aunts with a sweep of a couple of his arms.

Mel and Ludo struggled but the mechanics of Mr Habilis's coat multiplied his strength and they were held fast. Goldie leapt at Mr Habilis but yet another of his arms shot up and hurled her away.

'No!' screamed Wren. She felt the blades tighten against her wrist.

'Let her go!' shouted Mel.

Suddenly, Mr Habilis froze. 'What are you doing?' His arms went limp, releasing the children. 'Is that you, Thinkwell?'

Perched on Mr Habilis's right shoulder was Professor Thinkwell's hand. 'You didn't think I invented this coat for you without installing an emergency switch, did you?'

'And *you* didn't think that I wouldn't have planned for something like that, did you, Thinkwell?' The hand-bird on Mr Habilis's other shoulder let out a raucous screech and flew at the professor's hand, knocking it to the floor. It then began pecking at the emergency switch.

'That's my boy,' said Mr Habilis.

'Come on!' shouted Professor Thinkwell's hand. 'Quickly!'

By the time they got back to the Great Hall Hotchpotch was on his knees, engulfed in electric flames.

The friends broke open their sacks, releasing the hands, and rushed after them as they scampered to Hotchpotch's aid. Mel, Ludo, Wren, Goldie, Mrs Morel and Mrs Wood-Blewit each picked up an electric whip and began to lash out at the handymen. The hands seemed to gain the upper hand and the attackers fell back.

Hotchpotch rose from his knees and beat out the flames. 'Am I glad to see you,' he said.

Then came a raucous, chilling sound and into the hall flew a host of hand-birds. They were like a dark cloud and the whirring, flapping sound of their wing beats filled the air. Behind them was Mr

Habilis. At his bellowed command, they flew at the friends, pecking with their beaks, scratching with their talons and slapping and punching with their hand-shaped wings.

'This is hopeless,' yelled Goldie. 'There're just too many of them.'

Ludo took off his doublet and used it as a swat to beat at the diving birds with one hand while still wielding the humming electric whip with the other.

Mel tucked his quill and Cogito into his shirt and removed his own doublet. Wren copied him, but soon their doublets were in shreds, victims of the swooping birds' sharp talons. The three children in their white shirts and hose cowered before the onslaught.

'Look at Hotchpotch!' cried Wren.

The giant was covered in the strange hand-birds like a rash. They pecked, clawed and punched viciously at any exposed part of his massive form until he lost his balance and crashed to the floor, shattering into pieces. Professor Thinkwell, Bumnote, Shale and Shingle painfully picked themselves up from the workshop debris and retreated towards their friends.

Sensing victory, the handymen advanced towards them.

Then a new sound joined the mêlée. Screeching loudly and attacking the handymen from the rear was a horde of monkeys.

'It looks like the entire population of Monkey-Vlam,' said Wren.

'They're every bit as ugly and nasty as I remember them!' cried Goldie.

'And they're all drunk,' said Ludo.

'Better than that,' said Mel. 'They're fighting mad.'

'There you go,' panted Pilfer, out of breath. 'I thought you could do with some reinforcements.'

'You went back to Monkey-Vlam?' said Ludo.

'Brilliant!' shouted Mel. 'Thanks, Pilfer.'

'Come on, Mrs Morel,' said Mrs Wood-Blewit.

'We're right behind you,' said Goldie.

'Count me in,' said Pilfer.

'Come on –' Mel's voice was cut off in a strangulated cry as Mr Habilis appeared as if from nowhere and seized him around the throat with one of his hands. He grabbed Wren and Ludo too, and, before the others could react, hauled them towards the edge of the hall. He used another one of his hands to press a concealed catch. A secret door swung open and he dragged the three struggling friends into a large room. He locked the door after them. Their friends could be heard hammering on the door from the far side.

'Now I'll teach you to steal my hands and confront me in my own castle,' cried Mr Habilis. He reached into the pocket of his clockwork coat and withdrew the large pair of secateurs once more.

The children struggled but it was like trying to fight an octopus. Mr Habilis pinned them to the floor by their throats, squeezing ever tighter.

Mel fought for breath but none would come. Great black blotches began to blossom before his eyes and the sounds of his struggling friends faded until they seemed a long way away. The world started to spin and turn grey and he knew that he would soon lose consciousness. He could see Mr Habilis raise the secateurs and felt him position his hand between the cruel, curved blades. He felt the razor-sharp edges touch his bare wrist.

And then Mr Habilis stopped.

Mel, his eyes nearly popping from his head, cast a desperate glance about expecting to see Professor Thinkwell's hand once again. Instead, he saw a beggar in a turban replacing the stopper of one of his phials.

'That goo should clog up his works nicely,' said Doctor Sarcophagus.

'I think we'll take over from here,' said Scratchbeard. He prised Mr Habilis's hand from Mel's throat and hauled him, gasping for air, to his feet.

Doctor Sarcophagus grabbed Ludo and Nelly Buboes seized Wren. They were too breathless to put up a struggle.

'What about this one?' said Canker, kicking Mr Habilis.

'Bring him along,' said Scratchbeard.

'Let's get out of here,' said Nelly.

'Once we get back to Vlam we'll take these scrot-stain kids somewhere where we won't be disturbed,' said Scratchbeard. 'Then they'll tell us where this tree of theirs is.'

Mel looked at his friends. Any relief they felt at being rescued from Mr Habilis's separating vanished as they were bundled along by the beggars.

'OK, Octopus-Man, lead the way back to the docks,' said Doctor Sarcophagus. 'And keep your hands where I can see them – *all* of them! Any trouble and you'll never get this un-clogging potion.' He taunted Mr Habilis by waving a small phial under his nose.

Clutching Mel, Ludo and Wren, the beggars followed Mr Habilis along deserted corridors and down staircases. They came at last to the castle gates. From there they made their way to one of the transmogrificator docks and climbed to the top.

'This isn't the one we came out of,' said Nelly as she followed the others out on to the dock. 'It's that ghost train. The one from the freak market.' Puzzled, she followed the others inside.

'How're we going to get back to Vlam from here?' said Canker, eyeing a papier-mâché zombie suspiciously. He prodded it to reassure himself it was only a model.

'This is a *transmogrificator*,' snarled Mr Habilis. 'With the morphonium I can change it into something that will take you anywhere you want. But you must give me back the use of my arms.'

'You can have two of them for now,' said Doctor Sarcophagus as he poured his un-clogging potion on Mr Habilis's topmost set of arms. 'You'll get the rest back when we're somewhere safe.'

Mr Habilis lifted the seat of the organ stool. 'There should be more music here.' He picked up the sheets and leafed through them. 'There seems to be only one piece. And the ink's still wet.'

'So what?' said Doc.

'Without a title, I can't tell what the transmogrificator will mutate into,' said Mr Habilis. 'Still, beggars can't be choosers.' He sneered at his captors.

'Just get on with it,' said Nelly.

'Very well.' Mr Habilis sat at the morphonium and raised the lid. He propped up the music in front of him and flexed his fingers. As he started to play the ghost train began to tremble.

But that's all it did.

By the time the final notes of the cadenza faded away, it seemed that nothing had changed.

'What's your game?' snarled Nelly. 'You said the ghost train was going to change into something that would get us out of here.'

'I don't know what's happened,' said Mr Habilis. He scratched his head. 'Usually a piece on the morphonium is accompanied by dramatic changes. I can only imagine that –'

At that point a train with four cars rattled to a stop on the rails in front of the morphonium.

'Well, something's happened,' said Scratchbeard. 'The last time we were here nothing was working.'

'Do you think these cars will take us out of here?' said Doc.

'Well, will they?' said Nelly, thrusting her face at Mr Habilis.

'Where's your companion?' said Mr Habilis.

'Canker?' said Scratchbeard. 'He was here a minute ago.'

There was a horrible cry from behind the beggars. As one they turned. Canker was gripped around the throat by the papier-mâché zombie. He was desperately trying to say something.

'Quit fooling around,' said Nelly. 'We've no time for fun and games.'

Canker was going blue in the face. He pointed at the zombie and said in a strangulated voice, 'Ease eel!'

His dog fastened her teeth into the zombie's leg.

'Stop playing the fool and get that dog of yours under control,' said Doc.

'Ease eel!'

'We'll not tell you again,' said Scratchbeard. 'Now get your smelly carcass over here or we'll leave without you.'

Canker's dog leapt up and seized one of the zombie's hands in her jaws. The hand came away, freeing her master. Canker drew in a great gulp of air and croaked, '*He's real!*'

'Look behind you,' said Mr Habilis.

From out of the darkness staggered a number of horrible figures: zombies hung with rotting flesh, vampires with red eyes and glinting white teeth, foul ghouls with upside-down faces, and a pair of skeletons. They all had outstretched arms and were marching relentlessly towards the beggars and their prisoners.

'Something *has* changed,' said Mel. 'All of the dummies have come alive.'

Ludo and Wren gazed around them, their eyes open wide with fear.

'Quick!' shouted Scratchbeard. 'Everyone on board the train!'

The beggars shoved the children into the cars. Canker bundled Mr Habilis into the fourth. His dog jumped in after them. No sooner were they seated than the cars set off with a lurch.

'OK,' called Doctor Sarcophagus. 'As soon as we're out of the front doors we jump off and make a run for it.'

The train rattled off, passing now-empty alcoves. Mel's eye was caught by movement in the darkness behind them. It was too gloomy to see what it was but he was sure he could hear the rumble of another train over the racket their own was making.

'Here come the doors now,' said Scratchbeard. 'Get ready.'

But as the cars approached the doors there was a jarring noise and they switched tracks. With a lurch they sped off in a new direction.

'What's happening?' cried Doctor Sarcophagus, gripping Ludo in the second car.

'We're heading straight for that wall!' cried Nelly, throwing her arm up to shield her face.

The train struck the wall. But, rather than coming to a shuddering halt, it burst through amidst a blizzard of plywood splinters.

Mel looked up. They were now speeding along a track inside a colossal interior space. He blinked rapidly as his mind struggled to make sense of what his eyes saw. There were walls, floors, columns, arches, ceiling vaulting, domes – but none of them seemed to be in the right place or with any order about them. Ceilings occupied spaces normally reserved for walls or floors and countless arches threaded their ways through each other. It was as if they were speeding through a giant, three-dimensional maze, with yet more crazy spaces beyond in a seemingly infinite progression. As they hurtled on, they passed tall waterfalls driving giant waterwheels. Threading their way like swooping vines through this honeycombed architectural jungle were more tracks glinting in the half-light.

'We're going to die!' cried Nelly.

Mel's eyes widened. 'Look behind!'

As they turned they saw a second train of four cars hurtling along the tracks in their wake. It was packed with the zombies, vampires and other fiends that had chased them from the ghost train.

'And over there!' shouted Wren, pointing off to their left. More trains filled with ghastly monsters were running on tracks parallel to their own.

'And there!' called Ludo. Speeding towards them on tracks running at right angles to their own were yet more nightmare creatures.

'Let me off,' screamed Canker.

At that moment they all pitched forwards as the cars hurtled down an incline steeper than any rollercoaster.

'*Aaaaahhhhhhhhh!*'

At the bottom of the plunge, they levelled off and swung violently to the right.

One of the pursuing trains shot overhead and, as it did so, a vampire – his cloak streaming after him like bat's wings – leapt from it and landed in the rearmost car. He opened his mouth wide, displaying sickle-shaped teeth, and lunged at Canker.

Wide-eyed with terror, Canker thrust his dog at the bloodsucker. 'Here, take the mutt!' The vampire overbalanced backwards and, still clutching the dog, plummeted into the void. But the dog's leash snagged on Canker's wrist and pulled him after them. Their howls and the vampire's hideous scream mingled into a single piteous cry that faded and died as they disappeared into the depths below.

Another set of cars on parallel rails drew level with theirs and a zombie hurled itself into the front car. A second zombie landed right behind. Arms of shredded flesh reached claw-like hands towards the occupants. Scratchbeard was flung into the bottom of the car as the zombie grabbed Mel. Its hands sought his throat.

'Help!' cried Wren as she tried to stop the second zombie. It had hold of Doctor Sarcophagus with one hand and Ludo with the other.

Another car streaked by and a masked torturer

jumped from it to land in the third car. He seized Wren. She looked at Mr Habilis. 'Do something!' she screamed.

With an evil grin Mr Habilis reached forwards and withdrew the antidote potion from Doctor Sarcophagus's coat. He poured the contents on to his frozen arms. 'Hear the voice of Habilis!' he bellowed. With a swipe of one of his arms he knocked the torturer out of the car. 'How dare you attack me in my own transmogrificator!' With four arms he grabbed the rearmost zombie and flung him from the car. Then he clambered forwards and dispatched the second zombie in the same way. He watched the figures, their mouths wide in horror, disappear into the depths before he turned his baleful gaze on Mel, Ludo, Wren and the beggars.

At that moment another train of fiend-laden cars swooped down at an angle. 'How dare you!' Mr Habilis leapt into the train and began to throw the devilish passengers out. It sped away to the left, trailing bodies and screams as it went. The cry of 'How dare you! How *dare* you!' faded until it was lost in the rumbling of the friends' train on the rails and the rush of air in their ears.

Mel, Ludo and Wren gazed out at the mayhem, desperately searching for a way out and clinging on tenaciously. Their cars sped on, rising and falling and swerving to left and right until they suddenly came to a jarring halt and flipped over on to their sides, spilling the occupants out.

For a moment everything was silent save for the rumble of other cars on the rails somewhere out of sight.

They had ended up in a depression with steep sides that sloped upwards. It was a moment before Mel could work out that they had landed in a huge cup formed from an upside-down dome. The mad-angled architecture was like a giant, confused labyrinth above their heads. Before Mel, Ludo and Wren could get to their feet they were grabbed by the beggars.

'Oh no you don't,' said Scratchbeard.

'It's nice and quiet here. You're not going anywhere until you tell us where the miracle tree is,' said Doctor Sarcophagus.

'Right, Missy,' said Nelly. 'Start talking.'

A large shadow fell over the group.

Startled, everyone looked up.

'Oh, no,' cried Doctor Sarcophagus. 'More monsters! We're all going to die!'

The Mirrorshades

Looking down on them from the lip of the inverted dome stood Spiracle, Blinker, Gusset and Flob. The tattoos on Gusset's body were jumping up and down excitedly as they pointed down at the group below.

'We've caught up with you at last,' said Spiracle. He made a tick in his ledger with his peacock feather quill. As he did so, a blank sheet of music paper fell to the ground.

'*You* wrote the zombie music that brought us here,' said Mel.

Spiracle bent and picked the sheet up. 'Just one of our talents.'

'And part of the plan,' wheezed Gusset.

'You've led us a merry dance all the way from Deep Trouble,' said Blinker. He opened one of the many doors in his armour and lowered a rope ladder on a spool down into the depression. 'Be my guests – but one at a time. Just the children, and no sudden moves. Sudden moves make Flob very nervous. Believe me, you don't want to make Flob nervous.'

Flob growled and several fierce-looking creatures peered out from his ginger pelt.

'You scrots *know* these . . . these . . . whatever they are?' said Doctor Sarcophagus.

'Unfortunately, we do,' said Ludo. 'They're bounty hunters.' He shrugged and began to scale the ladder.

'What if we don't want to play your game?' said Scratchbeard. He grabbed Mel and drew his shiv.

Blinker shook his squeaky, armoured head. 'Bad move, Old Boy. *Very* bad move.' He formed his gauntleted hand into a fist which concertinaed from the end of his arm at lightning speed, fetching Scratchbeard a mighty blow to the jaw and knocking him head over heels backwards.

'Just a minute,' said Nelly. 'Can't we do a deal? Let us have the kids for a while. We'll give them back as soon as we've had a little word with them. We guarantee they'll be no trouble afterwards.'

'I think not,' said Spiracle. 'These runaways are the property of Deep Trouble until their trial. And for a long, long time after that would be my guess.'

Wren climbed from the bowl and her arm was firmly grasped by one of Flob's enormous, hairy hands.

'What are you going to do with *us*?' said Doctor Sarcophagus.

'It's none of our concern, Old Boy,' said Blinker, as his fist wound its way back on to his wrist. 'We're here merely for the fugitives.'

'But you can't just leave us here,' said Scratchbeard, getting to his feet and rubbing his jaw. 'We don't even know where we are.'

'And there are lots of hostile . . . *things* in here,' said Nelly.

'You're not part of our contract,' said Spiracle. 'Sorry.'

'So what did these little scrot-stains do that put a price on their heads?' said Scratchbeard.

Mel started to climb the ladder. 'We left our jobs early.'

Nelly snorted derisively. 'And you went on the run just for *that*?'

'A most serious crime,' came a voice. 'A delinquency of the gravest, nay, the *utmost* gravity.'

A train of four cars clanked to a halt behind the bounty hunters and out stepped the barrister Mithras Periwinkle in his black robes and legal wig. Trotting along behind him came Shrug, his ancient, baby-faced articled clerk, weighed down with a pile of casebooks.

'How did you know we were here?' said Wren.

'It's my job to know the whereabouts of my clients,' said Mithras Periwinkle. 'And to ensure their rights are protected.'

'These fugitives are being returned to Deep Trouble right away,' said Spiracle.

'Perhaps I may be permitted a short consultation with my clients?' said the barrister.

Spiracle nodded. 'Very well.'

Mithras Periwinkle beckoned Mel, Ludo and Wren over. In a low voice he said, 'Have you yet acquired that of which we spoke?'

Shrug sniffed. 'He means, have you found the mirrortree?'

Mel's shoulders slumped. 'No. I don't think it exists.'

'Doesn't exist?' said Mithras Periwinkle, his bushy eyebrows shooting up. 'Explain yourself.'

Mel told him what Cogito had written.

Mithras Periwinkle stroked his chin, deep in thought. 'This will never do.' He thought some more. 'You will need to come up with *something* to satisfy the court. I'll seek an adjournment while *you* seek a solution.'

'But . . .'

Ignoring Mel, Mithras Periwinkle turned to the bounty hunters. 'It seems an important new development has occurred that casts this affair in an altogether different light. I request a delay in the expedition of these individuals to their place of confinement.'

Spiracle shook his head. 'Out of the quest–'

'I can cite precedent,' interrupted Mithras Periwinkle. He snapped his fingers. 'Shrug? If you'd be so kind.'

Shrug stumbled forwards and the barrister took the topmost casebook from his clerk's pile and opened it. 'In the case of *Mirrorscape versus Orifice Slugg*, accused of wanton nefariousness, a postponement of seven days prior to immurement was granted to enable the accused to furnish the court with indisputable evidence of his non-culpability. My clients are entitled to no less.'

Shrug set the rest of the books down, took out a large handkerchief and blew his nose noisily. 'He means, give us a mo to sort this mess out.'

Spiracle, Blinker and Gusset went into a huddle, leaving Flob to glower menacingly at everyone else. After a while Spiracle looked up. 'Very well.' He produced a sandglass and upended it to set the sand running.

'But I must protest,' said Mithras Periwinkle. 'Protest in the most vigorous terms possible. That is not nearly enough time.'

'Protest all you like, Old Boy,' said Blinker. 'It's all the time you're going to get.'

'What are we going to do, Mel?' asked Wren.

'We're done for,' said Ludo.

'No we're not,' said Mel. 'There's only one way I know to get something that doesn't exist. You create it yourself!'

'But you can't make a tree,' said Ludo. 'Only trees can make trees.'

'In the real world,' said Mel. 'But we're not in the real world.'

'We're in the Mirrorscape,' said Wren.

'The Mirrorscape's made up from artists' imaginations,' said Mel. 'Everything we can see around us – the castle, the ghost train, all the transmogrificators, *everything* – they're all made up. So why not a tree?'

'But we'd need paints and brushes and a studio, just like the master,' said Ludo. 'And it'd take ages to paint a tree – trunk, boughs, branches, leaves.' Ludo glanced at the rapidly emptying sandglass. 'Even if you knew what this mirrortree looked like – which you don't.'

'Tick, tock,' wheezed Gusset, tapping the sandglass. It was about three-quarters full and emptying rapidly. 'Tick, tock.'

'But it's only the fruit we need,' said Wren. 'Is that what you're saying? Just paint the fruit?'

'No,' said Mel. 'I reckon that to get the fruit you'll need the whole mirrortree.'

Ludo looked again at the sandglass. It was more than half empty. 'Then we're skegged.'

Wren saw the twinkle in Mel's eye. 'What is it?'

'Just think,' said Mel. 'Trees don't always look like trees.'

'Really?' said Ludo. 'So what else do they look like? Birthday cakes?'

'Watch,' said Mel. He retrieved the much battered roll of parchment from inside his shirt and smoothed it out on the ground. He then took out his angel feather quill. 'Has anyone got some ink?'

Spiracle offered the small flask he had been using.

'First we'll need a mirrormark, to make it appear in the Mirrorscape.' He drew the strange, knot-like design on to Cogito with his quill.

'*Mel*,' urged Ludo, with a worried glance at the sandglass. 'It's nearly run out.'

'This won't take long.' Mel dipped his quill once more. He closed his eyes and let his mind drift into that strange yet familiar place he knew so well. The place where he felt truly at home and at peace with himself. The place where his ideas bubbled to the surface of his mind from somewhere far, far below. Mel's breathing slowed and the sounds all around him faded away. He opened his eyes. Slowly and carefully, he put his quill to the parchment and made a dot, no bigger than a full stop.

'Is that *it* ?' said Ludo.

'That's it,' said Mel.

Ludo put his head in his hands. 'We're skegged. We're well and truly *skegged*.' He looked up at Wren. 'What are you smiling about?'

'Don't you see?' she said.

'All I can see is a long stay for us in Deep Trouble,' said Ludo.

'Can't you see the tree?' said Wren, pointing at the parchment.

'All I can see is a dot,' said Ludo. 'A dot no bigger than . . .' Slowly, a smile spread across his face as well. 'No bigger than a *seed*!'

'All trees start out as seeds,' said Mel. 'The whole tree is locked up inside, waiting until it's time to grow. I just tried to put everything into that one seed.'

'So where is it?' said Wren, turning to scan the floor in all directions. 'It should have appeared.'

'It hasn't worked,' said Ludo, his smile vanishing.

At that moment everyone was startled as another train ran into the back of Mithras Periwinkle's train with a crash. Out jumped Mrs Morel and Mrs Wood-

Blewit, Professor Thinkwell and Bumnote, Goldie and Pilfer.

'You escaped!' said Wren.

'Thanks to the monkeys,' said Pilfer.

'The professor and Bumnote used their little fishbowl sphere to lead us here,' said Mrs Morel.

'Time's up,' said Spiracle, holding up the empty sandglass.

'Deep Trouble awaits,' said Blinker. 'Come quietly now.'

'Wait!' exclaimed Bumnote as he gazed into the sphere. 'You must look at this.' As he rushed forwards he caught his toe in a crack and pitched head over heels. The sphere went flying into the air and shattered on the floor. It was full of clear liquid, which seeped into the fissure.

'Stupid boy!' said Professor Thinkwell, helping his dazed assistant to his feet. 'Hello, that crack's getting bigger. And it's starting to glow. Stand back.'

The light from the crack grew brighter and then brighter still, illuminating everyone's face from below and causing them to shield their eyes. Giant black shadows were cast around the eccentric space.

'It's *lava*!' cried Mrs Morel as a glowing substance began to ooze from the crack.

'Oh, no!' wailed Nelly from the bottom of the dome. 'They've disturbed a sleeping volcano. We're going to fry. Get us out of here!' The beggars tried to climb out of the steep-sided hollow but kept slipping back.

'No, wait,' said Mel. 'I've never heard of lava that could do *that*.'

As they watched, the fierce light writhed and formed a tendril that started to grow. At first it looked like molten glass standing on end. It got taller and began to expand. Soon it was as tall as a man but still it grew. And as it grew it rippled with rainbow fire, creating colours like super-vivid mother-of-pearl. Branches sprouted and leaves appeared, each one more colourful and beautiful than the last. The branches grew into fat boughs that soared upwards, swelling as they filled the great space of the building. It was like watching an enormous firework explode in slow motion. More branches sprouted from these boughs and threaded their way into every nook and cranny until, enormous as it was, every part of the crazy, dizzying space seemed to be filled with the swaying rainbow fire of the mirrortree. Then, in the topmost branches, a huge, incandescent fruit appeared. It pulsated in and out with light as if it were a breathing, living thing.

'It's beautiful,' said Professor Thinkwell. He reached his hand forwards and yelped with pain as he touched the trunk.

'It *is* made from lava,' said Mrs Wood-Blewit.

'No, it's not.' Mel reached out his hand and caressed the trunk. It felt as cool as a spring breeze and tingled delightfully beneath his fingertips. He could hear sweet music like the most delicate wind chimes. It was as if the mirrortree were singing to him.

Wren stared upwards at the wondrous tree. She pointed. 'Mel, the fruit.'

'We'll help you get it,' said Ludo.

But as Wren and Ludo approached the mirrortree, they met an invisible wall of force that gently repelled them as if they were similar poles of a magnet. However hard they pushed they could get no closer.

'It's for you, Mel,' said Mrs Morel. 'For you alone.'

'Not entirely,' said Mithras Periwinkle. He waved his black legal robe in front of him like a great wing. When he lowered it, standing in his place was Spandangle. 'Before you ask, it's all part of the conjuror's art.'

Then, from their hiding place inside the train, rose the mirrorshades of Mel, Ludo and Wren.

'*That's* what I wanted to warn you about,' said Bumnote as he came to his senses.

The real Mel, Ludo and Wren stood staring at the new arrivals. It was like looking in a mirror – but a mirror that reflected back not only the physical image but the inner one, too.

Mirror-Mel stepped forwards, removed his mask and confronted Mel. 'I'm going to destroy this tree. Once it's gone, you will be too, and I'll be free of you forever. Free to go about my own business.'

Mel stared and stared. In his adventures in the Mirrorscape he had experienced some very, very strange things but nothing could have prepared him for this. As he stared he became uncomfortable, as if he had an itch he could not scratch. He was looking at himself, of that there could be no doubt. But alongside the fascination and the wonder there was something else. He felt uneasy. As he looked deeper he saw – and recognised – everything unpleasant about himself that he had always tried to keep hidden, even from Wren and Ludo. Then he looked yet deeper and saw something worse. Something feral and ruthless. Something that would be at home with the worst nightmare imaginings of the Mirrorscape. Could this be a part of him, too? He did not like what he was seeing. It scared him. He tried to look away but could not. His mirrorshade gripped his attention as securely as the finest painting of his master. He tried to speak, to break the spell, but his mouth hung open and no words would come.

Mirror-Mel shattered the silence. 'Get your filthy hands off my tree.'

The pleasant feeling from the mirrortree that had been coursing through Mel's fingertips instantly changed to searing pain. He cried out and whisked his hand away. 'It's not your tree. *I* made it.'

Mirror-Mel laughed derisively. He touched the tree. 'And now *I'm* going to destroy it.' Where his hand touched the trunk a black patch like an ink blot appeared and spread. The patch smoked and gave off the unmistakable stench of rot.

'What are you doing?' said Mel. He touched the black stain. A horrible pain shot up his arm but the tree healed beneath his fingertips.

Mirror-Mel laughed louder, sprang into the tree and began to climb. Wherever his hands and feet touched the beautiful tree it solidified and turned to rotting blackness.

'Mel! The fruit,' shouted Wren. 'He's going after the fruit!'

Mel began to climb after his mirrorshade. Each hand and foot hold was agony but he gritted his teeth and climbed as fast as he could. He had almost reached Mirror-Mel when the mirrorshade swung his foot and kicked Mel in the head. There was a blinding flash and Mel nearly toppled backwards but managed to maintain his painful grip.

Mel blinked hard and was astonished to see that the glowing branches all around him were bending and stretching. He was even more astonished to see that they were weaving themselves together to form faces. He saw his mother and father. Their images were smiling at him as if to lend him encouragement. Then he saw his mentor, Fa Theum. His image pointed upwards. The apparition mouthed the words, 'Go on, Mel.' Taking heart, Mel resumed his painful climb but was hampered by the rotting branches his mirrorshade was leaving in his wake. They crumbled whenever Mel tried to grasp them. As they rotted away they, too, formed faces. Faces Mel recognised. There was Adolphus Spute, the High-Bailiff of the Fifth Mystery, and that of Mumchance, his dwarf and torturer. He saw the rotting limbs assume the beautiful but wicked face of Ter Selen and that of the hideous Morg, her demon-sniffer. But the worst face of all was that of Groot Smert, the master's former head apprentice. He seemed to sneer and his venomous eyes glared at Mel, willing him to fail. *I'll show you*, thought Mel and he redoubled his efforts.

Mel was tiring fast and he gazed upwards to see that Mirror-Mel was halfway to the fruit. He could never beat him to it. He might as well give up. Then, more branches bent to form images and he saw his master, Ambrosius Blenk. His piercing blue eyes stared at Mel and Mel saw the steely resolve behind them. He knew in that instant that deep down inside himself he had the same resolve to beat his mirrorshade to the fruit. He fought back his pain, gritted his teeth and began to climb faster and faster through the incandescent branches.

Below, everyone stood speechless and transfixed, watching the progress of the two figures – one dressed in white, the other black. They seemed tiny against the massive mirrortree as they clambered ever upwards through the boughs and branches of shimmering rainbow light. Mel was clearly in great pain but Mirror-Mel was also hampered because each branch he grasped putrefied at his touch. The two figures climbed higher and the splendid tree became a patchwork of living, pulsating colour and black, rotting death. Slowly, Mel gained on Mirror-Mel.

Mel, gasping with pain, reached the topmost branches of the mirrortree at the same moment as Mirror-Mel did. Between them hung the huge, glowing fruit. Its surface was transparent and inside, as if floating, hovered a sleeping boy. He was dressed in grey.

It was Mel.

The boy rotated slowly in the weightless space but his face was twitching as if he were in the grip of a troubling dream. Then the boy awoke and opened his eyes. He looked first at Mirror-Mel and then at Mel and his eyes opened wider still. He looked from one to the other and then back again, the shock of recognition clear on his face.

Mel could barely keep hold of the tree as pain coursed through his limbs. Beads of sweat were stinging his eyes and it was hard to focus.

Mirror-Mel was forced to keep moving as each branch he touched rotted and disintegrated almost the moment he came into contact with it. The faces in the branches all merged into one.

Mirror-Mel reached out his hand to touch the fruit. 'Die!' he cried triumphantly.

At the same instant, Mel reached out his hand, too. 'Live,' he said softly.

There was an enormous, blinding flash. The mirrortree vanished!

Mel

Mel knew he must be dreaming. The strange scene was just too weird to be anything else. In his dream he had just woken up, as if from a dream within his dream. His viewpoint was from somewhere very high up. All around him were ribbons of light that rippled and swayed as if they were branches of some great, glowing tree bending in the wind. The moving branches seemed to form familiar faces. Then, suddenly, the tree was gone and he felt himself falling – but falling slowly, as if he were no heavier than a feather. He could see figures on the ground far beneath him. He floated down through the crazy, jumbled architecture until he could hear what they were saying.

'Mel? Are you all right?' It was Wren. She knelt and gently shook an unconscious figure lying on the floor.

'Are you sure it *is* Mel?' said Ludo.

'What do you mean?' said Goldie.

'We saw two Mels climbing the tree,' said Ludo. 'So where's the other one?'

389

'If that nasty mirrorshade's gone, who cares?' said Pilfer. 'Good riddance.'

The figure on the floor stirred. 'Where am I?' He sat up.

'You don't know where you are?' said Ludo. 'You've had a nasty fall. How many fingers am I holding up?'

The boy blinked. 'Eleven.' Slowly, a smile spread across his face.

'Mel? Is it really you?' said Wren.

Mel drifted closer and closer until he *was* that figure. He spoke. 'Yes, it's me.'

'Are you OK?' said Goldie. 'You look different – and not just your clothes.'

'My clothes?' Mel looked down and saw that his white shirt and hose had turned to grey. 'What happened?'

'You don't remember?' said Ludo.

'I remember getting here, in the ghost train,' said Mel. 'And before that I remember something about an old fortune-teller in a market.'

'There was no fortune-teller and no market,' said Wren. 'You must have been dreaming.'

Mel's brow creased. 'And before that there was a prison. You and Ludo were there, too.'

'That was Deep Trouble,' said Ludo, glancing over his shoulder at the bounty hunters. 'In the Mirrorscape.'

'The Mirrorscape?' said Mel. 'I could have sworn it was in Vlam. There was a beggar there as well.'

'No, Mel,' said Wren. 'You're getting everything muddled up.'

'No wonder, after a fall like that,' said Pilfer. 'Can you stand?'

Wren and Ludo helped Mel to his feet.

'Any broken bones?' said Spiracle. 'Not that it matters to me. Just as long as you can travel.'

'Travel?' said Mel.

'Back to Deep Trouble, Old Boy,' said Blinker. 'That bit was no dream.'

'Where did the other Wren and the other Ludo go?' said Goldie.

'They vanished along with the mirrortree,' said Pilfer.

'Who's he?' Mel nodded towards the tall, masked

figure dressed in black held by Flob.

'Allow me to introduce myself. My name is Spandangle. Conjuror of renown and prestidigitator without equal.' He inclined his head in a bow.

'But where's Mithras Periwinkle?' said Mel, looking round as events began to come back to him.

'It was him all along,' said Goldie. She pointed at Spandangle.

'And Shrug, as well,' said Spandangle. 'The double illusion is difficult but always a crowd-pleaser.'

'This scrot was helping those nasty mirrorshades,' said Pilfer. 'That's what Bumnote was trying to warn you about. Just give me the word and I'll treat him to a right royal dusting.'

'I think an explanation can avoid any need for violence,' said Spandangle. 'There's been enough of that already. Although it's true that I was helping the mirrorshades, I was also helping you.'

'Helping us?' said Ludo. 'The best thing you could have done was to keep those mirrorshades as far from us as possible.'

'On the contrary. My task was to bring you together,'

said Spandangle. 'I was certain that once I set you on your quest to find the mirrortree you would pursue it to the bitter end. I also knew that you'd work out that you needed to create the mirrortree yourselves for it to exist. Your mirrorshades, on the other hand, needed much more supervision. I popped the idea of the mirrortree into their heads soon after they sprang into existence and since then I have been ensuring they found it.'

'So where have our mirrorshades gone?' said Wren.

'They're back where they belong,' said Spandangle. 'At least, Mel's is. It's now a part of him. The boy inside the fruit of the mirrortree is the artist he was destined to become.'

'But what about Wren's and mine?' said Ludo.

'It's not your time yet,' said Spandangle. 'The fact that you have mirrorshades means that we will meet again, and I shall reunite you with your own dark halves. But not yet.'

'When?' said Wren.

'I can't say,' said Spandangle. 'Every artist has their own appointed time.'

'So we just have to keep an eye out for a tall, skinny

conjuror and a mirrortree?' said Ludo. 'Then we'll know it's our time.'

'You'll have no memory of these events,' said Spandangle. 'Not for a long time. Ambrosius Blenk forgot all about me for many years after I came for him. Not one of you here will remember anything.'

'Pull the other one,' said Goldie. 'We won't forget any of this in a hurry.'

'That's exactly what you *will* do,' said Spandangle. 'But first I can offer Mel, Ludo and Wren a small reward for their trials and tribulations. It seems the least I can do.'

The conjuror peered over into the upside-down dome. Sitting dejectedly in the bottom were Scratch-beard, Doctor Sarcophagus and Nelly Buboes, unable to climb out without Blinker's ladder. He turned to Spiracle. 'Would you accept these three malodorous miscreants in place of the children? They are far more deserving of a spell in Deep Trouble.'

Spiracle shook his helmeted head. 'Sorry. Our contract was for Mel, Ludo and Wren.' He showed Spandangle the entry in his ledger.

'Then have them you must. A contract is a contract, after all.' Spandangle gave a wave of his black cloak and there, sitting in the cup, utter surprise on their startled faces, were Mel, Ludo and Wren.

'What've you done to us?' said Mel with Scratchbeard's voice.

'Change us back this instant,' cried Wren-Nelly.

'You'll never get away with this,' said Ludo-Doc. 'It's *criminal*, that what it is.'

'It seems you're free to go, Old Boys, Old Girl,' said Blinker, turning to the real Mel, Ludo and Wren. 'We have our fugitives.'

'But what about all the trouble the mirrorshades must have caused for us back in Vlam?' said Wren.

'That will be taken care of,' said Spandangle. 'And now it's time for you to forget.' He raised his hands.

'Wait!' said Mel. 'Where're Mrs Morel and Mrs Wood-Blewit?'

'And Professor Thinkwell and Bumnote?' added Wren.

'Why, we're right here.'

Everyone turned and out of the fissure in the floor

through which the mirrortree had grown climbed Mrs Morel, her face and frock covered with earth. She was followed by Professor Thinkwell and Bumnote, equally dirty. Last of all came Mrs Wood-Blewit, carrying something. By the way she cradled it, it was obviously very precious.

'What's that?' said Ludo.

'It's a *mirror-truffle*,' said Mrs Wood-Blewit proudly. 'The professor and Bumnote helped us dig it out.' She held it in front of her for everyone to admire. It was the size of a melon and as covered with wrinkles as a brain. Rainbow colours rippled over its surface and it gave off the odour of pickled grass clippings mixed with rubber boots fried in butter.

'We just *knew* there would be something extraordinary growing in the roots of a tree as rare as the mirrortree,' said Mrs Morel.

'It'll be the pride of our collection,' said Mrs Wood-Blewit. She handed the mirror-truffle to Mrs Morel and began to dust the earth from her frock. 'Now, was this gentleman about to show us some kind of magical trick?'

'Indeed I was.' Spandangle raised his hands once more.

'Wait!' said Mel again. 'What about Shale and Shingle?'

'On their way home by now,' said Professor Thinkwell.

'And Mr Habilis?' said Mel.

'Oh, don't worry about Hector,' said Mrs Morel. 'He's indestructible. He'll soon find his way back to Castle Habilis.'

'Probably with a nice collection of zombie and vampire hands,' said Mrs Wood-Blewit. 'What a horror story they'll be when he reads them.'

'But what about our ghost train transmogrificator?' said Goldie. 'Where'd that come from?'

'Er . . . Actually, I designed it,' said Bumnote, blushing. 'I swapped it in Pennyweight Market for the canvas I painted Monkey-Vlam on. Pilfer must have bought it off the figment I sold it to.'

'*You* designed it?' said Professor Thinkwell. 'I think I may have underestimated you, my boy.'

'If everyone has *quite* finished,' said Spandangle.

'Wait!' said Mel. 'Who *are* you?'

Spandangle smiled his mysterious smile. He raised his hands and moved them quickly.

The World, the Mirrorscape and Everything

It was evening and Mel and Ambrosius Blenk were alone in the master's private studio, Mel's latest drawing resting on the large easel. He had made it with his angel feather quill, which had undergone a strange transformation. It could now both glow and suck in the light around it whenever he wanted it to. The drawing depicted an enormous tree fashioned from nothing more than light. All around its base grew giant mushrooms. Two had the faces of old ladies. The trunk appeared to have been formed from bundles of forearms and the branches were impossibly long fingers. Those to the left were dark and threatening, while those to the right were bright and welcoming. The branches on both sides wove themselves into faces. Perched on a branch was a tall, black bird with a masked human face, its wings wrapped around it like a cloak. A tiny white figure and a tiny black figure scrambled upwards through the branches of the glowing tree. A great transparent fruit hung in the top of the tree and inside it swam a foetus on the point of being born.

The master looked at the picture from close up and then stepped back to see it from further away. Then, to Mel's surprise, he turned it upside-down and spent some minutes looking at it that way, too. 'To better assess the composition, without the subject-matter interfering,' he explained, before turning it the right way up again.

After another long pause, Ambrosius Blenk said, 'You've matured greatly as an artist, Womper. What inspired this image?'

Mel blushed at such high praise from the greatest artist in the Seven Kingdoms. 'I don't know, master. It just came out.'

Ambrosius Blenk tore his eyes from the painting and looked at his apprentice. 'You know, Womper, I believe this is what's known as a "key work". Do you know what that is?'

'Is that "key" like unlocking something?'

'That's exactly what it's like.'

'So what's locked up inside this picture?' asked Mel.

'The only person who can answer that is you.'

'Me? But I don't know what it means. It's just a picture.'

'Oh, a picture's never just a picture, Womper.' The master was quiet for a long time. He looked down at Mel and fixed him with his piercing, blue eyes. 'Tell me, what do you think a picture is? What it *really* is?'

Mel thought before answering. 'I think it's like a window into another world. A world brighter and more vivid than ours. A place where dreams become real.'

'That's good, but actually a picture's rather more than that. Any work of art is. Art is a very special kind of *mirror*. It's a mirror that can reflect back to the observer a part of them that is otherwise invisible. A part of them that can only be seen with the heart. It reflects the very *essence* of the viewer.'

'Is that why the Mirrorscape's called the Mirrorscape?'

'Yes, Womper. That's why.'

They were quiet some more. The old master and his young apprentice shared the bond of silence in front of Mel's drawing as each drank in the nourishment that the small picture gave them.

Slowly, almost without him knowing it, Mel felt words rise to the surface of his mind like an idea bubbling up from deep inside. 'Sometimes, when I'm working, when I'm lost in what I'm doing, I feel that the things I'm drawing are real.'

The master nodded. 'But you feel more than that. I know you do.'

'Yes, master.' Mel was quiet again as he sought the right words. 'It's as if I'm not sure whether it's me imagining the things and the people in my picture, or them imagining me. Or . . .'

Ambrosius Blenk looked hard at Mel. 'Or?'

'Or . . .' Mel's brow creased. He tried to grasp the thought that was forming in his mind but it kept slipping away. For a moment he seemed to grab a bit of it but the rest eluded him as if it were too big to fit inside his head.

The master laid his hand on Mel's shoulder. 'Don't fight it, Womper. You're almost there. Just one, final step. It'll come. Now run along, it's supper time.'

Mel left the master's studio and joined Ludo and Wren in the refectory. They laughed and joked with their fellow apprentices and everyone ate well. One by one the others left until only the three friends were left around the long, oaken dining table.

'So?' said Ludo. 'What did the master want?'

'Did he give you a rollicking for us being away without permission?' said Wren.

'No, he seemed OK about that,' said Mel. 'I just wish I could remember where we'd been. But he liked my drawing.'

'Of course he did,' said Wren. 'It's the best thing you've ever done. Better than any of the other apprentices can do.'

'Yeah,' said Ludo. 'I *hate* you.' He winked at his friend.

Slowly, a smile spread across Wren's face and another across Ludo's. Then they burst out laughing. Soon, Mel was laughing with them.

Later, as Mel lay in bed, his mind drifted into that warm, delicious place between waking and sleeping and the slippery thought came to him the way the very best ideas do – unbidden and without any effort at all.

Or . . . said Mel to himself, letting the thought complete itself and taking the final step the master spoke of. *Or . . . that everything – the master, me, Wren, Ludo, Vlam, the whole world, even the Mirrorscape – is all a part of someone else's picture.*

And then, in the instant that sleep finally folded him in its familiar embrace, *And even that picture is a part of another.*

Glossary of Terms in the Seven Kingdoms and the Mirrorscape

Allopecopithicum – A fox/monkey hybrid

Arachnophant – A spider/elephant hybrid

Arpen – The capital of the province of Feg

Bestiary – A book describing animals

Bols – A village in Feg

Borealis – Northernmost of the Seven Kingdoms

Bridge of Smoke, The – Westernmost of Vlam's seven bridges

Cameleopard – A camel/panther hybrid

Castle Habilis – Home of Mr Habilis

Catoblepas – An imaginary beast

Chicevache – An imaginary beast

Chromophage – A colour-eating worm

Clinch, The – Vlam's prison

Cockatrice – An imaginary beast

Coloured Death, The – A wasting disease that colours the victim's skin

Coloured Isles, The – Chain of pigment-producing

islands off the west coast of Nem

Crippled Toad, The – A disreputable ale-house in Vlam

Crocotta – An imaginary beast

Diaglyph – Religious symbol worn by Fas

Deep Trouble – A prison in the Mirrorscape

'Empire of Sleep, The' – A place in the Mirrorscape

Fa – The title given to a priest

Farn – The river that runs through Vlam

Fas (pronounced Fars) Major – Second echelon of priests, above Fas minor

Fas Minor – Lowest echelon of priests

Feg – A distant province of Nem

Fegie – An insulting term for an inhabitant of Feg. A bumpkin

Fifth Mystery, The – Guild governing the sense of sight

First Mystery, The – Guild governing the sense of touch

Fourth Mystery, The – Guild governing the sense of taste

Frest – A port in Nem

Fugitive Garden, The – Experimental garden in the mansion

Fustinbule – An imaginary beast

'Garden at the End of Days, The' – A place in the Mirrorscape

Great Houses, The – The House of Spirits, the House of Thrones and the House of Mysteries

Grothling – An imaginary beast

Gryphon – An imaginary beast

Harlequin-Mangabey – An imaginary beast

Hierarchs – Third echelon of Priests, above Fas Minor and Major

High-Council, The – Ruling body of the Mysteries

Hill of Mysteries, The – Hill beneath the House of Mysteries

Hill of Spirits, The – Hill beneath the House of Spirits

Hill of Thrones, The – Hill beneath the House of Thrones

Hippardium – A horse/panther hybrid

House of Mysteries, The – Palace of the five

Mysteries

House of Spirits, The – Palace of the Maven

House of Thrones, The – Palace of King Spen

Iconium – A magical pigment that fades rapidly

Inspiration, Mine of – A place in the Mirrorscape

Interpellation, Instruments of – Torture implements

Issle – A province of Nem

Kig – One of the Coloured Isles. Home of the pigment mines

Kop – Mel's home village in Feg

Mansion, The – Ambrosius Blenk's house in Vlam

Manticore – An imaginary beast

Maven, The – The spiritual leader of Nem

Megaphine – An imaginary beast

Merrydrip's Theatre – A theatre in Vlam

Mines, The – Pigment mines on Kig

Mirrormark, The – The secret symbol that unlocks pictures

Mirrorscape, The – The world inside paintings and drawings

Mirrorshade – A double with the opposite personality

Mirrortime – The strange flow of time in the Mirrorscape

Mirrortree – A life-changing tree

Monkey-Vlam – A badly made painting

Morphic Interrupter – A device for opening transmogrification portals

Mysteries, The – Five guilds governing the senses

Nem – Westernmost of the Seven Kingdoms. Mel's country

Nemish – The language of Nem

Omniscope – An optical instrument with special powers

Pennyweight Market – A market where Nem and the Mirrorscape meet

Pleasures – The rights to anything beyond the bare necessities of life

Pyrexia – Southernmost of the Seven Kingdoms

Second Mystery, The – Guild governing the sense of smell

Service Passages – Secret passages that riddle the mansion

Seven Kingdoms, The – Nem and its neighbouring

kingdoms.

Separator – A guillotine for cutting off hands

Tabby – Plain, uncoloured cloth

Temporal Labyrinth, The – A place in the Mirrorscape

Third Mystery, The – Guild governing the sense of hearing

Thringle – An imaginary beast

Transmogrificator – A shape-changing vehicle

Vermiraptor – An imaginary beast that feeds on chromophages

Vlam – The capital city of Nem

Volm – A province of Nem. Home province of Vlam

Western Ocean, The – Ocean off the west coast of Nem

Winding Shed, South-Eastern, The – One of the winding sheds that power Vlam's trams

'World Turned Upside Down, The' – A place in the Mirrorscape

Some Artistic Terms

Achromatic Colours – Black, white and grey

Apprentice Piece – A picture made by an apprentice to graduate as a journeyman

Azurite – A blue mineral pigment

Background – Distant elements in a picture

Body Colour – Opaque colour

Canvas – Linen or cotton fabric used to paint on. Also a finished painting on canvas

Cartoon – A preparatory drawing

Cartridge Paper – Inexpensive white drawing paper

Charcoal – Drawing material made from burnt wood

Caricature – Exaggerated depiction of a person

Chiaroscuro – Bold depiction of light and shade

Cinnabar – A red mineral pigment

Collage – Picture made by sticking elements on to it

Composition – The visual organisation of a picture

Craquelure – Crazing on old paint or varnish

Easel – Stand or support for a painting

Foreground – Pictorial space close to the viewer

Foreshortening – The compressing distortion caused by perspective

Format – The shape and size of an artwork

Fugitive (colour) – A colour that fades in daylight

Gallery – A room or building used to display pictures

Gesso – White ground used to paint on

Gilding – Application of gold leaf

Glaze – Transparent colour

Golden Mean or Golden Section – Harmonious ratio for dividing a picture

Gradation – Smooth and gradual change of tone or colour

Graticulation – Grid used to enlarge, reduce or otherwise distort a drawing

Hatching – Tones formed by closely spaced parallel lines

Impasto – Thick, layered use of paint

Indian Ink – Dense black ink

Journeyman – Stage between being an apprentice and a master

Landscape – Picture of an outdoor scene

Landscape Format – Wider than it is tall

Lapis Lazuli – Blue semi-precious stone. Basis of ultramarine pigment

Linseed Oil – Oil commonly used as a medium with oil paint

Local Colour – The inherent colour of an object

Malachite – A green mineral pigment

Masterpiece – A picture made by a journeyman to graduate as a master. A picture worthy of a master

Medium – Liquid mixed with pigment to make paint. Also, materials used to make a picture

Middle Ground – Pictorial space between the foreground and background

Nocturne – depiction of a night-time scene

Ochre – A rich brown or yellow natural earth pigment

Oil Paint – Paint made from pigment mixed with oil

Opaque – Impervious to light

Orpiment – A yellow mineral pigment

Outline – The drawn boundary of an object or colour

Painting Knife – Small-bladed knife used to apply paint

Palette – Surface on which paint is mixed. Also, a range of colours

Palette Knife – Flexible knife used to mix paint

Perspective – Artistic technique for depicting depth

Picture Plane – The surface of a picture

Pigment – Natural or synthetic colouring matter

Portfolio – Folder for transporting drawings

Portrait – Picture of an individual

Portrait Format – Taller than it is wide

Primary Colours – Red, yellow and blue

Profile – Something rendered from a side view

Quill – A sharpened feather used as a pen

Realgar – An orange mineral pigment

Scumble – Pale, broken colour over a darker one

Secondary Colours – Green, orange and purple, made by mixing two primary colours

Sepia – Brown colour derived from cuttlefish ink

Sfumato – Technique of softly blending tones or colours

Sgraffito – Scratching through a layer to reveal another beneath

Size – Liquid glue used to prime a surface

Sketch – A rapid drawing

Spectrum – Red, orange, yellow, green, blue, indigo

and violet. Also, a range of colours

Stretcher – Wooden frame on which canvas is stretched for painting

Studio – Workplace of an artist

Swatch – A small sample of colour

Tertiary Colours – Colours other than primary and secondary colours

Tone – The lightness or darkness of a colour

Translucent – Allowing light through

Turpentine – Common solvent for oil paint

Ultramarine – Deep blue colour made from lapis lazuli pigment

Vanishing Point – Imaginary point in a drawing where parallel lines converge

Varnish – Transparent protective layer on top of a painting

Wash – Diluted paint or ink

Watercolour – Water soluble paint

Acknowledgements

My thanks to everyone at Egmont Books who worked so hard on Mirrorshade and in particular to Rachel Boden, who made sense of the many drafts that this story went through.